MW01253418

THE FOUR ENGAGEMENT RINGS OF SYBIL RAIN

ALSO BY HANNAH BROWN

Mistakes We Never Made

THE FOUR ENGAGEMENT RINGS OF SYBIL RAIN

HANNAH BROWN

with EMILY LARRABEE

FOREVER

New York Boston

Forever
Hachette Book Group
1290 Avenue of the Americas, New York, NY 10104
read-forever.com
@readforeverpub

First Edition: June 2025

Forever is an imprint of Grand Central Publishing. The Forever name and logo are registered trademarks of Hachette Book Group, Inc.

The publisher is not responsible for websites (or their content) that are not owned by the publisher.

The Hachette Speakers Bureau provides a wide range of authors for speaking events. To find out more, go to hachettespeakersbureau.com or email HachetteSpeakers@hbgusa.com.

Forever books may be purchased in bulk for business, educational, or promotional use. For information, please contact your local bookseller or the Hachette Book Group Special Markets Department at special.markets@hbgusa.com.

Print book interior design by Marie Mundaca

Library of Congress Control Number: 2025930346

ISBNs: 9781538756805 (hardcover), 9781538775929 (signed edition), 9781538775912 (Barnes & Noble signed edition), 9781538756829 (ebook)

Printed in the United States of America

LSC-C

Printing 1, 2025

To Adam, with love

THE FOUR
ENGAGEMENT RINGS
OF SYBIL RAIN

1

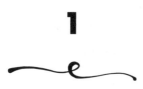

I'VE ALWAYS LOVED AIRPORTS. IF YOU'RE AT AN AIRPORT, IT MEANS something in your life is about to change. And there's no better glass of wine than an airport glass of wine: the first sip of adventure. Even if it's just a Kim Crawford from the Chili's at Gate 42.

Once I'm through security at LAX, I send a text to Nikki.

Good news: made it thru security in record time. Bad news: hot security guard nowhere to be seen.

Nikki hearts my text. *Good news: made it home just now. Bad news: I somehow drove in a circle through long term parking—twice.*

I laugh at her message. *Thanks again for the ride! Love you!*

Duh, happy to. Text me when you land!

I pop in my earbuds and weave my way through the crowded concourse toward my gate at the other end of the terminal with a smile on my face. It was actually at an airport that my best friends—the Core Four, as we call ourselves—all met each other for the first time.

The summer after freshman year of college, Nikki, Willow, Emma, and I went on an epic backpacking trip abroad. I've known Willow since I was a baby, and Emma since elementary school, but Nikki, as my college roommate, hadn't met the other two girls before. We were a bit of an eclectic mix. There was Nikki, in her Lululemon matching legging set, honey-blond hair pulled into a tight ponytail. Willow, with her handmade statement earrings and tousled brunette waves thrown into a heap on top of her head. Emma nervously twisting her red hair around her finger and covertly swallowing a couple of anxiety pills— though whether to ward off her fear of flying or the potential awkwardness of that first meeting, I couldn't be sure. I was also a little nervous about how everyone would mesh. I felt responsible as the group's connector to make sure everyone got along. But by the time we were cramming our overstuffed hiking backpacks into overhead bins, laughing about whether customs was going to have a problem with Willow's travel lube, I could tell everything was going to be okay.

The trip was even more magical than I could have dreamed: we started in Paris and spent most of the summer at Willow's family chateau in southern France, making trips to Milan, Salzburg, Budapest, and finally Istanbul. And somewhere between the midnight trains, bottles of Chianti, and hot Swedish guys in sketchy hostels, we became the Core Four.

When my boarding group is called, I unplug my phone from the outlet where I've been charging it and join the queue. Last year, I accidentally left my cell in a Vegas cab, prompting Emma and my other friend Finn to go on a multistate manhunt for me. Ever since then, I've been mildly obsessive about not losing my phone.

Once I'm settled into my window seat, I make small talk with the couple sitting next to me (Diane and Andrew from Santa Barbara, on their way to celebrate their fortieth wedding anniversary), then close my eyes for takeoff. The engines rumble beneath me, the cabin shaking back and forth as we pick up speed. Instinctively, I reach for the fourth finger of my left hand, rubbing at a ring that's not there.

We hurtle ahead, faster and faster, until finally, we lift off the ground, and the weightless feeling of being airborne settles my nerves. As we continue to climb to our cruising altitude, I let myself imagine I'm flying away from all my problems. From everything that happened last year.

Maybe my friends are right that this trip is going to be good for me. Maybe getting away from it all is exactly what I need.

THE IDEA FOR THE trip originated just a couple weeks ago, when the Core Four found ourselves all gathered in my little bungalow in Mar Vista for a celebration.

Or rather, the Core *Five*.

There's a new chick on the scene. I've known Nora for a little less than a year, and she's definitely shifted our dynamic. Her communication can get dicey, and she did throw up on me once, but I can already tell she's going to be a phenomenal addition to the friend group. (Besides, Nikki also threw up on me one night at a Phi Delt frat party, and I've never held that against her.) The birthday girl was currently cruising around my coffee table, a party hat with a number one on it cocked at a jaunty angle over her peach-fuzz head. Nora's *actual* first birthday was not until September, and it was only mid-June, but any excuse for a party, right?

Anyway, it was while we feasted on cupcakes and champagne—and a bottle of breast milk for Nora, which Willow dared me to try and Nikki begged me not to—that the idea for this trip came up. I wanted it to be all of us; in the end, though, it ended up just being me.

Willow had been talking about the nightmare of trying to find affordable day care for Nora, and Nikki told us about the producer who was hounding her to appear on the next season of *LovedBy*, the dating reality show she'd been the lead of a few years back. Emma was filling us in on her latest high-maintenance design client, and I could see she was physically struggling to rein in her impulse to redecorate *my* entire one-bedroom. (When we lived together in New York, she'd move pieces of furniture in and out of my room at whim. One time, I came home from a weekend in the Hamptons, and my whole bed had been lofted. So the fact that she didn't immediately start styling my bookcases the second she walked into my place was evidence of real personal growth.)

And then it was my turn to update everyone. It felt weird; we used to spend so much time together, with so few gaps, that updates weren't really required, but as I looked around, I had this sudden fear that if we weren't careful, getting older—getting busier with our careers, falling in love—could cause us to drift apart. Or rather, could cause *them* to drift away from *me*. Emma was engaged, Nikki was basically a celebrity influencer now… I mean, Willow had an actual, real-life *child* to take care of. Sometimes it felt like they had all achieved a level of adulthood that I was still grasping for.

"Honestly, there is nothing to catch you guys up on," I told them. "You know everything, I promise."

Willow picked Nora up and plopped onto my couch. "No good Meredith stories lately?"

Meredith is my boss at Flowies, LA's hottest women-owned period underwear start-up. I've been running their socials for the past ten months. The founder is amazing but definitely has her...quirks.

"Actually, there was the Flowies-by-Buzzworthy collab launch party," I told the girls.

"What's Buzzworthy?" Emma asked.

"Vibrators," Willow and I answered in unison.

"Right," I continued, "and this was, like, a two-hundred-person event with all the board members, and long story short, we found out the hard way that Meredith was *wearing* the product at the party."

Emma threw a hand over her mouth as Willow laughed and demanded to know, "What do you mean you 'found out the hard way'?"

"I truly do not need to hear the answer to that," Nikki declared, swigging her champagne.

But of course, I was going to tell them anyway. I was in my element. "Okay, so the creative director at Buzzworthy is this girl Christina, right? So Christina takes the mic, and she's about to start talking, and the room goes quiet, and that's when all of a sudden, we all hear this, you know, *buzzing* sound. I'm not joking, like, everyone in the vicinity turns around, and we all realize at the same time that the sound is coming from *Meredith's pants*."

Nikki spat out her champagne, and Willow started laughing

so hard I was briefly concerned she was going to drop Nora into a bowl of tortilla chips.

"Anyway," I went on, "we have since been talking to them about an updated model that doesn't make so much noise. So, you know, in the end, it was useful market research."

Emma shook her head, red hair swishing like a shampoo commercial. "Sybil, for real, you *have* to get the *LovedBy* producers to do a show about your office. It's such a good idea."

I sip my drink. "Ha. I would definitely watch that, if it wasn't, like, my *life*."

"But it sounds like things are going...okay? Generally, I mean," Emma said.

"Yeah, everything's great!" I assured her. But from the way she was looking at me, it seemed like she didn't quite believe me. I turned to the other girls, and they, too, had quieted.

"You should tell her," Nikki said to Emma. She then exchanged a glance with Willow, who in turn raised an eyebrow at Emma. None of them said a word.

"Tell me what?" I asked. "You guys, what is this, some kind of intervention?" I gave an awkward laugh.

"No!" Nikki exclaimed at the same time Emma said, "Not at all!" and Willow, more quietly, said, "Well, sort of."

Finally, Emma came out with it. "Sybil, tomorrow, it will have been exactly one year."

The words hung in the air like she'd uttered a curse.

I knew what she was talking about, of course. I'd had the date mentally circled on my calendar for weeks now. On June 18, it would be exactly one year since my wedding.

Well—my *almost* wedding.

My friends would be the first to tell you that my life is full of epic, sometimes charming and sometimes horrifically mortifying catastrophes, but that one really took the (three-tiered, strawberry bagatelle with Bavarian cream) cake.

I swallowed, trying to push down the lump in my throat that bobbed up every time I thought about what happened with Jamie. My stupid *Runaway Bride* routine. His callous coldness when I returned, finally ready to bare my soul to him. Our fight at the altar. The shocked look on all the guests' faces. The chaotic, messy tears. My girls helping me stuff my gown into the back seat of an Uber as I fled the Malibu wedding venue. I've tried to tell myself that things falling apart between us was inevitable. That a failed engagement is better than a failed marriage. But that doesn't mean remembering that day doesn't still tear my heart to shreds. Especially since it wasn't even my first broken engagement but my *third*. Two had always just seemed like bad luck, but three? It was starting to seem like some sort of jinx.

"We just want you to be happy, Sybil," Nikki said. "And it feels like you haven't quite been the same since . . . since then."

In that moment, it suddenly became clear to me why the girls had all converged upon LA for this "impromptu, early first birthday" celebration. I was simultaneously annoyed that Emma and Willow had lied to me about "just happening to be in town" and immensely grateful that they all wanted to be here with me on the anniversary.

Emma tucked her hair behind her ear. "Also, I got an alert that those refund vouchers for the hotel and flights are going to expire at the end of June if you don't book something." She glanced at Nikki and then back at me. "We really think you should use them and take a trip."

A trip. The idea wasn't unappealing. I'd been working like a dog for months, developing a new Flowies social marketing campaign and training the Spring interns. I hadn't even made it home to Dallas for Easter, much to my mother's disappointment. Spending a week lying on a beach—okay, a *different* beach than the ones that surrounded me on the west side of LA— sounded pretty great, actually. Except...

"Wait, are you saying I should go to Halia Falls—as in, my *honeymoon destination*—alone? Now? After everything?"

"Totally!" Nikki nodded emphatically. "It would be such a waste not to."

"I would love to go with you, Sybs, but, you know—baby." Willow shrugged, bouncing a cooing Nora on her hip.

"And I think Mrs. Perry might literally murder me if I don't get her kitchen remodel done on time," Emma said with a cringe.

"Niks?" I turned back to her with desperation in my eyes.

"My filming schedule is unpredictable," she said apologetically, before plastering on a megawatt smile honed from many years on the pageant circuit. "But I think this could be so good for you, Sybs! You love to travel, and it's been ages since you got out of town. I actually started looking, and it seems like the resort has availability the first week of July—"

"That's in two weeks!" I protested. "I know my office is a little less formal than some, but I still have to get approval if I'm going to take vacation."

"Maybe it could be a working trip!" Nikki said.

Emma smiled encouragingly. "Yeah, Sybs, you do content creation—can't you do that from anywhere? If you're going to be working, you might as well be working from Hawaii."

I felt a prickle of defensiveness. It's one thing to admit to yourself that your life hasn't been that great lately. It's another to have that fact unceremoniously thrown in your face by your best friends. "Why are you guys doing this? Do I really seem so depressed that you needed to stage a coup to get me on vacation?"

Once again, they all responded at the same time.

Emma: "This is so not a coup!"

Willow: "Because you deserve it?"

Nikki: "We just want the old Sybil back."

I USED THAT SAME argument—the one about this being a working trip—with Meredith when I pitched the idea to her the following Monday. To my surprise, she was immediately on board— once I confirmed that the company wouldn't have to pay for my hotel or flights.

"Really?" I asked, sitting across from her in our offices on Wilshire Boulevard. "I do have lots of ideas for content. I saw there's supposed to be this eclipse thing happening while I'm there. They call it a 'blood moon.' I was thinking maybe we could lean into that? Do a post about femininity and the moon, maybe even do a live stream during the eclipse? We could connect it back to the fertility campaign we did—"

Meredith held up a hand to stop my rambling.

"Sorry," I said meekly. "I used to be really into space as a kid; it was kind of my thing."

Meredith smiled. "Sybil, that all sounds great. I trust you."

I let those words wash over me. Honestly, it's something I'm still learning to accept. That my boss trusts me to do my job well. That I am actually *good* at this. Before Flowies, most of my jobs were a bit more...shall we say, eclectic? I was a temp receptionist at an art gallery for a while. I was briefly a barista at a bespoke coffee shop. I even served as a personal assistant for a D-list soap star, which mostly entailed bringing her beloved dog to regular grooming appointments. (With all those treatments, Gigi the cocker spaniel definitely had healthier hair than me—better natural highlights too.) Flowies isn't a *Fortune* 500 company or anything, but my role with them is the most legit, most stable job I've ever had. And I desperately want to do well.

"Go ahead on the trip, and try to have some fun while you're there too," Meredith said.

So that night, I pulled up the website for the Halia Falls Resort. The photos were as gorgeous as I remembered—plunge pools and natural hot-spring spas, five-star restaurants and fun tiki bars. I clicked through to the page that described their adventure excursions, trying to get myself excited about horseback riding and sea kayaking.

This is good, I told myself. *This is proof that you're moving on.*

And with a few clicks, it was done. The confirmation email from the hotel and the airline made it official.

So now, two weeks later, I'm finally going on my honeymoon.

I just happen to be going alone.

2

GOLDEN LIGHT STREAMS THROUGH THE AIRPLANE WINDOW. BELOW US, emerald mountains rise up from the turquoise sea. Even from thirty-thousand feet up, the view is stunning. I watch as the landscape grows more detailed with little winding roads and palm trees as we descend toward an airstrip along the shore. Then there's a rumbling beneath us as the wheels emerge and a shuddering jolt as we touch down. I hear the pilot's voice over the intercom, welcoming us to Kahului Airport, Maui.

The resort has sent someone to greet me. A friendly man holding a sign with my name takes my luggage and directs me to an enormous black SUV. As we drive along the coast, I can see the dramatic peaks of the neighboring islands set against the bright blue morning sky. With the time difference, it's only ten a.m. here, and I feel refreshed and energized as I roll down my window to the humid island air, trying to capture some footage of the scenery on my phone.

The road is curvy; palm trees bend and sway in the breeze.

After leaving the airport behind, we drive along the stunning Maui coast. The west side of the island has some of its most famous beaches, and a bunch of the big-name hotels line Wailea Beach to the south, but Halia Falls is on the east side, one of the more remote resorts on the island, surrounded by a national park and forest reserve. At one point, the driver directs my attention away from the beaches to a waterfall cascading over the side of a mountain. "This road is iconic," he tells me. "One of the most wondrous drives you'll ever experience."

I lean out the window and grab some more video for the Flowies feed. Forty minutes into the trip, and I'm already crushing this content.

The road slips away from the coastal views, in and out of rustic little towns, and then twists through miles of lush rainforest, crossing over narrow bridges and weaving between mountains. I've never experienced anything like this rolling sea of greens. It's breathtaking, just as the driver promised.

Eventually we turn off the narrow road and wind through a secluded dirt pathway. As we crest the top of a hill, the ocean appears before us again, its clear green water breaking against a white sand beach. A small wooden sign welcomes us to Halia Falls Resort.

The car slows to a stop beside an estate nestled into the cliffside with plumeria shrubs lining the entrance, heavy with hot pink blossoms. The scents of fresh flowers and ocean air greet me as I step out of the car. I take a deep breath, the warm breeze making me feel slightly more human after my long flight, and the dappled sparkling of the sun through palm trees giving everything a magical, slightly surreal look.

A beautiful woman who looks about my age, with light

brown skin and a lemon-yellow flower tucked into her long, dark hair, welcomes me. The two men beside her are both holding silver platters: one piled high with purple flowers, the other holding a lowball glass. The woman grabs a handful of flowers, which tumbles down to reveal a lei.

"Aloha. Welcome to Halia Falls." She walks toward me and places the lei over my head. "I'm Ash. I'll be your personal concierge throughout your stay. I'm here to make your time with us unforgettable, so if there's anything you need, please don't hesitate to ask."

She pulls a tablet from the inside pocket of her suit jacket and scrolls until she finds something on the screen. "I've got your info right here. Sybil Rain, right?"

I nod, still taking in the views from every direction, itching to snap photos of it all.

"A beautiful name. We have more than two hundred words for rain here in Hawaii," she says. "We see it as a blessing. And it always brings rainbows." Then she turns toward the man behind her holding the drink tray. Ice clinks as she plucks the glass from his platter. "This is the hotel's signature cocktail: a passion fruit mai tai. Welcome to island time." She winks, handing me the drink.

I lift the glass to her in a mock "cheers," then take a sip. It's tart and bright, the bitter bite of alcohol stinging my tongue before breaking open into sweetness. I let out an indecent groan. This drink tastes like vacation in a glass.

"If you'll follow me, I'll take you to your room." She nods to one of the men behind her, who takes my suitcase. "We'll make sure your bag meets you there."

The hotel's even more beautiful once I've stepped inside.

The lobby, lined in creamy marble, has a view straight to the ocean. The tableau is framed by potted palm trees that sway gently as a warm breeze blows through the open-air atrium. I trail behind Ash, past an infinity pool lined with private cabanas and through an archway that leads us to an elevator bank.

When we reach the third floor, Ash leads me to a door at the end of the hallway. There's a soft beep as she unlocks the door with a smile. "Welcome to your room."

It's easily the most stunning hotel room I've ever been in. The walls are clad in a light blond wood that makes the space feel like it's glowing from within. There's a king-size bed piled high with plush white pillows, its four posts draped in a gauzy fabric that flutters as the breeze wafts in through the open balcony doors. I take a deep breath and inhale the scent I'm already beginning to associate with Halia Falls—fresh basil and mandarin orange—sweet, but with enough sharpness to give the impression of sophistication and finery.

Ash leaves, and my bag is delivered only a few moments later. A bellhop lifts my bright, lime-green BÉIS roller from his cart, and I notice there's a second bag—a navy Away suitcase—waiting to be delivered to its owner.

A shiver travels up my spine. Jamie had that bag. Of course, *thousands* of people have that bag—a fact Jamie and I actually fought over when he bought his. I said a suitcase should stand out from the crowd, be something that's easy to spot at baggage claim. "Says the woman whose luggage looks like a family of exotic parrots," Jamie had responded.

For the record, he wasn't wrong.

I tip the bellhop, and after he leaves, I'm alone. For a brief moment, I feel a pang of sadness. Probably from seeing that stupid suitcase. If things had gone differently last year, I would have been here with Jamie, having a romantic honeymoon. An image flashes before me of the two of us holding hands on this balcony, him turning to kiss me, laughing as we both stumble inside and fall onto the bed... I quickly blink the fantasy away and remind myself that everything happens for a reason.

Flopping onto the gorgeous bed, I pull out my cell phone to check that today's scheduled Flowies post has gone live. The reel at the top of the feed is a fast-motion sequence of me sorting through a mountain of clothes in my room back in LA. I hit the volume button and listen to the voice-over.

Have you felt the sudden urge to clean out your closet lately? It might be because of the impending lunar eclipse. This instinct to purge the clutter—both physical and emotional—from your life could be your subconscious preparing for the start of a new celestial cycle. With the upcoming blood moon, it's time to reflect deeply on what needs to go, release it, and never look back. One thing we're definitely ditching? Tampons and pads. Check out the caption to learn more about how Flowies period undies are a healthy, comfortable, and sustainable alternative to other period products!

I can admit that Flowies has kind of taken over my life, but honestly, it's been a much-needed distraction this past year. Throwing myself into brand aesthetics and content calendars and post queues has created this semblance of order and predictability that I've never really had before.

I click over to my personal account and impulsively snap a much less curated pic—a selfie of me holding up my passion fruit mai tai—and post it to my feed, tagging the location.

It took a while for me to come back online at all after the

shame of my wedding debacle. Before the Wedding-That-Never-Was, my account gave the impression of a body always in motion—streaks of windblown hair covering my smile, silly TikTok dance trends turned laugh-fests, reels shot shakily in one hand while biking down the crowded Venice boardwalk. I scroll down further and a lump in my throat rises as I land on a picture of me kissing Jamie's cheek outside of Wabi on Rose, fairy lights dangling behind us, casting our faces in shadow.

I never had it in me to totally scrub Jamie from my grid. Maybe I should get rid of these pictures. Make a clean break. Purge these relics of my past and fully embrace this new cycle of life.

I'll bring it up with Gwendolyn in our next session. She's my holistic feminist positivity coach (which is LA for therapist).

I scroll a little faster to get past anything from the Jamie Era of my life, which accidentally catapults me into the Sebastian Era. Suddenly, my grid is full of pictures of beaches and mountaintops, hole-in-the-wall bars and indie rock concerts. When the two of us were dating, we were always on an adventure or on our way to one. For a long time, I thought he was my perfect partner. The two of us just *made sense*: Syb and Seb, two knuckleheads who could be relied on for a good time, as long as you didn't expect them to arrive *on* time.

That kind of freewheeling chaos was exactly what I needed at the time. Before Seb, my last serious relationship had been with my high school boyfriend, Liam, the golden boy pastor's son. Liam was always on time. Always pressed and polished—and he expected the same perfection from his girlfriend. After Liam, being with Seb felt like a breath of fresh air. Like a judgment-free zone where I could let my wildest impulses run free.

I stare at the cute pic of me and Sebastian licking each other's cotton candy at Coney Island, and casually tap over to Seb's profile. Now *this*, I really haven't scanned in a while. There are *thousands* of new pictures—so many you'd never be able to go back far enough to find any of us together. Which isn't surprising since Seb is a professional photographer. I scroll through pictures of breathtaking landscapes and sun-kissed models, mixed alongside shots of political rallies and war-torn cities. Without thinking much of it, I "like" one of his more recent shots of an erupting volcano. Then I cross to the luggage rack and unzip my suitcase.

I'm fishing around for a bathing suit when my phone pings with an incoming DM.

Hey neighbor

It's Seb. I freeze, instantly panicking. Why is he DMing the second I liked one of his pics? We haven't talked in *years*! Then again, maybe it's also been that long since I liked one of his pics.

And come to think of it, why is he calling me "neighbor"? Last I knew, Seb was living in Tokyo.

As if intuiting my confusion, he adds: *I'm wrapping up a shoot on The Big Island. You're on Maui?*

That's when I spot the other phone notification, alerting me that Seb has liked the selfie I posted.

Yes! Just got here today. Staying @ Halia Falls Resort. You been? Seb's been pretty much everywhere.

No! He types back. *But always wanted to. That place is supposed to be incredible. My buddy Tim shot a spread there for AD. Who are you there with?*

I freeze. We've never talked about it, but I'm sure Seb knows by now that my wedding to Jamie fell through.

Just me! Hanging on the beach solo. Unless you were planning to hop over on a puddle jumper lol

I have no idea why I hit send. I look pathetic, desperate. Am I really so incapable of being alone that I need to recruit an ex-turned-friend to come keep me company? I see that he's typing something, but nothing appears. Then, a minute later: *Sybil, Sybil, Sybil* is all he writes.

What what what

Oh nothing. You just haven't changed at all have you?

Lol, I text back stupidly, for what feels the millionth time. I can feel it—how I'm just trying to keep the conversation going because the attention feels good. But his question gnaws at me a little bit.

Haven't I changed? I have a new job, a nice new place—my first time living alone, even—and my friends keep telling me how proud they are of me, of how far I've come in the past year since everything fell apart.

While I'm still scrambling to think of something else to say, he messages again: *Listen, I gotta run but save me a spot on the sand ;)*

I consider replying again, but he's already logged off.

Quickly, I close the app and throw my phone on the bed. My face is warm, my palms a little sweaty. I decide to blame this on the open balcony door, letting the warm air in—and not on any physical reaction to that stupid flirty convo with Seb. His banter means nothing, and I, better than anyone, should know this. The man could hit on a rock and make it blush.

It's funny—the men I've dated don't fall into any one "type." Where Sebastian was a natural-born flirt, Jamie was endearingly awkward. And my high school boyfriend Liam—always-correct, always-in-charge—could not have been more different from the other two. Yet, there seems to be a common denominator to all these past relationships: every single one ended disastrously.

I pull myself off the bed and return to my bag, riffling around for my bathing suit and cover-up. I want to get out to the pool before the heat of the day really sets in. But as I'm rummaging, my hands land on a small black velvet pouch. At first, I'm confused. I packed my jewelry for the trip in a larger polka-dot travel case. I lift the pouch from my suitcase with shaky hands as I realize what this is. I've barely traveled in the last year, not since the wedding-that-wasn't. I haven't gone anywhere long enough to warrant my full-size suitcase. The last time I used it, the luggage was hastily packed by Nikki while Emma was dealing with all the cancellation logistics and Willow rubbed my back as I sobbed. Nikki must have tossed the pouch into the suitcase that June day with everything else—my rehearsal dinner dress, the lingerie I was supposed to wear on my wedding night. And I must have missed that it was still in here when I was packing to come to Hawaii.

I take a deep breath and pull the drawstring of the pouch, emptying its contents into my cupped hand. It's like my entire past glares back at me: in the form of three little rings.

Engagement rings, to be precise. One's a simple gold vintage band with a small citrine stone in a filigreed setting, then beside it there's the delicate strand of kelp twined around itself into a makeshift ring, and finally, the third: a shiny new platinum band with a massive teardrop diamond. My three perfect messes, my almosts.

A voice in my head—one I've been working on ignoring—whispers softly: *good enough to fall in love with, but never enough to last.*

No. I'm not going there. Not right now, while I'm at one of the most beautiful resorts on the planet. This is a time for sun-bathing, not wallowing. I pour the rings back into the pouch, pull the drawstring, and toss it unceremoniously back into my suitcase. In the bathroom, I splash my face with cool water, pat it dry, spritz a little face mist, and dab some lip gloss. Pull out the braid I wore for the flight and let my hair hang loose and wavy, not bothering to comb it. Then I locate my tangled pile of swim-suits and yank out a casual, nautical-striped two-piece along with a white linen button-down, not minding if a few other items tip out of my bag in the process. I'll deal with the cleanup later.

With my straw beach bag slung on my shoulder and my worn-in leather thong sandals on my feet, I retrace the path I took with Ash, back toward the infinity pool. I've barely sat down on one of the lounge chairs when an attendant appears to hand me a fluffy white towel. I thank him, then take a deep breath, letting the warm breeze drifting in off the ocean blow away the weird anxious energy I'd been feeling in my hotel room. I allow my mind to go blissfully blank like Gwendolyn taught me to do when my feelings threaten to overwhelm me.

Breathe.

This is going to be a great week. I'll enjoy the pool, maybe do some hiking, check out the eclipse, and try to get inspired for some fresh social campaigns for Flowies. Who cares that this trip was once supposed to be a honeymoon? I'm not going to let that pesky detail ruin what would otherwise be a phe-nomenal vacation.

Who knows, maybe I'll even meet a guy here!

Once I'm settled, I snap a quick selfie for the girls with the pool and ocean in the background.

Nikki: looks amazing sybs! [heart-eye emoji]

Willow: gorgeous—you and the view!

Emma: don't forget sunblock!!!

I grin down at my phone and dutifully start applying some SPF, though Emma is the one who burns just running outside to grab the mail. I'm a natural tanner, but she's always telling me the damage is just as bad.

I'm just about to lean back in my chair and pull out my e-reader when something stops me.

A deep voice, coming from the near end of the pool. "You must be kidding me."

A deep, *familiar* voice.

I pivot my body toward it.

It can't be...

But it is. The dark hair, dripping wet as he emerges from the pool. The broad shoulders and rippling chest and slightly scruffy, day-after-a-shave shadow...

For a minute, I'm afraid my fantasy from the bedroom earlier has come to life, that I'm hallucinating.

My voice gets trapped halfway up my throat as I blurt out in surprise, "Jamie?"

3

My mind goes blank. But not the serene, calm blank I'd been feeling just moments before. More like computer-short-circuiting blank. Jamie shakes the water from his hair as he climbs the stairs out of the pool, staring at me like I'm staring at him.

I take in Jamie's warm brown eyes, adorably crooked nose, and perfectly full lips... and his bare chest, still dripping wet, pool water running down the rivulets of his abs.

I'm rooted to the spot, trying to make sense of what I'm seeing. Maybe I had too much of that welcome mai tai and this isn't real—I'm just passed out in my hotel room having a deranged daydream that my ex-fiancé is actually here in the same hotel as me.

"I—you—What are you doing here?" I choke out.

It takes a few seconds for Jamie to respond, and I can tell he's just as taken aback as I am.

"Sybil. Wow. Hi." He runs a hand through his hair. "Um, I'm here to—"

There's a splash behind Jamie, and a woman with sun-kissed skin and glistening jet-black hair exits the pool to stand beside him. He motions toward her. "This is my colleague, Genevieve Lee."

"I—" I start, but it sounds more like I'm gargling my own saliva. "I mean, um, hi." *Great recovery.*

I watch as a bead of water descends from his face to his chest and further down.

What. Is. Happening.

Jamie starts to describe the specifics of the work trip that has brought him here, but I'm still in ex-fiancé shock and can't make sense of any of it. Something to do with portfolio diversification and leveraging existing client relationships. Truth be told, I was never really able to grasp what Jamie does for his family's equity firm. The finance lingo always sounds like gobbledygook to me. Plus, I'm hung up on what he called Genevieve just now...his *colleague?*

A colleague in a tangerine string bikini? Yeah, right.

My heart twinges, and I suddenly feel annoyed with my choice of bathing suit; the nautical stripes and little anchor decals scream cute and quirky, not hot and effortless, like hers. *Breathe.* I tell myself, *It's not a competition.* And just because my love life has been DOA since we split up doesn't mean that Jamie's would be. It's been over a year; it's only natural that he'd be with someone else by now. Guys like Jamie don't stay on the market.

Obviously sensing the sheer awkwardness of this interaction, Genevieve steps forward gracefully and offers her hand.

"It's a pleasure to meet you..." She lets the words trail off in a question.

Slowly, I reach out to shake her hand. "Sybil. Sybil Rain."

"Nice to meet you, Sybil." There's no look of horror or recognition in her eyes, so they either must be newly dating or Jamie didn't feel I was worth mentioning.

I suppose I shouldn't be surprised. Jamie clearly wants to forget that period of his life ever happened. But seriously, he's never once said my name? Not even in the context of "Oh yeah, my crazy ex Sybil used to work at that art gallery—you know, before she ran off days before our wedding and completely ruined everything."

He squints his eyes, like he's having trouble seeing me—like I'm standing miles away and not a mere few feet from him. "What are *you* doing here?" he asks.

"Um, just, you know, vacationing."

"Here?" I see a spark of something flicker in Jamie's dark eyes. It almost looks like anger? Or maybe *betrayal?*

A prickle goes down my spine, and the pure and utter confusion that had been fogging my brain since first seeing him starts to fade away, making room for something sharper.

"Yes, *here.* I've always wanted to visit this resort," I say stiffly.

"I remember." Jamie's mouth is a grim line.

My brain conjures images of the two of us poring over travel websites, sending each other pictures of various getaway destinations: Santorini, Thailand, the Azores... but when we came to the homepage for the Halia Falls Resort, we both knew in an instant that this was the one.

"Look," I had said, coming to sit on the couch next to him

with my laptop. "It has all kinds of activities for me, like ATV-ing and sea caves, plus a bunch of art galleries and heritage sites for you—and seriously, have you ever seen more beautiful beaches?"

"It's perfect," Jamie had agreed. "But hey, don't count me out for all the adventurous stuff."

I put my laptop on the coffee table and climbed onto Jamie's lap, carding my hands through his brown waves. "Mmm, so what you're saying is, you want to go spelunking the Hana Lava tubes with me?" I said, slowly lowering my face to his.

Jamie gave me a crooked grin. "That sounds like hell."

"Parasailing?"

"Let's start with horseback riding," he whispered before meeting my lips for a kiss.

The Jamie standing in front of me on the pool deck now clears his throat, and I'm forced back to the present.

"Anyway," I say pointedly, "I had some unused vouchers laying around, so we figured we'd—"

"We?" His voice is sharp as he glances around. "So you are here with someone?"

I'm about to correct him—by *we*, I meant the Core Four—but the hard look on Jamie's face is just so infuriating, and Genevieve is standing there, an awkward, but still beautiful, smile on her pretty face, and I don't know—something evil possesses me, and I can't keep the words from tumbling out. "My boyfriend." Jamie blinks. "Yeah. I'm um, here, vacation-ing, with my, you know. My boyfriend."

Boyfriend? What the frick?

Jamie blinks once, and his jaw tightens. Something shut-ters in his eyes. "Right."

We all stand there silently for a beat. Jamie and I are close enough that I can smell the chlorine on his skin. Feel the warmth radiating off his body . . .

"Well, we're only here for a few days," he says, clearly trying to break the tension. "Leaving Friday afternoon, so not sure we'll run into you again." His voice is matter-of-fact. "Hope you have a good stay, Sybs."

I inhale sharply. *Sybs.* It's just a nickname—the one all my closest friends use—and yet hearing Jamie casually toss it out now feels like a blow to the chest.

"Thanks," I manage to say.

He nods, like this makes it official. Then he gestures for Genevieve to walk ahead of him, back toward the gate that leads out of the pool area. She gives me a small smile and walks away. Her gait is confident, like she knows the view of her from behind is just as good as, if not even better than, the front.

Jamie trails behind her, presumably enjoying said view. Then, just before he reaches the gate, he turns back and glances at me, just briefly. His face is inscrutable. The same placid blankness I remember staring back at me from the end of the aisle last June. When we first started dating, he used to joke that he had a slight problem of RAF (Resting Asshole Face). I always said his reserved nature—the way he held his cards close to his chest and was so intentional about who he let in—was one of the things I loved most about him. Now, it just makes me feel every inch of the distance between us.

"Goodbye, Sybil."

And then he's gone.

Thankfully. So I can die of mortification in peace.

Because it's one thing to say I have left the shame and sadness of that breakup behind me and quite another to be trapped in the most beautiful place on earth with the man I once thought I was going to spend forever with.

THE DAY OF OUR wedding, I arrived at the venue a little late. Okay, very late. So late, everyone feared I might not show at all.

And I very nearly hadn't.

I knew I needed to talk to Jamie about what happened. Why I'd missed our welcome party and rehearsal dinner. But my mother assured me there'd be time for that later. Everything was still, by some miracle, on schedule for the ceremony. But only if we hurried.

I remember arriving to the ceremony site, with its breathtaking ocean views and the floral arrangements that looked even more perfect than the pictures we'd consulted beforehand. And rows and rows of white wooden folding chairs, with the backs of all our friends and family members.

I took a deep breath, trying to center myself, but before I could exhale, the bridal music started up, and my father was wrapping my hand around his crooked arm and leading me down the aisle.

Was it all like I'd pictured it would be? Not exactly. The wind kept catching up my veil, and the roar of the ocean mostly drowned out the cellist—or was that just the roar of my pulse in my ears?

But when my eyes landed on Jamie, relief surged through me. I had to squint because he was a little bit backlit by the sun. The breeze picked up his dark hair, making him look like a lead in a James Bond film, his perfectly tailored tux hugging his body just right. Just looking at him waiting for me at the end of the aisle sent a wave of calm through me. *With Jamie, I'm safe*, I told myself. With him, everything was possible.

"Sybil," he whispered when I reached him. "Thank god. Are you all right?"

"I'm... fine." I felt my pulse tighten in my throat, though. There was so much to explain. "Should we maybe talk?"

His shoulders stiffened. "Here? Now?" He looked to our officiant, who also happened to be his older sister, Amelia.

"It'll just take a second," I said, then turned around to face our gathered guests. "Hey, y'all!" I flashed them my brightest smile. "Thanks so much for coming! Grandma G, you look fab in that yellow dress!"

The crowd tittered with laughter, shaking their heads, as if to say, *Classic Sybil.*

"I need to have a quick word with my gorgeous husband-to-be, so if you could just give us a moment, that'd be great."

More laughing from the crowd, but in my periphery, I could also see looks of concern painting my bridesmaids' faces. In the second row of chairs, my friend Finn seemed ready to jump to his feet and assist with whatever disaster was about to unfold. But I ignored him, and the girls, and grabbed Jamie's sleeve.

"Great, thanks, y'all!"

Jamie followed, clearly flustered, as I pulled him a few yards back, over to a spot half-hidden behind the floral arch that served as an altar.

"Sybil, what the—" Jamie cut himself off. His brown eyes widened as he swallowed. "Wow," he whispered. "You look beautiful. Really beautiful."

"Thanks," I whispered back, my lips forming a smaller, sweeter smile than the glowing one I'd tossed to our guests. A smile that was more real, and just for Jamie.

But this little bubble of happiness didn't last long.

"We should get back over there," he said stiffly. "Everyone's waiting for us."

"Jamie, no, they'll be fine. We need to talk," I said with a gentle hand on his arm. "I tried to find you in your hotel suite just now, but they told me they'd already brought you down to the altar."

"We were running behind schedule," he said flatly.

"I know. I know it's all my fault." I swallowed down the guilt. "Can we talk about where I went?"

"Well, I know it wasn't to Vegas for an impromptu bachelorette party," he said.

I felt a stab of guilt and gratefulness toward Willow, Nikki, and Emma for fabricating that story to cover for me, even when they had no idea what I was up to either.

"Did you know I went out there to be with you?" Jamie said. "I thought, 'sure, I'll blow off the welcome party and sneak away for a night in Vegas too. I can be spontaneous and fun, like Sybil.' But when I showed up with the guys, you weren't there. You weren't *anywhere*. No one could reach you."

"I know, I'm sorry. I left my phone in an Uber."

A crease formed between Jamie's brows—the same one that always appeared when I misplaced things, which, yes, happened pretty often. Keys, lipstick, my wallet, even once my left running shoe—while I was actively at the gym. But in this moment, his exasperation wasn't tempered with its usual fondness.

"Losing your phone isn't an excuse for being unreachable for *two whole days*. Were you even in Vegas at all? Or was that just a lie?"

I sucked in a breath. Jamie had every right to be upset with me, given the way I had just disappeared, but it still hurt to see him so readily think the worst of me. "Yes, I was actually in Vegas."

I could feel everyone's eyes on me; could hear the dull murmur of their whispers, wondering what was holding up the ceremony. My gaze drifted upward, as if the right words might be somewhere in the cloudless sky.

"Sybil," Jamie said imploringly, bringing me back to the present moment. "Why? Why did you go?"

"I went to see Gwendolyn Green." It was the most surface-level answer to his question, but it was the only place I could think to start my explanation.

Jamie looked at me like I'd grown a second head. "That woo-woo woman?"

"She's a wellness coach," I said, trying to push down the prickle of annoyance at Jamie's dismissiveness. "I should have told you I was going to see her, but I was just so in my head. I—it's been a really, really hard weekend for me." I tried to find the right words, where to begin. "I needed some advice. Some clarity, I mean."

"Clarity?" he repeated, and I could see he was getting fed up. It was all coming out wrong.

"Everything has been moving so fast, and then this

weekend I just—something happened. I started spiraling and wondering if I could even *do* this, because—"

"Good," Jamie said, his voice sharp and brittle. It was like something inside him had snapped. The Resting Asshole Face evaporated, leaving raw emotion in its wake. I'd never seen Jamie look so broken. Not even when his grandfather died. "Because I'm not sure I can do this either, Sybil."

My heart plummeted to my stomach.

Jamie ran a hand through his hair, turning over his shoulder to look back at our family and friends. "You completely abandoned me this weekend. Everyone was asking for you, and I was forced to lie to them. It was humiliating."

The truth hit me like a ton of bricks. I'd been so focused on my own drama, and then on the fear of ruining everything, that I ended up doing exactly that. "I'm so sorry, Jamie."

"And you know what the worst part is? Part of me wasn't even surprised."

I flinched as if he'd reached out and slapped me.

"Don't say that—I love you, *I'm here*, Jamie."

"For now," he says, "but what about five years from now? What about when you get bored? What about when we have *kids*, Sybil? You can't fuck off to who-knows-where when there are people counting on you."

His words landed with the same dizzying force they always did whenever Jamie spoke of us being parents one day.

"You say this is all moving too fast, but that's because of *you*," he continued. "You wanted to get married here, so we grabbed the date. I've never been impulsive like this. God, it's like"—he barked out a bitter laugh—"it's like you put some sort of spell over me so I make crazy decisions."

"Well, if you didn't want to get married so soon, why did you propose?" I couldn't help but snap back at him. "Or is that my fault, too, since apparently, I'm some 'woo-woo' witch who manipulated you into loving me?" The defensiveness was seeping out of me. I came here prepared to explain my absence, to apologize to Jamie on my hands and knees for running off this weekend, but I never expected him to cast doubt over our entire relationship. Over who I am as a *person*.

"That's not what I said—"

"Maybe I *am* crazy. Crazy for thinking that you actually understood me."

"I *do*. But all this running away—it's not normal behavior, Sybil. Do you even see that?" he said tightly.

"Well, maybe I'm just not a 'normal' person, Jamie!"

"No fucking kidding," he muttered, piercing me with those three words. He used to love my weirdness. Used to be charmed by all my little idiosyncrasies—how I knew the number and name of every planet's moons, or that my karaoke song was always an a cappella version of the *Duck Tales* theme song. But in that moment, he just looked disappointed, almost disillusioned. He ran a hand through his hair, again turning away and speaking more to himself than to me. "My family was right. Amelia told me you weren't ready, but I didn't listen . . ."

"Oh, so your family doesn't think I'm good enough for them?" I spat out. Because, *of course*.

"My family are the only ones looking out for me," Jamie said fiercely. "They know me better than anyone." He sighed, shaking his head. "The truth is, Sybil, it feels like the other shoe has finally dropped. All this time, I've been looking for a reason, and now you've given me one."

"A reason for what?" I asked, an ominous feeling building in my gut.

"A reason not to marry you."

Just then, Amelia appeared over Jamie's shoulder, her pashmina flapping like a dark cape about her shoulders. "Hi. Sorry to interrupt"—the daggers she was sending my way suggested otherwise—"but are we going ahead with this wedding or not?"

Jamie looked at his sister, then back at me, anger, confusion, and hurt all swirling in his coffee-brown eyes.

Then, as if I wasn't even there, Amelia turned to Jamie, her voice concerned, urgent: "Jamie, are you really going to put up with this?"

And that's when I risked a glance at the crowd. Though they couldn't hear every word, they could see what was going on here. The looks of cringe and horror were blatant on everyone's faces. All of them were looking at me like I was a monster. A horrible, horrible human being, selfish enough to risk the love and patience of a man like this. I looked back at Jamie, and he was wearing the same expression. Amelia's eyes said it all. *Disappointment. Failure. Disaster. Not good enough.* As if she knew it all along, could have predicted this outcome.

And really, shouldn't I have known it too? *Third time's a charm!* I'd said cheerfully anytime someone alluded to my history of failed engagements. But the truth was more like *three strikes, you're out.* How could I let myself think this time around was going to be different?

"I'm sorry, Jamie," I whispered one last time, willing him to believe me.

But Jamie didn't look me in the eye. His eyes remained on

his shiny black shoes as he said, "I'm sorry, too, Sybil. But I can't do this."

And that was when I felt it—physically, like it was actually happening right there in my chest—the splintering. The stabbing pain. I never knew a heart breaking could feel exactly like that. But the *breaking* was so real, I could almost hear it, the shattering.

So I did what I do best. The only thing I *could* do with all those faces staring me down, knowing that I'd ruined everything.

I ran.

4

HELP. SOS. CODE RED. My thumbs fly furiously across my phone's keyboard as I sit hunched over on the lounge chair.

Nikki's text is the first to come through. *Oh no. What's wrong?*

Breathe, babe, Willow says.

Emma chimes in with, *I told you to put on sunscreen!!!*

Not sunburn. JAMIE. HERE.

Moments later, my phone is ringing.

"Hey, Niks." I can hear the hysteria creeping into my voice.

"Sybil, oh my gosh. Are you okay?"

I take a deep breath. I don't need Nikki spiraling off the deep end with me. "I'm all right," I tell her. "It's just *weird*. It's weird, right?"

I still can't believe Jamie and I are both here, at this hotel, on the very same off-season weekend. The odds must be astronomical.

Actually, I suppose, in a way, they *are* astronomical. Our universe is full of cosmic coincidences. The whole reason we're able to experience the phenomenon of a solar eclipse is because the sun is four hundred times bigger than the moon, but also just so happens to be four hundred times farther away, making them appear the same size to us in the sky. Weird, unlikely things happen all the time. Without them, life on our planet wouldn't even exist.

I wrote a science report all about this in tenth grade.

And yet, knowing these factoids doesn't do much to lessen the blow of unexpectedly running into Jamie with second-day hair and a schmear of sunblock on my nose.

"Totally weird," Nikki agrees. There's a pause, and then she adds, "Except, maybe not?"

"Explain."

"Well...his cancellation vouchers were probably expiring around the same time, so..."

"Oh, right."

I suppose that explains the coincidental timing. Maybe he got the same alert. Maybe he figured he'd kill two birds with one stone: meet up with some high-net-worth individuals for the firm (Jamie and his father were always jetting off to luxury locations to schmooze with potential investors) while also treating his new girlfriend to what was essentially a free Hawaiian vacation.

"I'm sorry this is so weird for you, Sybs," Nikki says through the phone. "I hope it doesn't ruin your trip."

"It won't," I say with one hundred percent more conviction than I feel.

"So, you're not going to...leave?" Nikki asks tentatively.

"Of course not." I don't admit to her that open on my phone right now is a Safari tab searching for flights back to LAX tonight. After running into Jamie, the urge to flee was strong, but it turns out that even my impulse to run can be schooled by hefty change fees. It would have cost me over a thousand dollars to return home early. My wallet won't let me do that. And neither will my pride. I'm not going to go running with my tail between my legs just because Jamie is here.

"Good, that's good," Nikki says. "Also, I don't know, but maybe things happen for a reason?"

"Reason? What do you mean?"

"I mean, you could, like, talk to him?" Nikki's voice tips up at the end. "You guys never really talked."

"Oh, trust me, we talked." Memories of the ugly words exchanged behind a flower arch in a beautiful field in Malibu flood my mind.

"You fought, Sybil. That's different," Nikki says, as if hearing my thoughts. "And now, more time has gone by...you've done some great work in therapy. You've changed. Maybe he has too. Maybe you guys could—"

"Niks," I cut her off. "I'm still me. And Jamie is still... Jamie." I sigh. As much as I tried to deny it when we were together, the fact was, Jamie and I were like oil and water. (Me: glitter-infused, strawberry-scented body oil, him: distilled, ethically sourced alkaline water.)

We just didn't work.

"It's whatever," I say to Nikki. "I probably won't even run into them again. And if I do, I'll be perfectly pleasant."

"Them?" Nikki asks.

"Yeah, he's here with a coworker from The Kauffman Group.

Genevieve Something. She seems really lovely, actually... and also gorgeous. I'm, like, ninety-nine percent sure they're dating."

Nikki groans into the phone.

"Yuuuup," I say, popping the P, as I acknowledge the truly batshit scenario I've found myself in.

But it's not just the fear of running into Jamie again that's got me rattled...it's all the memories that are getting unleashed in his wake. The cozy Saturday brunches at home and Sunday movie nights. The gallery openings and upscale dinners with his fancy business colleagues and the way that, no matter how big the crowd, he'd always lock eyes with me across a table or a room, and I'd just feel held, seen. Like he was there for me and only me. And, of course, the way he kissed me—every time, for as long as we were together, he kissed me like it was the first time. Tentative yet hungry. Like he couldn't believe he had won me over somehow. How he could be the perfect gentle-man that everyone in both our circles looked up to but still just the right amount naughty behind closed bedroom doors—or shower doors, or car doors, or that one time behind a stone wall on a grassy cliff overlooking the sea somewhere between Big Sur and Monterey...

"Okay, well, keep me posted," Nikki says, interrupting my thoughts.

"I will. And oh, hey—when does shooting start?"

"Shooting?" Nikki sounds totally confused.

"For that *LovedBy* special. Didn't you say you had that coming up?"

"Oh, um, yeah," Nikki says, and I swear I can hear her

chewing on her thumbnail through the phone. "They're still working out the timing."

It was surreal to watch my best friend fall in love on television, but that's exactly what happened. She and Aaron seemed perfect for each other, with their matching golden hair and flawless teeth. But then, on the live New Year's Eve finale when they were supposed to say their vows, Aaron revealed that he'd actually been seeing another woman the whole time. He'd gone on the show in the hopes that Nikki's connections in the athletic wear world would help him gain sponsorships—he was a pro golfer looking to up his celebrity status. Nikki had, of course, been shattered. I honestly can't believe she's willing to go back on the show after what happened, but if there's one thing I know about Nikki Bennett, it's that she's a professional. With her, it's always *the show must go on!* But of course, that doesn't mean she doesn't feel pain.

That's why she was the one person I wanted by my side after my own heartbreak. I knew she'd understand. It must have been so hard for Nikki to watch my wedding implode, just like her own engagement did. But she was there for me every step of the way. Helped me get settled in my new rental house, brought me dinners, and reminded me that she was just a fifteen-minute drive away in Venice if I needed her, day or night. Thinking about it, I'm angry and devastated all over again—for both of us. We both thought we were going to get our happily ever afters only to have the rugs yanked out from under us.

"I love you, Nikki," I say to her now. "Thanks for calling. I'll be fine."

"Love you too, Sybs."

I'll be fine, I repeat to myself after Nikki and I hang up.

I just need to survive a few more days without running into Jamie again. Halia Falls is a big place—it should be easy to avoid each other, right?

"Do you need another Diet Coke, Miss?"

"Derek, I told you to call me Sybil," I tell the poolside waiter as he deposits the poke bowl I ordered for lunch onto a little side table beside my lounger. Derek and I go way back. Okay fine, we go back about twenty minutes, but already we've chatted about the best items on the outdoor bar menu (the lomi lomi salmon salad), the most secluded beaches only locals know about (and how to actually get to them without falling off a cliff), our astrological signs (him Aries, me Gemini), and his mom's Etsy shop (she's a collector of rare books and antiques). "And no, I'm great! Thank you!"

I'm not sure what the tipping etiquette is here but I leave him a few extra because I know firsthand how absolutely exhausting working in the service industry can be—and, well, also because I may need his help in the near future, like to physically hide behind if Jamie returns to the pool area.

An hour later, after I've finished my meal and sent off a few emails to the interns back at Flowies, reminding them not to forget Meredith's preferred nondairy creamer and the phone number for her dry cleaner, I make my way back to the lobby.

Ash, the woman who greeted me earlier, is there at the

concierge desk. "Wow, I love your earrings!" I tell her, admiring them.

She smiles back and shakes her long, wavy dark hair, letting her delicate gold hoops with green beads sway. "Thank you! I actually got them from a little shop in town."

"Really? Oh my gosh, you have to tell me where. I will definitely go check it out. I love your style." *And I could also use some modest retail therapy.*

She laughs. "Ninety percent uniform, ten percent personal choice, but thank you. You'll love the sweet town of Hana. It's just down the road. Can I help you with something?"

"Yeah, I was just wondering if you have a resort map? I'd love to check out the grounds, but my sense of direction is absolutely insane. Give me a GPS to find the gym and I would probably still somehow end up walking straight into the ocean."

She laughs again. "No problem!" she says, pulling a pamphlet from behind the desk. "There's also a QR code for the digital version."

"Great, thanks!" I'm about to walk away when I remember another question. "Sorry, one more thing—are you guys planning to do anything for the lunar eclipse on Friday?"

"Yes, there's actually going to be a watch party out on the lawn that overlooks the beach. We'll have music, cocktails, and passed hors d'oeuvres."

"Great, thank you!" I make a note to do some Googling about what camera settings I'll need to adjust on my phone to get a good picture of the moon turning blood red as it passes through Earth's shadow. After coming all this way, it would be a serious fail if I ended up just posting a blurry red smudge to the Flowies feed.

I cross the lobby, pausing in the center of the atrium to study the map. I'm curious about the sculpture garden, thinking vivid flowers and bird baths would make for a great setting to stage some products, so I decide to head there after a quick change.

Already, my skin is looking more vibrant; tropical air suits me. I throw on a fresh bathing suit—this one decidedly sexier, an all-black bikini with beaded straps—and an airy cotton mini-dress that you can see through in the light. I run a brush through my hair and dollop another bit of lip gloss and I'm good to go.

I'm feeling a lot more like myself again when I descend back down to the main floor. But I've barely passed through the hedges that line the perimeter of the gardens when I spy Jamie and Genevieve sitting on a stone bench, tucked among lush, flowering pink ginger. Their heads are bent together as they read over a binder resting on their laps. She's now in a fuchsia wrap dress that hugs her curves and sets off her sleek dark hair. Jamie's changed into shorts and a T-shirt, and his hair has dried in soft waves. One piece keeps falling into his eyes as he leans in to point to something in the binder. My fingers itch with a Pavlovian instinct to reach over and smooth it back.

I think about just passing through anyway, give them a good look at my outfit change, act like I don't care. But I'm not ready for that. I can't handle another potential interaction this soon.

Then, as if he can sense my presence, Jamie's head darts up, his eyes instantly finding mine.

My face flushes, and I turn on my heel to exit the way I came.

I'll check out the sculpture garden another time.

FOLLOWING THE RESORT MAP, I take a path instead that goes past a putting green and a barbeque and picnic area before eventually winding its way down to the beach. I turn the corner, and the vista that opens up before me is absolutely breathtaking. Soft white-gold clouds on a brilliant blue sky, waves swooshing rhythmically in long white lines, the bright sand dappled with sunbathers.

I rent a chair under one of the hotel beach umbrellas and settle in to read a few eclipse articles. But I end up drifting off instead—probably thanks to the mai tai earlier, or the jet lag, or else the mental breakdown I'm fighting off.

When I wake up an hour or so later, the afternoon sun is glittering off the sea. Everything is cast in peachy-pink light. And there, head crowned in a halolike glow, is Jamie once again. I rub my eyes, convinced for a second that I'm still dreaming, but no.

His hair is wet again, this time with seawater, and his rash guard is plastered to his chest. He's got a surfboard tucked under his arm—since when does *Jamie* surf?—as he emerges from the sea like a Greek god and makes his way up the beach.

As in, straight toward me.

I slump down to hide my face but overestimate the width of the chair and end up sprawled in the sand. *Dear lord.*

For a moment, I seriously consider just staying here and "owning my space and my stance," as Gwendolyn would say, but the thought of faking my way through another painfully awkward interaction with Jamie has me back on my knees, stuffing my sunscreen into my tote and jamming my straw hat onto my head.

When I make it up from the beach, I make a beeline for the lobby lounge, figuring Jamie's headed toward the elevators at the opposite end of the atrium to return to his room and shower off. He looks good sandy, but I have clear memories of the fact that he does not like to *stay* sandy.

But I'm wrong.

I no sooner step inside the marbled foyer than I spot him passing through one of the many arched entrances. He's bypassing the elevator bank and heading straight for the lobby bar. I don't think, I just act. Seconds later, I've ducked behind the bar, crouching beside a pair of very practical sneakers.

Above me, the bartender, an early-thirties chick with olive skin and a shaved head, doesn't even pause wiping down a highball glass. She just glances down at me and says, "Can I help you find something?"

"My dignity?"

Her lips quirk up in a smile, but she doesn't say anything as she reaches for another glass to dry.

"I'm trying to avoid my ex-fiancé," I explain, looking up at her. "He's here with his new girlfriend."

She pauses and cocks her head at me. "How did you and your ex end up at the same hotel?"

"Ominous lunar energy? Or maybe just simple bad luck?"

Her eyebrows (both pierced) shoot up, but the smile doesn't

leave her face. "I'm not sure I want you behind my bar if you're trailing luck that bad."

"I don't blame you." I pull at the ribbon on my hat. "I promise to leave and take my doomed vibes with me in a sec. I just can't seem to find anywhere in this hotel where he *isn't*."

Just then a man's Boston-accented voice comes over the bar. "Can I have a piña colada?"

"Of course." The bartender starts making the drink, and then I hear the man's voice again.

"How about you guys? Pat? Gary? Fellas? What can I get ya?" There's a cacophony of responses, and I peer out from behind the bar to see a mass of middle-aged men in Hawaiian shirts and name tags. "Okay, yes. We'll do three piñas, two mai tais, four lava flows, a hibiscus daiquiri, and three Coronas. With lime."

From my spot on the floor, I can see the bartender's stricken face. She's trying to hide it—no doubt her managers having drilled into her that at an upscale place like Halia Falls, the customer is always right—but I can tell she's a little overwhelmed by the large order. Seems like they only have one person on duty down here before five p.m., and these guys are ready to hit the afternoon like it's Vegas.

Not even pausing to consider if Jamie might still be in the lobby, I whip off my straw hat and pop up from my hiding spot, startling a balding white guy in a guayabera who jerks back and nearly knocks over a barstool.

"All right, who had the Coronas?" A couple hands shoot up, and I quickly locate the mini fridge that contains the beers and start pulling out bottles. "Got an opener?" I say to the bartender. She looks at me dumbfounded but pulls a bottle opener

HANNAH BROWN

from her apron and hands it to me. I pop off the caps and top each bottle with a wedge of lime from a container of fruit garnish in front of me, then start handing the beers off. Beside me, the bartender is mixing punch, piña coladas, and mai tais at record speed. I pass off each drink as it's completed. "Oh, Gary, you *would* be a daiquiri guy," I say with a grin, handing the beverage to the man I'd heard that other guy call Gary. He's short with small round spectacles and graying hair at his temples—and little-to-no hair on his crown—and he looks surprised, but pleased, that I somehow know his name.

"What makes you say that?" he asks.

"Because daiquiri guys are the most fun, obviously!"

The mood of the crowd brightens as I continue to hand out drinks, all with cocktail umbrellas and bright decorative flowers floating on top, making playful banter with each customer as I go. And then, in just a few minutes, everyone's got their orders, the bartender is swiping a credit card, and the group is heading off.

When they're gone, the woman leans her lower back against the bar and looks at me. "So much for bad luck." She flings a white towel over her shoulder. "What are you, some kind of guardian angel?"

"No, but I worked for a wedding caterer one summer." I pick my hat up off the floor. "Pure hell. Don't know how you do it."

The bartender grins. "I'm Dani, by the way."

"Sybil."

"Well, thank you, Sybil."

I laugh. "Thank *you* for letting me hide down there."

48

"No problem," she says. Then she raises a studded eyebrow. "So, ex-fiancé, huh?"

"Yep," I say, wincing. "And if you can believe it, he's not my first."

"What do you mean?"

"I'm oh-for-three on engagements turning into actual marriages. My friend Finn jokes that I'm allergic to the altar."

Dani gives a low whistle. "Wow, that's gotta be some kind of a record."

"I never do anything halfway," I say with a shrug and a half grin.

"So why did you leave this one?"

I'm momentarily taken aback by her frankness, but at the same time, I appreciate it. Even my best friends have been wary over the past year of asking too many questions about the failed wedding. I'm sure they think they're just giving me space, and I appreciate the intention. But sometimes, it also feels like they're not asking because they already know the answer. *Sybil Rain is a bolter. That's just who she is.*

"Jamie is actually the one who called it off," I say to Dani. "I did something stupid over our wedding weekend, and he couldn't forgive me for it. So he cut me loose."

"Something stupid?" Dani asks, and I can see wariness in her expression. Her lips have gone tight, and her eyes narrow. "As in . . . cheating?"

"No!" I say quickly. "Not like that at all. Maybe stupid is the wrong word. More, just . . . I handled myself all wrong." Of all my many transgressions, at least I can say infidelity has never been one of them. I sigh and look up toward the beautiful blue-tiled ceiling, wondering how much of my baggage I want to spill to this bartender. "Essentially, I started not feeling well, and I guess I just got major cold feet and skipped town for a few days. I mean, it's a little more complicated than that, but that's the gist. I came back in time for the wedding, but at that point, the damage was done."

Dani gives me a sympathetic nod. "I'm sorry."

I wave off her sympathy. "It's fine. Anyway, what's in the past is in the past. I just wish it would *stay* there."

"I still can't believe you're both here," Dani says, shaking her head. "Truly, what are the chances?"

"Well," I tell her, "it's not that much of a coincidence since we both had airline vouchers that were about to expire. We were supposed to come here on our honeymoon last year."

Dani looks like she wants to ask me another question, but a customer comes up to the bar, and she turns to start fixing them their drink.

"Sorry, I'll get out of your hair," I tell her, coming out from behind the bar. "Now I just need to find a new hiding spot. Is there anywhere at this resort where I can be sure not to run into him?"

Dani smiles as she pours rum into a cocktail shaker. "Listen, if you really want to avoid this guy, I can think of one place to go. Out to sea."

I look at her to see if she's joking.

"There's a snorkel boat," she explains. "I think the last trip heads out at 4:30 and it's...4:15 now. Want me to call down and have them hold you a spot?"

"That's perfect." I startle her by giving her a swift hug. "You're a saint!" Then I race out of the bar toward the docks.

It isn't until I'm hurrying across the white-sugar sand to the snorkeling shack that I wonder if I've been overhasty. Maybe instead of avoiding Jamie like the plague, I should just grin and bear it. We're both adults. There's no reason why we can't be cordial to each other. Talk, even, like Nikki suggested. But Jamie's face from this morning—cold and distant—flashes through my mind, and I shut down any thoughts of cordiality with him. The past should stay in the past. That ship sailed and sank. There's no point trying to salvage anything from the wreckage.

5

THE GUY MANNING THE SNORKEL SHACK IS STRAIGHT OUT OF A QUIKSILVER surfing catalog. He's all bronzed skin and windswept dark brown hair, and he looks like he's about to lock the doors of the shed behind him.

"Sorry I'm late! Is there still room on the excursion?"

He returns my smile. "No worries. We were about to pull anchor, but Dani called down to let me know you were coming. I'm Mason, and I'll be taking you out."

"Dinner and dancing?" I say, but Mason just wrinkles his brow, clearly not picking up on my dumb joke. "Sorry, never mind. Um, so do I need equipment of some kind?"

I accept an armful of flippers and goggles from Mason and make my way toward the boat, a small, sleek catamaran bobbing in the low surf. Mason hops onto the boat deck after me, and I whip off the silk dress and roll it into a ball in my bag, then put on the gear and take the bench seat next to two older men holding hands. Across from us is a mom with her two teenage daughters. I smile at them, wondering what it's like to actually get along with your mom at that age. I have a good relationship with my parents now, but as a teen, I was a nightmare, a square peg in a round hole. I couldn't do anything right in their eyes, and we all knew it. Maybe if I'd had a sister, like these girls, it would have been better. Someone to throw them off the scent of disaster.

Piling my snorkeling gear in front of me, I give the family a friendly wave, trying to put myself back into vacation mode. Who knows, maybe we'll spot some dolphins on this excursion.

"Okay, folks! Who's ready to see some amazing sea life?" There's a cheer from the other five or so people on board. Mason bends to untie the ropes that are keeping us tethered to the dock.

"I know I am!" a woman's voice—throaty, but in a sexy way, not a three-packs-a-day way—calls out.

I whip around to see Genevieve, now dressed in a chic white one-piece with tasteful cutouts. A lot more snorkel-appropriate than my current get-up. Beside her, Jamie stands there on the catamaran, looking completely at ease with a childhood's worth of sailing lessons, bobbing easily with the waves like he owns the freakin' ocean. That is, until he sees me. Jamie's mouth drops open as he stares. They must have been on the bow of the boat when I came on board, hidden by the central mast. Jamie closes his mouth, then opens it again, like he wants to say something but has no idea what.

I'd make a crack about him looking like one of the fish we're about to see, but I feel like I'm having a slow-motion heart attack.

There's a roar and a lurch as Mason ignites the engine.

Jamie looks back toward the dock, but we're already sailing into deeper waters, rapidly moving away from the shore, away from the dock, and, apparently, away from all hope of me escaping Jamie and Genevieve on this trip.

"Hold on tight, folks."

Mason pulls back on the throttle, and we cruise through the glistening aqua water.

Genevieve motions toward the only available seats. The ones directly across from me. She and Jamie sit down, and Genevieve, who either still has no idea who I am or is the most well-adjusted woman on the planet, shoots me a genuine smile.

The crashing of the waves is loud in my ears, and I move to cross my legs without remembering that I have flippers on both my feet. I manage to knock over my bag and send my sunscreen, phone, wallet, discarded sandals, crumpled-up dress, and e-reader spilling out onto the deck. *Oh god.*

I lean forward to try to stuff everything back into my tote bag, but I'm once again tripped up by my own flippers. My knee hits the deck with a sharp crack that has me wincing.

Jamie bends over to help, and I jerk back before our hands can touch. "Thanks," I say. It comes out more breathlessly than I mean it to as I scramble back to my seat, clutching my tote bag to my chest.

Just think about dolphins, think about dolphins.

The boat is moving with speed now, the coastline streaming past, a blur of lush greens and swaying palms. I grip the side of the boat with one hand while my other crushes my hat to my head to keep it from flying overboard.

Mason points out a narrow spit of land sticking out into the ocean. "Just on the other side of that headland is a little cove. That's where we're headed," he calls out over the rushing wind.

My stomach lurches, and not just because the boat is now bobbing over ocean waves as Mason drives us farther out to sea. Jamie is back in his seat beside Genevieve, and I chance another look at them. They look good together. Like tall, all-American, sun-kissed Ralph Lauren models. Her dark hair is cut in a bob that I could *never* pull off. And what exactly are they doing having a "business meeting" on a snorkel boat?

Either Genevieve has a sixth sense and can tell I'm thinking about her, or I haven't been subtle enough with my glances, because she looks up at me and smiles. "Did your boyfriend not want to go snorkeling?"

Jamie's back straightens, and his hand curls into a fist, but his eyes never leave the horizon.

"Oh." I wince and start digging through my bag to give myself a minute to think. "He got held up with some work stuff," I say casually as my hand closes around a bottle of sunscreen.

I chance a glance at Jamie, and he seems to have relaxed a bit. "Work stuff?" he asks. The first words he's said to me since I got on the boat.

"Yes, work stuff." I make myself as busy as possible rubbing sunblock onto my legs, even though this is now a very thick second coating.

"Oh, that's too bad. I had to drag this one away from his spreadsheets." Genevieve rests a hand on Jamie's arm, and the casual intimacy of it punches through my chest like a harpoon. "So, what does your boyfriend do?"

I freeze, my mind drawing a complete blank. What would be an impressive job for a fake boyfriend to have?

"He's, well…a, um, an, ah…" I let my eyes drift around the boat, frantically looking for inspiration. All I can think is *boat, fish, betrayal, maybe dolphins?* "A marine biologist!"

Genevieve lifts her eyebrows. "Wow. That's…such an interesting vocation."

I nod vigorously. "Yeah. There's a species of, ah, squid out here that has him really fascinated." *Good lord.* This fictional boyfriend is sounding less and less appealing by the second.

"Oh," Genevieve says pleasantly, though a slight crease has formed between her brows. "I'm surprised he wouldn't have wanted to come on the snorkel boat then…"

I want to slap my forehead for my stupidity. *Duh, Sybil.*

"Oh, well, he—"

"Oh, silly me," Genevieve says with a sheepish smile, before I can come up with an explanation. "I bet that species hangs out in much deeper waters, right?"

"Exactly!" I'm grateful to Genevieve's undersea knowledge for saving me from my own dumb lie. Even though it just highlights how brilliant she obviously is. Smart *and* helpful. Just great.

"Hey, Gen, let's go talk to Mason," Jamie says abruptly. "I want to ask him about the parasailing excursion they offer."

I'm so shocked, I can't stop the words—or the accusatory tone—from spilling out of my mouth. "*You* want to go parasailing?"

"Maybe." Jamie folds his arms across his chest.

"Since when?"

He shrugs. "A lot can change in a year." He turns to Genevieve again. "You coming?"

Genevieve darts a glance between the two of us, then smiles a little awkwardly and gets up to follow Jamie, offering me a little wave as she goes.

I stalk over to the edge of the boat (carefully, so as not to trip over the flippers again) and lean my forearms lightly on the wire railing. My temples are pounding, and there's a twisting in my gut. I try to focus my gaze on the horizon to settle my stomach. I can't get over the fact that Jamie apparently *parasails* now. My eyes drift toward the bow of the boat where Jamie and Genevieve are chatting with Mason. Jamie has his arm casually slung around Genevieve's shoulders. There's that lurch in my gut again. But it's not seasickness, I realize.

It's *jealousy*.

I sigh and close my eyes. The breeze lifts my hair, and the sun warms my face. I try to anchor myself in the here and now, like Gwendolyn taught me. To let the feeling wash over me without letting it consume me. After a few minutes, I open my eyes and pull out my phone, snapping a few pictures to use on a future post about Flowies's upcoming line of period-safe swimwear. *See, everything's fine. You can handle this.*

But my moment of Zen is interrupted by a voice, raised over the roar of the motor.

"So not to be weird, but—she's your ex, right?"

It's Genevieve. I glance up to see that she and Jamie are sitting on the stairs to the flybridge. From where I'm standing on the deck below them, they can't see me—but I can hear every word they're saying.

"Yeah, we were...we were engaged."

"Oh."

There's a pause. The boat begins to slow. We've reached the little cove, surrounded by a crescent-shaped beach. When we're less than half a mile offshore, Mason drops the anchor and calls out for everyone to gather around for a lesson on how to use the snorkeling equipment. Genevieve and Jamie begin to make their way down the stairs. Without the motor running, I can hear Genevieve clearly when she says softly, "I'm sorry things didn't work out. She seems nice."

"Everyone loves Sybil." Jamie's voice is flat. "But I dodged a bullet on that one, trust me."

My stomach drops to my knees.

Their flip-flops thwack down each step, in time with the hammering of my heart.

Shit. I can't be here. Can't see the look on Jamie's face when he reaches the bottom of the stairs. I don't know if I'm going to cry or scream at him or keel over and die from embarrassment. But I'm not sticking around to find out.

I make my way toward the stern where the group is gathered in a circle watching Mason explain how to use our snorkel for breathing and the best way to swim with the flippers. I get the basics, but I'm barely listening, my body humming with anxious energy.

A memory sparks. It was three days before our wedding, and my nerves were frazzled, but my spirits were high—until I went to drop off welcome bags at the hotel reception area and overheard Amelia, Jamie's older sister, talking to Jamie in a hushed voice. They were inside his suite, but the door had been left open. When I heard my name uttered, I did the obvious, normal thing and ducked to the side of the entrance, trying to hear. "Are you really sure she's marriage material?" Amelia asked her brother. "Can you seriously see this woman as the mother of your children someday?"

I froze on the pathway outside Jamie's hotel suite, the monogrammed tote bags spilling from my arms as I pressed a hand to my stomach. As if my small, manicured hand was enough to keep my soft insides safe from the dagger of Amelia's words. I lingered long enough to hear Jamie mumble something in reply—it sounded a lot like *no*, or *I don't know*, but I wasn't quite close enough to make it out over the roaring in my ears. I'd always known that Jamie's family weren't my biggest fans. It was clear the Kauffmans found me a bit cringeworthy as a match for their brilliant, handsome, successful, highly-accomplished Jamie—how could they not? Even *I* thought it!—but I truly hadn't realized the depth of their disdain, their distrust of *his* judgment in choosing me.

Now, on the boat deck, Mason starts gesturing out to the shoreline, describing some hiking path that leads from the cove beach back to the resort's main beach on the other side of the headland, when suddenly from behind me, there's a familiar scent. Cardamom and sandalwood carried on the breeze. I'd recognize the smell of Jamie anywhere, and despite the overwhelming surges of mortification and anger spreading through me, a spark of desire makes its way into my gut. Maybe there are some things you just can't shake, no matter how much "evolving" you do.

Okay, that's it. Gotta go.

Without waiting for the okay from Mason, I swipe my goggles from the seat and jump straight over the side of the boat into the ocean.

6

WATER CLOSES OVER THE TOP OF MY HEAD AND THE ROAR OF THE WIND cuts off.

Beneath the waves everything feels calmer. For a whole minute, I feel solitude. I feel safe. The disaster above the waves can't reach me down here.

Without my goggles on, I keep my eyes squeezed closed, losing myself in the soft pull of the current. My lungs start to burn from lack of oxygen, and I kick my way back up.

Breaking through the surface, I suck in a gasp of air and get a face full of saltwater. I hear both Jamie and Mason calling after me, but the idea of returning to the boat feels impossible.

I swivel to face the shore instead, seeing that it isn't *that* far. I tread water, trying to calculate if I can make it. I'm an extremely good swimmer. I was always decent as a kid, but I really picked up a lot more technique and stamina when I briefly dated a swimmer at USC.

Another illustrious era of my romantic past I don't like to spend too much time dwelling on. But at the moment, I'm grateful, at least, for the skill.

Because there's no way in hell I'm getting back up on that boat. I'll just get my bag from Mason later, back at the resort.

Mind made up, I take another deep breath, put on my goggles, and start swimming toward the half-moon-shaped shoreline.

Is it a little bit unhinged? Sure. But can you blame me? Besides, Mason said something about hiking trails that lead from the cove back to the main beach, so it's not like I'm venturing into unknown wilderness.

Seconds later, there's a splash behind me, and I turn to see Jamie shaking the water from his hair. My mouth falls open, and a swell of water splashes me in the face. I cough on saltwater, unable to believe what I'm seeing.

The whole reason I jumped out of the boat was to get *away* from Jamie. And it seemed like he wanted to be near me about as much as I wanted to be near him, which is to say, not at all. *I dodged a bullet on that one.* So what the hell is he doing out here?

I continue to swim toward shore. Jamie tries to match my pace. I ignore him and kick harder, congratulating myself on the forethought to escape while wearing a pair of flippers.

But eventually, my body begins to feel the results of all this exertion, and I slow down my strokes, allowing Jamie to come up alongside me.

"I don't need a babysitter," I grit out through clenched teeth.

"Could have fooled me," he mutters, treading water. It gives me some satisfaction that he seems out of breath too.

"Besides," I continue, "even if I did need help, that's not your job anymore." The words are laced with bitterness. My mind is still swirling with memories of all the times Jamie's family made me feel like a burden, like an ill-behaved puppy that Jamie was struggling to housebreak.

"Look, I couldn't let you swim all the way to land alone!" Jamie insists. "It's much too dangerous." He seems... angry, actually. As if he doesn't want to be out here, treading water in the Pacific, but he's powerless to make any other choice. Being the dutiful guy who does the right thing is embedded so deeply in Jamie's DNA that he'll make himself miserable just to prove himself honorable.

I roll my eyes at him. "It's not *that* dangerous, and I don't need rescuing." Before he can respond, I splash away from him toward the shore.

But soon enough, Jamie begins pulling ahead of me with his long strokes, and much to my annoyance, he beats me to dry land, then stands there, gathering his breath and waiting for me with his hands on his hips.

I'm almost tempted to turn around and swim right back to the boat, but it was a farther swim than I'd judged from out at sea, and my limbs are shaking with exhaustion. So maybe it was a *tad* impulsive of me to swim to shore on my own.

As I clomp onto the beach with my flippers, panting and out of breath, I try not to show how much effort that took, lest Jamie suspect he was right.

"Classic Sybil," he mutters.

"What's that?" I snap, unable to stop myself.

"Nothing, it's just, you know. It's quite a skill," he says, squinting out over the water, refusing to make eye contact with me.

"What is?"

"Running away instead of facing your problems."

"I don't know what you're talking about," I say defensively, even though I know exactly what he's talking about. "I don't have a problem. I just wanted a swim."

"Uh-huh, sure."

Ignoring his sarcasm, I turn back to face the boat and can make out Genevieve's concerned face bobbing up and down with the waves. She offers a small wave. A childish part of me wants to ignore her, but guilt slices through me, and I raise my hand to wave back. Then drop it when I realize she's waving at Jamie.

Taking stock of the beach, desperate to figure out how to get out of here, I notice a path that cuts through the swaying grasses, winding a route along the sand, back to the other side of the headland.

Jamie nods. "The resort is that way, but we'll have to make it up that trail first. And we should hurry if we want to get back before dark." Then he gestures down at my bright yellow flippers. "Think you can hike in those?"

With as much dignity as I can muster, I bend down to peel them off and start down the trail, slinging my swim fins over my shoulder.

"You coming?" I ask without looking back "I might need more *rescuing*."

★ ★ ★

JAMIE AND I HUFF up the trail in silence for a while, the only sound the occasional scuff of dried palm bark underfoot. My hair is still soaked, and the only thing keeping it out of my face is the sticky plastic strap of the goggles I've pushed up onto my head like a headband. As we round a bend and lose sight of the boat and the cove beach, I try to swipe surreptitiously beneath my eyes to mitigate any rings left by the goggles. I don't need Jamie to see me looking like a manic raccoon.

"I think we need to bear left here," he says.

I twist my neck to look back at him. He had his shirt on when he jumped into the water after me, and it's still wet. Very wet. And clinging to every dip and swell of his chest and stomach. The same chest and stomach I used to run my hands over, my *mouth* over. I swing my gaze forward and start walking faster, pulling the goggles from my head and running a hand through my tangled waves. I'm half tempted to look around for hidden cameras. I'm no stranger to the odd uncanny coincidence or unexpected disaster, but this is some *LovedBy*-level shit. I'm on an island, alone, with a man who has seen my naked body from every angle imaginable. I can hear Nikki's voice in my head. *Sorry, Sybs. This is no reality show. This kind of craziness could only happen to you.* At the thought, a slightly unhinged laugh bubbles out of me.

"You okay?" Jamie's looking at me warily, like I'm a feral animal about to snap. Which, given the noise that just escaped my mouth, I guess he can be forgiven for thinking.

"Oh, I'm just peachy, you?" I start walking again and can hear Jamie's footsteps close on my heels.

"This isn't funny, Sybil."

"Oh, I know it's not, James."

Jamie hates his full name.

"You could have gotten seriously hurt, jumping into the water like that and just swimming away. What were you thinking?"

I stop and turn to see his arms crossed against his broad chest, a deep crease forming between his eyes.

"I *wasn't* thinking, okay? I just needed to—"

"Well, that much is clear," Jamie huffs. "Forget it. Let's keep walking. I don't want to fight."

"Of course you don't." I roll my eyes. With the exception of our blowup at the altar, Jamie and I almost never fought. If we disagreed about something—like what to order for dinner or which movie to stream—he would present his opinion with coolheaded logic, while I'd argue my side passionately. In the end, Jamie usually agreed to go with my choice. But inevitably, I'd get distracted watching *him* watch the movie, wondering if he was actually enjoying it or if he had just given in to avoid a fight. Which is exactly what he's doing now. I know Jamie is furious at me. Not just for jumping out of the snorkel boat but for everything that happened last year. But he won't let himself get worked up beyond mild disappointment. The irony, of course, is that all his restraint is just making me *more* upset. "You never say what you're really feeling," I tell him. "You shove all your feelings down—"

"And *you* let yours run completely wild. Following every impulsive whim without—"

"Well, good thing you didn't marry me then, huh?" I interrupt. "Really *dodged a bullet* there."

For a moment Jamie looks confused, but then realization dawns. The annoyance on his face evaporates. Pink blossoms on his cheeks as he looks down at his bare feet.

"You...you heard that?"

THE FOUR ENGAGEMENT RINGS OF SYBIL RAIN

"Yup. Oh, and tell Gen thanks; she seems nice too." I don't know why I'm so stung by his words from the boat. I should be glad. This is all just proof that I was right all along. That we were wrong for each other—even at the best of times. Even when it felt right.

"Listen, Sybil—"

"It's fine. Forget it. That's what you wanted, right?" I turn on my heel and begin to walk up the path again, but before I can take another step, Jamie's hand closes around my wrist, stopping me in my tracks.

"It's not fine," he says in a low voice. His grip is loose, but I'm rooted to the spot.

This is the first time he's touched me in over a year.

Electricity surges up my arm, burning through my whole body. Every cell is on alert and focused on the few square inches where Jamie's skin is in contact with mine. He might as well have used titanium handcuffs to hold me in place.

"I shouldn't have said that," Jamie whispers. "I'm sorry."

My eyes lock with his. The warm brown has darkened to molten chocolate, and the sizzling current in my body settles into a languid heat. His thumb absently grazes the inside of my wrist, and my pulse skyrockets. Memories flash through my mind of other times Jamie took my wrist and pulled it above my head, hovering over me, then pressing into me...My eyes drop to his hand. There's a pause as he looks down, too, and, as if realizing he's overstepped, he releases me instantly. He clears his throat and steps back.

I feel the lack of him immediately. The warmth he left roils inside me, crashing up against my skin, begging to be let out. I shake my head and take my own step back.

It's just lust, I tell myself. It's just hormonal muscle memory responding to the last non-battery-operated thing to give me an orgasm. It's just a year's worth of sexual frustration finally coming to a head at the most inopportune time possible.

I croak out, "Apology accepted." Jamie blinks at me in confusion, and then, a moment later, nods again as if finally processing my words.

We continue along the path as it makes a steady incline. The tender pads of my feet sting every time I step on a rogue pebble or rough piece of bark. I can feel the tendrils of hair tickling the nape of my neck. It's like every inch of my skin is aware of the man just a few steps behind me. *What the hell is happening to my body, and how do I make it stop?*

Finally, we reach the crest of the hill we've been climbing, and the view unfolds before us—Halia Falls laid out like the Emerald City twinkling in the distance. Beyond the resort, you can see the curve of the bay where the water sparkles, steady breakers landing softly on the shore. And you can see even farther, to the more mountainous part of the island. I think I can even spot the rushing waters of the beautiful waterfall the driver pointed out to me this morning.

"Wow," Jamie breathes out. It's the first thing either of us has said in thirty minutes.

"Yeah," I can't help but agree.

Jamie finds a seat on a fallen log, catching his breath. "You know, I didn't actually want to come here," he says quietly, like he's talking to himself more than to me. "I thought it would be too hard, given everything…"

I swallow and nod, even though Jamie's not looking at me. His eyes are still trained on our bird's-eye view of the resort.

"It was Amelia who encouraged me to come down," he continues. "She kept telling me I shouldn't let the past stop me from moving forward with my future. And she always gives the best advice."

Yeah, like telling you not to marry me.

The memory of what happened last year is too much for me to handle right now. I need to change the subject away from Jamie's older sister and her opinions about how I wasn't *marriage material.* I turn away from Jamie, pointing toward the sky. "Hey, look! You can already see the moon. A waxing gibbous." Jamie's brow crinkles in confusion as he follows my gesture up to the pale, nearly full smudge of a moon. "Did you know that the waxing gibbous signifies a time of reflection on the mistakes of the past?" I blurt out.

"Um, no, I didn't." Jamie's looking at me like I've swallowed a deck of tarot cards.

"I've got all this content lined up about the blood moon eclipse on Friday," I say. "Did you know we're in the path of totality? I'm the social media manager for a brand called Flowies, and my boss is actually letting me do a whole campaign about—"

"Wait, what?"

Yes, Jamie, I know I've gone around the bend. Just go with it.

Except, Jamie's no longer looking at me like I'm ridiculous. He's got his "working out a tough logic puzzle" face on.

"I thought you were here with your boyfriend so he could study the squids?"

Shit.

"Um, yeah, no, I am." I drag my fingers through my hair in a failed attempt to tame some of the snarls. "It's a vacation-slash-work trip for both of us, actually." *Smooth save.*

Jamie studies my face for a moment. His dark eyes can be so expressive, but right now, they look guarded. I can't tell if he's buying my explanation. Then he looks away, turning back toward the path.

"We should probably get going. It'll be nightfall soon."

I nod. The sky *is* rapidly darkening.

We walk a few minutes in silence, then come to a fork in the path. I pause, not sure which way leads back to hot showers and fluffy towels. "I think we need the left one again," Jamie offers after a beat. Then he looks down the other fork. "Although, it does look like the trail levels out to the right..." He seems hesitant.

"So...right, then?"

Jamie closes his eyes for a minute. Then opens them. "No, it's left. I remember it from the resort map. Going left each time will bring us back to the hotel. No use risking a shortcut. We should follow what the map said."

I nod once—lord knows I have no sense of direction—and head left.

We go a few yards down our chosen path and pretty soon find that this trail does *not* level out. If anything, it gets steeper.

And right as the path becomes filled with boulders, rain dumps out of the sky like someone's turned on a water hose. I'd been mostly dry, but in seconds, my hair and my cover-up are nearly as wet as when I stomped out of the ocean.

"We should have gone right," I mutter.

"Excuse me?" Jamie's words are punctuated with puffs of air as he exerts himself up the hill.

I stop in the middle of the path and take a step toward him.

"I'm just saying, if you had listened to your gut, instead of obsessively following the—"

"And if *you* had given one ounce of thought to your plan before you jumped off the boat, we wouldn't need to rely on my memory of the map." He takes a step toward me, and we're nearly chest to chest. The closeness sends another jolt of energy burning through me. Or maybe it's the unrestrained anger in his voice. "I did what I thought was right," Jamie spits out. "Sorry I didn't want to risk us getting stuck in the wilderness overnight just so that—"

I bark out a bitter laugh. "You never risk *anything*."

"I jumped out of the damn boat, didn't I?" Jamie shouts. "I suppose your squid man boyfriend always takes the risky bet. I suppose he probably has the patience of a saint and never asks questions even when you disappear for days on end."

"That's not fai—" I try to object, but Jamie is not finished.

"I'm sure he's just a perfect specimen who always shaves his sideburns..." I almost laugh at that—I *did* used to criticize Jamie for those overabundant sideburns—but I'm struck by the intensity of Jamie's gaze. It's a little unnerving, but it also feels like a veil being lifted. Like we're finally breaking through the wall that's been built between us.

Rain falls down heavily, plastering our bathing suits to our skin, making me shiver. Drops of it meet his forehead, his cheeks, his jaw, before trailing toward his mouth. I dart out a tongue to lick my own lips. Jamie blinks, as if gathering himself up for something.

Finally, he speaks, his voice softer now but still just as raw. "But Sybil, I was never that man, and you knew it when you agreed to marry me. You knew that I like structure and order and certainty. That I only let the people closest to me see the real me. I thought you were one of those people. But obviously, I was wrong."

He turns around and continues hiking, leaving me standing there stunned. He thinks *I* didn't accept him for who he really is? That couldn't be further from the truth.

"And I thought you knew *me*," I call to his back. "I told you everything, Jamie. About what happened in my past. About my...episodes." *Panic attacks*, Gwendolyn has explained to me. Though until I started seeing her, I never had a name for those moments when my heart would race and my breath would turn shallow and it would feel like my mind was unspooling. "You knew, and you said you understood," I say to Jamie, raising my voice over rain. "You said that even if I sometimes had to run away, you'd always be waiting for me when I came back. But that was a lie, wasn't it?"

"You mean like the lie about where you went on our wedding weekend?" Jamie tosses over his shoulder. "You were gone for two whole days, Sybil. How stupid do you think I am? And don't act like that's the only thing you ever hid from me."

I swivel around. "What's *that* supposed to mean?"

But before he can answer, I yelp as my foot twists on a root and my knee hits the ground hard.

The rain has made everything slick. We've come to the other side of the hill, and the trail has descended into a steep drop. I skid into Jamie, toppling him over with me.

As he falls, he manages to use some of his momentum to roll us. We come to a stop with my body sprawled on top of his.

My face is once again just inches from his, and the rest of

his body is pressed along my entire length. The warmth from earlier rushes back to me, and I have to stop myself from rolling my hips against his.

"Are you okay?" The anger is gone from his voice, and all that's left is concern.

My mouth falls open again. "I'm fine," I lie. There's nothing "fine" about nearly dry humping your ex-fiancé on a public hiking trail.

I roll off Jamie, brushing a few leaves off my shins and straightening up. Pain shoots through my left ankle and I instinctively pick up my foot to rub the sore joint.

"Can you put any weight on it?" he asks.

I try but let out a sharp hiss. In an instant, Jamie's arm is around my waist, supporting my weight. I let myself lean into the broad warmth of his body.

"Let me help you." He's tall enough that he has to crouch down a bit. We take a few more steps, but the angle must be awkward enough for him that he gives up. Before I realize what's happening, he's pulled me up, cradling me in his arms. I'm overtaken by the scent of him again. Even soaked with rain, his T-shirt once again drenched and sticking to him, the distinct smell of Jamie pulls me back and sends a rush of familiar adrenaline through me, and the feeling is intoxicating. As I look up at the firm line of his jaw, a wave of nostalgia rolls through me. For a moment, I let myself sink into the sensation of it. A damsel in distress, lost in the woods and rescued by a familiar stranger.

"Do you remember when you carried me over to the stables in Napa?" It was our first trip home to meet Jamie's family. It was also the trip when Jamie proposed. Craning my neck to look up at him for an answer, I inhale sharply at the look on his face.

"Of course," he says softly. There's a strained note in his voice.

Like maybe our nearness is having the same effect on him as it's having on me.

Or maybe the heat and the pain in my ankle have just gone to my head.

The trail begins to level out—finally—and the gently rolling lawn of the hotel comes into view. It's easy going the rest of the way, and as we make it back to the resort grounds, he sets me down gently on the path and flags a passing golf cart.

"Are you going to be okay from here?" he asks.

"I'll be okay. I just need to rest it for a bit, and I'll be fine."

But will I? I wish all it took to wash you free of your past was an evening rainstorm.

I hop over to the golf cart and start to slide into the passenger seat but lose my balance on my wobbly ankle.

Jamie takes my hand and helps me up, and for some reason, just the spot where our palms meet tingles, as if a shared language has passed between us.

I look up into his eyes.

"Make sure you put it on ice," he says. "Your ankle, I mean."

And then I'm watching—again—as he walks away.

7

THE THIRD RING

Jamie waited so long to introduce me to the Kauffman clan—more than a year!—that I had started to worry he was actively trying to keep me a secret... or else that *they* had some terrible secret he didn't want me to find out about. Like maybe his father was a cult leader with eighteen wives, or maybe they didn't live on a former vineyard at all but some sort of chinchilla farm—just cages and cages full of shaved rodents. But a few weeks before Christmas, I was finally about to find out the truth.

We flew from LA to San Francisco then rented a car to drive the final hour up to his parents' house in Napa. My nerves were shot by the time the car crunched up a long, gravel driveway—well, really more of a private road than a driveway—and the house came into view. Though *house* might not be the proper word for it. *Estate* might be more appropriate. The idea of this being home—as in, the place where you built pillow forts as a kid and watched Sunday cartoons and did homework and got in trouble for drawing on the walls—was a little hard to picture. The enormous chalet of creamy yellow stone was surrounded by garden paths that led out across the sweeping grounds. The house was surrounded by acres of grape vines—remnants of a once-thriving winery that now served as a playground for Mr. Kauffman's amateur winemaking hobby. I knew Jamie's family had money, but it hadn't really registered for me how *much* money they had until someone greeted us at the door and took our luggage, like we'd arrived at a boutique hotel, before leading us inside.

Jamie's voice echoed as he called for his parents, but no one answered. "Looks like we have the place to ourselves." He grabbed my hand and led me back out the front door. "Let me give you the tour."

Jamie pulled me around the side of the house where the perfectly manicured lawn gave way to a wilder expanse. Rows of grapevines stretched in every direction.

"Wow," I breathed, taking in the scale of the vineyard. "This is incredible."

Jamie ducked his head in embarrassment, but I could see there was a hint of pride in his eyes. "Come check it out." We walked down a set of stone steps and crossed the lawn until we were standing in front of the rows of grapes. Jamie gestured toward a rustic barn nestled amongst the vines. "That's where all the magic happens."

I raised an eyebrow. "Magic?"

He chuckled. "Yeah, you know, the fermenting, the aging,

all that stuff. It's pretty fascinating, actually." He plucked a grape from a nearby vine and popped it into his mouth. "Open up," he said, before slipping a grape between my lips.

It burst with sweetness, a hint of tartness lingering on my tongue. "Delicious."

"Right?" Jamie grinned. "And the wine tastes even better. I've been telling my dad for years we should expand our sales beyond wine country. It's off-menu at the Michelin-starred restaurant nearby, and the som there is a huge fan. He says it's a total crime that no one can find it outside of Napa because of our limited distro." He paused, his gaze sweeping across the vineyard. "I think it could be a much more significant piece of our business one day, and a really meaningful part of our portfolio, you know? It's exactly the type of venture our Kauffman Group clients would love to invest in." Jamie was practically glowing with this idea. He looked way more excited about it than he usually did when speaking about The Kauffman Group's investment machinations. "Anyway," he said with a shrug, "I just think maybe it could be something special."

I couldn't help but smile at his passion. I knew about as much about winemaking as I did about private equity—which is to say, basically nothing—but I knew one thing for sure. "If you're behind it," I said to Jamie, "I *know* it could be something special."

Jamie squeezed my hand then led me toward a large meadow where half a dozen horses roamed leisurely, stopping every now and then to bend over to munch some grass. He leaned against a wooden fence gone silver with age, and for a second, he looked not quite real. Too perfect, like a photo in a catalogue.

"So, are you going to teach me to ride?" I asked, pulling myself up to sit on the top rail of the fence.

"Maybe. If you play your cards right." Jamie's hands left the fence and started to trail beneath the hem of my sweater. "I did try to teach Sadie and Milo once—with very mixed results," he added, referring to his niece and nephew. "Milo insisted I hold the reins and walk him the entire time; Sadie took off at a canter after about five seconds in the saddle."

I grinned, thinking eight-year-old Sadie sounded like my kind of girl. Though I hadn't met her or her brother yet. "Are they here this weekend?" I asked, pulling the sleeves of my sweater over my hands.

Jamie shook his head. "They're doing the first half of Christmas break with their dad and the second half with Amelia."

"Oh, that's sad."

"Not really. They do Hanukkah with him and Christmas with us. And Amelia and Dan still get along really well. It's very low drama."

"I would definitely not be low drama after a divorce."

"Oh, I know." Jamie huffed out a laugh.

"What does that mean?"

"Sybil, nothing about you is low drama. It's just one of the many things I love about you."

Before I realized what was happening, Jamie had plucked me off the fence and swung me into his arms, holding me bridal style. I let out a delighted shriek as he carried me along the meadow and behind the nearby stables, then into a thin patch of trees. When the world turned right side up again, he'd set me down beside a little hidden creek, barely more than a foot wide.

"This was always my favorite spot to hide as a kid," he said, a bit sheepishly.

We sat down in the shady grass. "I can't imagine wanting to hide if you lived in a place like this," I told him.

"You'd be surprised," he said. And then he added with a sly grin, "The creek is very peaceful, and has the added benefit of not being visible from the house. No one can see us right now."

I was already leaning into his shoulder but then he pulled me on top of him, my legs straddling his waist, his hands on the waistband of my jeans.

I leaned forward, my hair dancing into his eyes. "I had this fantasy of having sex tonight in your childhood bedroom," I said to him. "Is that perverted?"

He smiled. "A little. But in a good way."

I smiled, bending forward into his kiss.

"But I don't want to wait until tonight," he whispered, his lips moving to my neck. "Do you?"

I let myself get lost in the feeling of his hands as they slid under my sweater and gently lifted it up and off me. I shivered against him, the desire for him so powerful, so certain, it was almost out-of-body. It was like being here, in this place where he'd been raised, made me even more connected to him than I'd ever felt before.

"No, I don't want to wait."

THERE WERE VOICES COMING from beyond the foyer when we stepped back into the house forty minutes later. The current of nervous energy that had calmed when I was alone with Jamie whipped back up as we entered the grand living room.

I'd known that Jamie took after his dad, but seeing them side by side, it was uncanny how similar they looked. They had the same chestnut-brown hair and tall build, but where Jamie's eyes were the warm brown of his mom, his dad's were a dark blue. His sister, Amelia, had the same coloring as Jamie but not the height. She barely reached Jamie's shoulder wearing three-inch heels, but she still managed to seem incredibly intimidating. Probably because, as a district court judge, it was literally her job to project a sense of authority. Seated in a wingback was an elderly woman with a snow-white bob, a nearly empty wine glass, and a well-worn Judith McNaught book balanced on the arm of her chair.

Jamie led me over to her. "This is my Grandma G," he said, bending over to give her a peck on the cheek.

She squinted at me playfully. "Jamie tells me you and I share a love of happily ever afters." She tapped the book beside her. "Are you a fan?"

I nodded and smiled. Grandma G stood from her chair and looped her arm through mine, placing a delicately bony hand on my arm. I noticed her large ruby-and-diamond art deco ring—I had seen it in a picture of her on Jamie's desk once. He'd said it was called a "Toi et Moi" ring—*you and me*. I always loved that idea, and how unique the ring looked. It was even more beautiful in person.

"Truth be told, I'm actually more a Johanna Lindsey girl," I admitted as Grandma G began steering me toward the dining room—with an incredible amount of force for a woman of her age and size.

"Ah," she said, "so you like a pirate."

"Love a pirate," I agreed.

"Our Jamie's a little more of a Mr. Darcy type, you know. He's not swashbuckling; he's strong and silent."

"Well, no one's better than Darcy—not even a pirate."

Grandma G gave me an appraising glance. She must have been satisfied with what she saw, because she patted my arm twice and released me. "Good luck, dear." I could've sworn she added, *You're going to need it* before settling into her chair at the far end of the dining table.

As I settled into my own seat, a woman in a black button-up shirt and slacks appeared and asked what I'd like to drink.

"We have everything," Jamie said encouragingly, sensing my awkwardness. I'd never been waited on like this in someone's home. "Patty makes amazing cocktails, and we have wine, of course."

"Oh, um—could I get a vodka martini, please?"

"She likes them extra dry," Jamie added with a sly smile. "And extra dirty."

"Jamie!" I hissed at him. It was true, that *was* my preferred cocktail order. But asking for anything with the word "dirty" in the name in front of my boyfriend's parents was mortifying. "I'll just do a glass of wine."

"Try the cabernet, Sybil," Mr. Kauffman said from his seat at the head of the table. "It's our specialty."

Red wine usually gave me a headache, but turning down Mr. Kauffman's prized passion project seemed like a terrible way to make a first impression. So I just nodded and said, "Cabernet sounds great, thank you."

Moments later, the woman returned with a bottle and began pouring everyone a glass.

"So, Sybil, did Jamie give you the full tour?" Mrs. Kauffman asked.

"Yes, we checked out the grounds when we arrived this afternoon—it's so beautiful here."

"Isn't it?" Amelia said. "I'm dying for a good ride in the meadow."

I choked on my cabernet, my face turning as red as the beets in the salad. Had Jamie's sister seen us cowgirl style in the meadow? Jamie *swore* we weren't visible from the house.

"*Horseback* riding," Jamie muttered to me under his breath, a devilish grin quirking at the corners of his mouth.

Amelia raised an eyebrow at her brother, then turned back to me.

"Do you love riding? I'm sure Jamie could never date someone who didn't like horses. He's such an animal lover."

This was actually news to me—our life in the city hadn't afforded many interactions with wildlife. I looked to Jamie for help, but he just smiled and shrugged, saying, "I was known to rescue a stray here and there, back in the day."

Grandma G leaned in conspiratorially. "He insisted we hold a funeral for a dead skunk once."

"At least it wasn't a funeral for a live skunk?" I said, but no one laughed.

From across the table, his mother rolled her eyes. "Yes, my dear son does have a habit of dragging adorable little mongrels into our home and expecting them to be fed."

The way she said it, with her eyes grazing over me, I could have sworn she was not talking about a stray puppy or lost rabbit but about *me*.

"So, Sybil," Amelia said, taking a swig of her wine. I silently thanked her for interjecting to change the subject. "You went to USC, right?" Amelia's glass of wine flashed ruby as she set it back down and looked at me with a smile that felt... professional. "One of my clerks went there; I wonder if you know her. Kendra Davies?"

I shook my head. "Sorry, it doesn't sound familiar."

"What year did you graduate?"

Oh god. I had chosen that moment to take another long pull from my own glass of wine, but didn't want her to think I was avoiding her question, so I tried to swallow it quickly—and ended up choking and coughing.

Jamie handed me the cloth napkin from my lap, which I wished I could disappear behind like a magic trick, and answered for me. "Sybil was a year behind me in school."

Amelia continued to look at me expectantly, so I did my best to strangle what remained of the coughing fit and shrugged apologetically. "It's a really big—ahem, excuse me—school. I'm sure I crossed paths with her at a Delta Gamma party at some point!"

"Probably not," Amelia said with a tight smile that didn't reach her eyes. "She was a double major in English and poli-sci. Not much time for frat parties."

She said the words "frat parties" with approximately the tone you might use to tell someone to watch out for dog poo. I didn't bother correcting her that DG was a sorority, not a fraternity. Nor did I mention that Ruth Bader Ginsburg, who was a member of Alpha Epsilon Phi at Cornell, somehow managed to find time to attend a Greek party or two while also becoming one of the nation's greatest legal minds.

Eager to change the subject, I was about to compliment Mrs. Kauffman on the beautiful centerpiece when Amelia cut in again. "And what do you do for work, Sybil?"

"I'm actually between things right now."

She sat silently, expecting me to fill in more. When I didn't, she just gave a small "oh!" of surprise. "But your career is in the field of..."

I could feel myself sweating nervously. Amelia may not have been behind the judge's bench, but her version of casual conversation felt like a formal inquisition.

"I'm really a dabbler!" I said helplessly, knowing anything I added by way of embellishment would probably not impress her. She didn't seem like someone who appreciated the merits of high-end dog grooming or who would understand my promising-yet-failed entrepreneurial line of leopard-print scrunchies. I had greater ambitions...I just didn't quite have words for those yet.

"I'm sure something will turn up for you soon," Mrs. Kauffman said. Though she didn't sound sure at all.

The conversation moved on, thankfully, with Jamie and his dad talking shop and Amelia and Mrs. Kauffman discussing some apparently high-profile court case I'd never heard of. I nodded vigorously and gulped nervously at my wine, and when Mr. Kauffman said something about a former client that made his wife laugh, I laughed, too, even though I had no idea what was funny about his comment. But somehow my laugh came out about as loud as a five-piece jazz band, and everyone suddenly went silent again and looked away as if I'd committed some horrid faux pas.

It was truly one of the more painfully uncomfortable meals of my life, and that's saying something considering my own parents aren't always the warmest and fuzziest.

I took a sip of the cabernet, trying to think of a contribution to the conversation. "Wow, this wine really is nice," I said to the table at large. "Jamie mentioned y'all were thinking about expanding production? I could totally see ordering this at any of the best restaurants in LA and New York." I turned to Jamie, "Babe, what were you saying about client investors?"

Before Jamie could even open his mouth to respond, his dad cut in. "Jamie knows it's just a pet project. I've told him, there's no real business model in a vineyard this size." His voice had a disinterested air, but I could still detect a note of finality.

Jamie cleared his throat. "Yeah, my dad's right about that," he said, though his eyes were focused on his glass, I noticed, not on me or his father.

I was surprised—I knew Jamie didn't like to argue, but it seemed so strange that he wouldn't even push back a little bit. Jamie's face in the vineyard earlier had been pure excitement, but now it was just quiet resignation.

An awkward silence descended over the table. I turned my attention to my plate, willing the meal to be over soon and wondering what else Jamie was quietly resigned to.

★ ★ ★

THE MOMENT JAMIE CLOSED the door to our room, I whirled around, covering my face with my hands. "What an absolute nightmare."

He put his hands on mine, pulling them away from my face. "What, dinner? Did you not like the food?"

"The food? The *food*? You let me walk in here totally unprepared for—for *that*!"

"By 'that,' I'm guessing you mean my family." He sighed, dropping his arms. "Look, I know they can be tough to impress. It doesn't mean they didn't love you," he said, with a notable lack of conviction in his voice. "It just takes them a while to warm up."

"Warm up? The way they spoke to me, it was like they're shocked you'd even spend time with me. Like I'm some pathetic rescue you've just adopted." I was trying to stay composed and not betray how much I had loathed every single one of his relations, but I could feel myself growing more and more anxious. The last thing I wanted was to burst into tears and humiliate myself even further. "And what the hell was with the third degree from Amelia? She knows we were at dinner and not in court, right?"

"Babe, come on." He tried to wrap an arm around me, but I pulled away.

"Why is she so obsessed with where I went to school anyway?"

Confusion painted Jamie's face. "She's not—she was just trying to make a connection. I know she's intense, but that's just Amelia. It wasn't anything personal. Trust me."

"And what was that with your dad?" I barreled on. "He just completely railroaded your whole vision for the vineyard, didn't he? Do you really not care about expanding on this place that you love, or did you just not feel like facing up to him? I swear, the only delightful part of your family tree is Granny G."

He closed his eyes and took a deep breath, and when he opened them, he pulled me to him in a hug. This time, I let him. "I'm sorry, Sybil. You're right. I didn't speak up because I was embarrassed."

"*You* were embarrassed? How do you think I felt?" I leaned my face into Jamie's chest, letting his shirt muffle my words. "You, and Amelia, and your parents...you've all got letters after your name, and I don't even have a measly diploma."

"Wait, what?" Jamie pulled me away from his chest, stretching his arms out but keeping his hands gripped firmly on my shoulders.

I sighed, looking down at my feet and not into Jamie's eyes, sure I would find disappointment there. "I never graduated, okay?"

When people asked where I went to school—like Jamie had when we first met—it was easy to rattle off USC. Because I *had* gone there...I just never got my diploma. The fact that I never graduated wasn't something I offered up freely. Don't get me wrong, I know there are plenty of good reasons why a person might drop out of school, or not go to college at all. The problem was, I didn't have any of those good reasons. A week before graduation, my ex-boyfriend Liam had shown up at my dorm, drunk, spewing the same hateful things that had driven me to break up with him three years earlier. With the help of Nikki and campus security, I'd gotten him to leave. But the experience had shaken me so much that I ended up spiraling into a depressive state. When my parents arrived for graduation weekend, they found me in bed crying, having missed all my final exams. The disappointment on their faces still haunts me. I had let myself fall apart because of a boy, which was the really mortifying part.

Especially given the impressive, high-powered career women in Jamie's family (in addition to his sister being a judge, Jamie's mother was a partner in a white-shoe law firm).

I stood there, in Jamie's childhood bedroom, feeling his eyes boring a hole in the crown of my head. Finally, he spoke.

"Sybil . . ." His voice was strained. "Why didn't you ever tell me you didn't graduate?"

"Because I knew you'd think less of me—"

"I wouldn't. I don't."

"—and clearly I wouldn't measure up to your perfect family."

"How many credits were you short?" Jamie asked, ignoring my barb and transitioning swiftly into problem-solving mode. "Maybe you could go back and—"

"I don't need you to fix me, Jamie."

I pulled away from his grasp and crossed toward the closet, looking for something warm to put on.

"What are you doing?" Jamie asked.

"Grabbing a jacket. I need to go outside and get some air."

"We're in the middle of a conversation, Sybil."

"A conversation? Sounds more like a fight to me." My eyes landed on Jamie's Barbour coat—the one he'd been wearing on the drive up. I reached for it, and in an instant, Jamie was at my side.

"Forget the jacket; we need to talk about this."

"Fine. I just need a second to clear my head." I began to

slip my arm into the jacket's right sleeve, but then Jamie was pulling at the left one. "What the hell, Jamie?" He had never been territorial over his clothes before. He was the king of boyfriend sweatshirts, always happy to lend me something to wear. He even admitted once how hot he thought it was, the sight of me in his clothes. So why was he acting so weird now?

"Don't take the jacket!" Jamie's face was white.

"What is the big deal?"

"Just leave it—"

And with that, Jamie tugged, and I let go, and suddenly, the jacket was flung across the room, something small dislodging from one of the pockets and landing with a thud on Jamie's childhood bed.

For a moment, we both just stared.

Then my brain whirred to life, putting the pieces together.

It wasn't just any small item. It was a small box. A small *velvet* box.

"Is that..."

Jamie hastily crossed the room and grabbed the ring box, stuffing it into his pants pocket, his expression unreadable.

I turned my back on Jamie and the little black velvet box, as if removing them from my field of vision could make this whole moment disappear. "I'll just, um...I can forget I saw that. Whatever it was."

I was giving Jamie an out. Surely he wouldn't want to talk about marriage now—in the middle of a fight, during which it was revealed that not only was I a college dropout, but also I'd been lying to him about it for the length of our relationship.

"Sybil." Jamie's voice was soft now, and there was something almost plaintive in his tone that made me turn around.

And when I did, I found him down on one knee in front of me. He was holding the box, which was now open to reveal the most beautiful, sparkling diamond I'd ever seen.

"What are you doing?" I whispered.

"Sybil, you were right. My family *did* suck tonight. They're just overly protective of me. I'll talk to them. They'll do better. And anyway, fuck what they say." A little shiver ran down my arms. I loved it when Jamie let out a swear; it happened so rarely. "I want to marry you. I hadn't meant to do it like this, but none of this changes how I feel about you."

"It doesn't change how I feel about you either," I said quietly. "But Jamie, are you really sure you want to be with me . . . *forever*?"

Jamie reached out one of his hands to grasp my own. "Sybil, when I'm with you, I feel like I've caught lightning in a bottle. You bring color to my world. You have the biggest heart, and you feel things more strongly than anyone I've ever known, and it's contagious. I've spent my whole life doing what was expected of me, following the path they've laid out for me. My family may not be pleased at first, but we'll deal with that later. Right now, all I know is you make me feel happier and more alive than I've felt in a long time, and I never want to lose that. I never want to lose you."

Despite the disaster the evening had turned into, it moved me that his family's bad opinion of me hadn't swayed him. At the time, it seemed like a sign, like maybe we really could be strong enough to overcome that. I'd been engaged twice before, and both of those relationships had spiraled out of control before we made it anywhere near the altar. But this felt so different. It had to be different. I knew how much I loved him. And I wanted to believe in us, to believe it could work this time.

I wanted, above all, to believe that I deserved the love of someone like Jamie.

Which was why I looked into his warm brown eyes and said yes.

8

I REGRET THE *MOHALA* PEPPERMINT BODY WRAP THE MOMENT THE aesthetician starts slathering it on my body the next morning. She told me *mohala* means "heart opening" and described the treatment as "cooling and reinvigorating," which had sounded exactly like what I needed. After saying good night to Jamie last night, my whole body had been left hot and tingling— and I knew it wasn't the twisted ankle. I barely slept. I woke up this morning feeling almost hungover, even though all I'd had to drink was that one mai tai when I first arrived. It was clear I needed a detox, something to douse the feelings racing through my blood. The spa, with its private treatment rooms, seemed like a safe place to spend the day. Not that I'm hiding exactly, but...

Okay fine, I'm hiding. It's the only rational thing to do.

Now, however, I just feel like I've been rolled in a snow-drift. My skin is so "invigorated" I can't relax. All I want is to let the tranquility of the spa room lull me into a soft doze where, for a few minutes at least, I can forget running into my ex-fiancé with his gorgeous girlfriend and then panic lying about being on a romantic vacation with a nonexistent boyfriend of my own.

Where I can even forget Jamie carrying me—somewhat begrudgingly, yet with gentleness—the rest of the way down the hike yesterday. Our bodies smashed together that close, the wetness of his shirt, the sharpness of his jaw, the way his eyes, so determined, looked ahead at the path but occasionally, I caught him glancing down at me...Memory morphs into imagination. I see Jamie press me backward until my spine scrapes along the bark of a palm tree, my arms pinned above my head. I grind against him the way I wanted to before, willing him even closer. Jamie pulls my bathing suit top to the side before his mouth closes around my peaked—

I jolt my eyes open.

Finally, after what feels like an eternity, the aesthetician returns and pulls off the Saran Wrap that has kept me swaddled up like a Christmas-flavored Swiss roll. After she leaves, I rinse off in the shower attached to the service room, and the hot water is a welcome relief. It sluices off the rest of the peppermint wrap, and warmth suffuses me. Stepping out of the shower, I *do* feel invigorated, and my skin feels more supple and soft than I can ever remember it being. I guess it was worth twenty minutes of suffering to feel this good.

I slip into another cozy bathrobe and head through the locker room door to the spa pool. Water trickles down a carved stone wall, and the soothing sounds of a reed pipe play over the crashing of the ocean waves just a few yards away. There's a spread of healthy treats laid out, so I grab a glass of cucumber-infused water and a small ramekin filled with almonds before seeking out an empty lounge chair.

Across the pool, I see a woman with two teenage daughters—the same ones I saw on the snorkel boat yesterday, though I leapt off and swam away before getting a chance to actually meet them. One is more like a preteen, maybe eleven or twelve, and the other sister's older, probably sixteen or seventeen. I can't help but see myself at both ages: the carefree seventh-grade Sybil who still believed in backyard faeries and alien conspiracies, and the senior-year Sybil—rebellious, confused, constantly ashamed of something, and rapidly getting swallowed up in a relationship with Liam. At the time I was dating him, I felt so mature, but looking at this teen girl now, I am struck by how young and clueless I really was. Too much happened too quickly, and I still have the scars today, though they're invisible to pretty much everyone else. If things had gone the way Liam had wanted, I'd be married to him now. In that version of reality, *I* could be the one here at the spa with an eleven-year-old daughter.

I don't even realize that I'm crying until a spa attendant appears at my elbow, silently offering me a tissue.

"Sorry," I say, dabbing at my eyes. "Must have some peppermint oil in my eye or something."

"There's no need to apologize," the attendant says. She has a kind face and calm energy. Something about her reminds me of Gwendolyn Green—maybe it's the linen shirt and pants. "People often have strong emotional responses after their treatments," she says. "It's a natural reaction to your body feeling a sense of relief. Of peace. Please don't be embarrassed."

I nod, thanking her again for the tissue, and watch as she

walks away. But it's not peace I feel washing over me in waves. It's that same wobbly uncertainty I remember from my wedding weekend.

ON THE THURSDAY MORNING before I was supposed to get married, I hopped in an Uber to LAX and boarded a flight bound for Vegas. Cliché, I know, the runaway bride escaping to Sin City, but I wasn't going there to gamble, or party, or even elope. I was going to center myself.

The night before, at my last-minute, pseudo-bachelorette party, the reality of what I was about to do hit me like a freight train. I, Sybil Rain, was getting married. For real this time. This wasn't a hormone-fueled teenage mistake, like it had been with Liam. It wasn't a half-baked flight of romantic fancy like it had been with Seb. This was the real deal.

This was forever.

And my body was full-on rejecting it. I'd felt off all night, seizing up with cramps in my abdomen, and despite trying to distract myself with the company of my closest friends, I returned to my hotel suite a weepy, mascara-dripping mess, trying on my wedding gown in the middle of the night because I was convinced it wouldn't fit. But it wasn't the dress that was the problem.

It was me.

And the secret I'd been holding in from everyone.

Which was why I had to talk to Gwendolyn Green. She's my therapist and a renowned wellness coach, but she's more than that. She's the one person who knows every detail about my history. What happened with Liam back in high school, and everything since. She was the only person I could think of who could help stop my spiraling and understand the source of it.

Only the problem with renowned wellness coaches is that they're in very high demand, and as I frantically dialed her office over and over with no answer, I began to realize I might not get ahold of her. Which was when I looked her up on social media, and saw she was giving a talk in Vegas.

For anyone else, I understand that it might seem a little *not normal* to ditch your wedding to fly out and see your therapist give a speech on women's health and wellness in the hopes of cornering her for a private session after... but I'm not normal.

In more ways than one.

So, heart beating out of my chest the whole way, I told my mom a little white lie—that I needed a special spa treatment—and instead flew to Vegas, touched down, and went straight to the MGM Grand.

By some miracle—and a ticket vendor who was a *very* good listener—I scored a last-minute pass for the conference and slipped into Gwendolyn's talk minutes before it was about to start. Just seeing her take the stage at the MGM Grand in a cream linen top with matching flowy pants put me instantly in a better place. Her ash-blond hair hung in waves to her collarbone. Her sharp gray eyes surveyed the crowd from behind her green-rimmed glasses.

The speech was brilliant—funny, moving. She spoke about the power of self-commitment amid the toxic messaging of society, how no advances in women's health and medical research can be achieved without committed large-scale action. But, to be honest, I wasn't listening that hard. I fidgeted the whole time, waiting for it to be over so I could corner her alone.

As soon as the speaking portion of the event wrapped, I hurried to the book-signing line. I needed to talk to Gwendolyn face-to-face. Finally, I reached the front, and she blithely held out her hand to sign my book, when suddenly, she looked up and saw it was me. "Sybil! So nice to see you! But... what are you doing here?"

"I need to talk to you. I—" I looked over my shoulder at the line behind me, feeling out of place and foolish. But I barreled on. "I know it's not your policy but I'm hoping we could have an emergency session later today? Something has come up."

"Sybil, aren't you supposed to be getting married this weekend? I—I really don't think this is appropriate. Of course I want to help you out, but this isn't the right place and time."

I think that was when I started crying.

She stood up from behind the table and hugged me. I grabbed her shoulders and whispered something quietly in her ear. I needed her to understand how urgent this was. What I was most afraid of in the world.

She hugged me again, tighter this time, then stood back, and said in words that rang something deep within me:

"Sweetheart. I'm so sorry. But I need you to hear me, Sybil. What you need isn't a therapist right now. What you need is a doctor."

AFTER THE SPA, I go back to my room and order room service for lunch. I'm not risking running into Jamie and Genevieve again at one of the resort restaurants. I just need to make it to the day after tomorrow, when he said they'd be leaving.

While I wait for the food to arrive, I unzip the luggage that I have yet to unpack. When I used to travel with Jamie, he found it insanely annoying that I would take so long to settle into our hotel rooms, usually letting my clothes spill out of my open luggage for days until I couldn't tell what was clean and what was dirty.

I can't help it; I'm a messy person. Always have been. My childhood bedroom was a constant disaster of stuffed animals and half-finished science projects. But it was my safe place. The one place where I could really be *me*. Well, there, and my tree house in the backyard. I used to escape there when my "big feelings" got to be too much. My parents weren't therapy people—Mom found the whole thing distasteful, said it was like airing your dirty laundry to a stranger—so I didn't know then that what I was experiencing was a form of panic attack. I just knew that if I wanted to avoid being grounded, I had to make myself scarce until I calmed down. My mom and dad are the sweetest people ever, truly, but their expectations of me have always been high, and their values old-fashioned. Conservative, in the traditional sense of the word. They expected a daughter who fell in line, and instead, I think from a very young age, I was just a little too much for them to grasp. They did their best to polish up my bright sides, and they hid the dark, complicated stuff as well as they could— even from themselves.

I slide my laptop from my tote bag, brushing off some crumbs from a granola bar that disintegrated in my bag somewhere between leaving my place in LA and right now, and spend a few hours editing videos, drafting vlog content for later, doing a little research, and responding to emails. I'm surprised to find it's nearly six p.m by the time I finally look up from my screen. Including my time in the spa, I've basically been indoors all day, which seems like it should be illegal when you're in Hawaii. Maybe I'll do dinner at that cute outdoor tiki bar I passed by on my way to the beach yesterday morning.

Before I go, I do one last check of my work emails. There's a new one from my boss, Meredith, telling me that the reel I posted yesterday with curated video clips documenting my arrival here to Halia Falls is getting great engagement.

The place looks beautiful! Reminder—we also want to do more casual, straight-to-camera reels to encourage people to tune in for the eclipse live stream on Friday where we will be doing the limited discount for channel subscribers only. Thanks, Sybil!

Well, I guess now's as good a time as any. I do a quick mirror check and dab on some blush and a light coat of mascara, just so I don't look totally washed out on screen.

I grab my cell and start recording.

"Okay, so, is anyone else dealing with seriously ridiculous life events right now? Weird things from your past popping up when you least expect them? Feelings you don't know what to do with? Well, we might have Friday's blood moon to thank for that. These kinds of eclipses are often described as wild cards. During this cosmic cycle, anything's possible, so I guess you just have to go with the flow—which I know is easier said than done, trust me. And speaking of going with the flow, don't miss out on Flowies 50% off sale this week! And don't forget to tune into our Instagram live this Friday where your first month with Flowies is free if you subscribe during the live stream!"

Meredith always says our brand needs to reflect authenticity... let's hope she means it. Because I basically just spilled my guts to our ninety-five-thousand followers. Though the only followers who will have any idea what *thing* from my past is popping up are Nikki, Willow, and Emma.

While I'm still holding my phone, a text comes in from Nikki.

Updates?

I had filled her in on my rain-soaked hike with Jamie when I got back to my room last night. How angry he'd been... even when he was carrying me in his arms after I hurt my ankle. She'd been quick to say that maybe beneath the anger was lingering hurt—on both sides. But what did Jamie have to be hurt about? He'd wanted an out, and I'd given it to him. Now he's moved on and he has Genevieve, the kind of woman his family probably adores. What's left to be mad about, really? Nikki's response gutted me. All she wrote back was: *you guys loved each other. It hurts when there's that much love lost.* After that, I silenced my notifications and went to bed.

No sightings today, I tell her now. *#Blessed*

Nikki sends back a praying hands emoji which I "heart."

Just remind me never to get engaged again unless it sticks. I can't have another ex-fiancé roaming the earth hating me. I already have three.

Oh Sybs, she writes back. *None of them hate you. Especially not Jamie. I bet all three of them will always love you. Everybody loves you, Sybil.* Six heart emojis.

I swallow, thinking of what I overheard Jamie say on the boat yesterday. *Everybody loves Sybil.* Like it's a slogan for a TV series. Everyone loves the *performance* of Sybil Rain. That's because I put on a great fucking show. But the guys who get close enough to actually know the real me? Every single one of them is disappointed in the end.

9

THAT'S IT. I CAN'T WALLOW IN MY ROOM ANYMORE. I'M STARVING AND, TO be honest, I could use one of those strong cocktails I helped serve up yesterday. When I get to the beach tiki bar, I spot the same bartender from yesterday wiping down the driftwood bar top. I wave at her, and she raises a glass at me in question. I nod.

The bar is quiet, with only a few patrons sipping predinner cocktails. There are cozy groupings of rattan chairs ringing the bar and even a hammock strung between two posts. A gentle breeze drifts in from the bay, making me shiver.

Dani greets me as I slide onto one of the barstools. "Hey! Sybil, right?" I nod. "Thanks for helping me out yesterday."

"It was no big deal."

"It *was* a big deal," Dani insists. "We're down one third of last year's staff, and we're almost fully booked. Which is great for this time of year, but . . . " She rolls her eyes and then brightens. "Oh, hey—how was snorkeling?"

"It was... fun! *So* fun!" There's no point in telling Dani about my run-in with Jamie after she was nice enough to get me a last-minute spot on the boat. She couldn't have known that she was sending me straight toward the one person I was trying to avoid.

Dani places a glass of water on a dark green cocktail napkin in front of me. I hadn't realized how thirsty I was. The various spa treatments must have left me a little dehydrated. I immediately down half the glass.

"Any suggestions for an excursion I can do tomorrow?" I ask her once I've swallowed. I don't want to lose another day hiding inside.

Dani considers, leaning on the back bar and folding her arms. "The horseback riding is pretty amazing. You go on this path through the mountains to a gorgeous waterfall. Our friend Kaia leads it—she's great."

"Sounds awesome! I love horseback riding!"

In truth, my experience with horses has been pretty limited—a few birthday parties when I was growing up back in Dallas, plus a tour of the stables at the Kauffmans' Napa house, which turned into a literal romp in the hay.

I can feel myself blushing as Dani pulls out her order pad and asks me, "Do you know what you'd like to eat?"

The menu here is fantastic, and I've been eating healthier meals than I usually do at home—but I'm suddenly craving a heaping basket of mankind's greatest triumph over nature: chicken frickin' nuggets. All this dwelling on the past has me wanting comfort food, I guess.

"Do y'all have chicken tenders?"

"I'm sure we can make something like that happen," she says, doing me the decency not to look aghast at my request.

"Thank you! You are a goddess."

"You got it," Dani says as she tops up my glass of water.

"Also, could I grab some ice?"

Dani gives me a look. "There's ice in the water."

"No, sorry, for my ankle. I twisted it yesterday, and it's still a little sore." The spa treatment temporarily numbed out the pain, but it's creeping back in now.

"*Oh*," Dani says. "Should I call the medic—"

"No, no, I'm fine. Just some ice would be great."

"Of course, let me grab you some." I lose sight of Dani as she moves to the other end of the bar that curves around an enormous semicircle of glass and brass shelves filled to the ceiling with liquor bottles.

A few seconds later, she returns with a Ziploc filled with ice. I fold my leg so my ankle is resting on my knee, and balance the bag of ice on top.

"Cool tattoo," I say to Dani, noticing the ring of waves inked around her finger.

"Thanks," Dani says. "Ash has a corresponding one—my wife," she clarifies.

"The concierge? Oh, cool! I didn't realize y'all were married."

"Two years next March." She gives a little one-sided grin. "Hers is the moon, mine's the sea."

"That's so romantic," I say, feeling a tiny twinge of jealousy. For some people, love is just smooth sailing.

Dani's grin turns a little goopy and lovestruck. "We'd been

together for a month, and then one day, I woke up, looked over at Ash, and knew I never wanted to wake up without her. So I popped the question, and we went to the courthouse that morning."

"Wow, so no engagement?"

"I guess we *did* have an engagement. For, like, three hours?" Dani laughs.

I laugh. "Taking your time's overrated," I tell her.

Jamie and I planned our wedding over a whirlwind six months, and he thought *that* was fast. He proposed at Christmastime and our dream venue, usually booked two years out, happened to have a June opening. We jumped at the opportunity—*jumped* being the operative word, because from the moment we signed the contract with Cielo Ranch, I felt like I'd flung myself off the beautiful Malibu mountains and was hurtling headlong into the Pacific below. As someone who struggles to commit to so much as a dentist appointment more than a few days out, I found the entire process intensely stressful. I agonized over passed apps for cocktail hour. I stood baffled in the dress shop, wondering how I should be expected to know what kind of fashion mood I'd be in six months from now. I could see myself feeling the mermaid vibe, but then again, I'd also always been drawn to the flowy fairy princess look…

In the end, I chose a tailored, understated gown that my mother-in-law-to-be said reminded her of her own. It had dozens of buttons and a structured eggshell fabric. It reminded me of a straitjacket. But I'd wanted so desperately to please Mrs. Kauffman that I'd said yes to the dress…and to the orchid boutonnieres, even though they felt too fussy. And to the smoked whitefish puffs even though I thought the mini fish tacos sounded yummier. I'm almost never shy with my opinion, but something about this monumental commitment made me want to show Jamie I could be the bride he and his family wanted me to be.

"Let me know if you need anything else," Dani says, jolting me back to the present, and then she goes to check in with a couple at the far end of the bar. I pull my phone out.

There's a text from Emma in our group chat, sharing some updates on the latest reno she and Finn are working on. In exchange, she asks for more pics of paradise. I snap a quick selfie and turn on my stool to capture a picture of waves crashing onto the shore. Then I pull up the Halia Falls guest page and sign up for tomorrow morning's horseback riding excursion. Soon after, Dani returns with my order, placing in front of me a plate of the most delicious-looking crispy tenders and golden fries.

"Thanks, could I also get some—"

Dani slides a small bowl of ranch dressing beside my plate. I'm about to be incredibly impressed with Halia Falls's commitment to intuiting guests' condiment choices when Dani says, "From the gentleman across the bar," and nods to her right. My spine straightens.

It's Jamie.

My fight-or-flight instincts kick in, making me want to bolt to avoid anything unpleasant or painful. It's the same part of my brain that had me jumping over the side of a boat yesterday afternoon and running down a rose petal–strewn aisle back in Malibu. But surprisingly, as quickly as it came, the feeling passes. Maybe it's because I've already spent so much of the past two days attempting (and mostly failing) to dodge him. Maybe it's the pain in my ankle. But I find that I can't bring myself to push away from the bar and head back to my room.

"Thanks for the ranch," I call down to the other end of the bar. Jamie's head pops around the corner, and I toast him with my ramekin of ranch.

"I can leave." Jamie stands up and comes into full view. He's wearing a short-sleeved linen button-down, his damp hair is curling around his ears, and even after only being here a few days, his skin is already burnished in a deep tan. "If you're waiting for your boyfriend, I mean."

"Oh, no, I—I'm eating alone." I blush, wondering if it's obvious by now that the boyfriend is fake. I haven't even bothered to give him a name. "His, um... he's having gut issues."

"Oh he is, is he? I'm sorry to hear that..." Jamie says, but his lip quirks up to the side, and suddenly I realize the mistake I've made. *Gut issues* was always our code phrase for getting out of events we didn't want to go to. "Well," he adds, clearing his throat. "I'll leave you to your solo tenders date."

"No, it's fine." I motion to the chair next to me. "I mean, you can sit if you want. It's just chicken tenders." Heat rushes to my cheeks, and I feel like I'm inviting my middle school crush to join me at the lunch table.

Jamie's movements are slow, like he's not sure if he trusts that I'm serious. He pulls the barstool out carefully and sits. He takes a moment, looking at me, as if calculating something in his head. Calculating, perhaps, the chances that I've lied completely about having a boyfriend in order to save face...

"How's the ankle?" he asks finally.

"Oh, it's—" My voice breaks off when I feel the ghost of

Jamie's fingers trail along my lower leg. At my sharp intake of breath, he whips his hand away, his cheeks flushing red.

Dani returns with another plate of chicken tenders and fries. She pauses, noting Jamie's new seat, and gives me a questioning look, nodding her head ever so subtly in Jamie's direction as if to say, *you cool with this guy?* But all she says is, "Would you guys like something a little stronger than water?"

The roughness in Jamie's voice surprises me. "Absolutely."

She checks with me first, and I give her a nod.

"What can I get you?"

"How about two dry vodka martinis, extra dirty," Jamie says.

My heart lurches. "Hey," I say softly. "That's my drink."

"You don't say." Jamie gives me a small, bittersweet smile, like maybe this martini is a peace offering after what he said on the boat the other day. And our fight on the hiking trail.

I feel the need to offer up one of my own.

"Um, but you shouldn't feel the need to get a martini just because I want one," I say. "You should get what *you* want to get."

"I know," Jamie responds. "But right now, I want what you want."

Images of exactly what I want flash like a neon sign in my brain, and I blush as Dani returns with our cocktails.

"Thanks," I say to her. She gives me a little salute before crossing to the other end of the bar.

There's an awkward silence as Jamie and I take tentative first sips from our martinis, careful not to spill the liquid that Dani has filled right to the rim of the glass. I can't help wondering what has happened to Genevieve. I haven't seen her since the snorkel boat, though that would make sense since I've been hiding out all day. Still, my imagination has them fighting later that night. Over me. Over why Jamie leapt off that boat to come after me. Why *did* he jump, really? I'm dying to ask, but I don't want to somehow tripwire the argument we already had about it. Not when it feels like we've reached some kind of fragile truce.

Finally, Jamie breaks the quiet by saying, "I watched some of your social media content for that Flowies brand."

I choke a little on my cocktail, olive juice going up my nose.

"You did?" It's not at all what I expected him to say.

He nods. "I was curious after you mentioned them yesterday, so I looked them up. Obviously, I'm not their target demographic, but even I can tell it's really good. *You're* really good, Sybs."

I swallow my next sip of martini, vodka and warmth sliding down my throat. "Thank you, Jamie."

It's not like I've been looking for validation from him. I get that from my boss, from the followers, from my own sense of accomplishment after I nail an edit that goes on to get tons of engagement. But still, it doesn't hurt to know that Jamie sees that I'm good too. That he might even be proud of me.

"They're so funny," he continues. "That one where you're in an Uber asking the driver to take you to all those different stops in a failed search for a lost tampon? Hilarious. And they're honest. They don't feel like an ad, you know? They just feel like...you."

"That's the goal," I say with a shrug. But my heart is pounding, remembering how it feels to be seen by Jamie. To be known by him. "I've been there for almost a year—kind of a record for me." I give an embarrassed little laugh. "But, um, I feel like I've gotten into a groove with the content creation. I really love the work."

"Good for you, Sybs." Jamie reaches a fist over to lightly bump my knee. Then he sighs down into his martini glass. "Honestly, I'm kind of jealous."

"You should be." I nod, adopting an expression of mock solemnity. It's a ridiculous notion, Jamie being jealous of my job given the success he's had in his own, but I play along anyway. "Everyone knows that the hallmark of a high-powered career is free underwear from your employer," I say. "But last I heard, The Kauffman Group was still just doing those complimentary travel mugs. *Lame.*"

"Actually, we've moved on to tote bags."

"Oh!" I throw a hand to my heart. "I had no idea. Well, that's just one step away from Kauffman Group–branded portable chargers, so sounds like things are looking up!"

Jamie smiles, a soft one that crinkles the corners of his eyes. For a moment, I just smile back, wondering how, after everything, we came to be here, in this moment, joking together on an island in the middle of the Pacific.

"Seriously, though," Jamie says, leaning his forearms on the bar. "I think it's really awesome that you found a role where you can shine. Be yourself. Do things your way." He starts tearing at his cocktail napkin. "I don't get to do a lot of that these days." As quickly as it came, his smile has faded.

"Your dad?" I ask tentatively. I know how complicated his working relationship with his father is.

"He just..." Jamie sighs, running a hand through his hair. "He likes things done how he likes them done. He never wants to try anything new."

"Sounds like someone else I know," I say a little coolly. 'Structure and order and certainty...'"

Jamie frowns and starts to twist a little on his barstool, turning to face the ocean—and away from me. "Fair enough."

"Sorry," I say. "I know you're not like your dad. Would your dad have 'jumped out of the damn boat'?"

Jamie grins. "Not a chance." He sighs and runs a hand through his hair. "I have been listening to my instincts more these days, instead of my father's. At least, I've been trying to. My family is great, but sometimes I feel like they have a very specific picture of who I'm supposed to be, what my life should look like—where I should live, what I should do for work, even who I should lo—" He cuts himself off, but the unspoken word lingers between us. *Even who I should love.* Jamie swivels back toward me on his stool. His eyes meet mine, and my pulse quickens. "I just wish—"

"What?" I try to breathe, but the air feels trapped in my lungs. Does he wish what I wish?

Jamie looks at me, fondness and something like regret in his warm brown eyes. "I wish I had started listening to my instincts sooner." He pauses, his eyes studying my face.

"How come?"

"If I had, we would be married right now, Sybil Rain."

The directness of it sends a shiver through me. Does this mean he regrets being with Genevieve? Or, is it possible, maybe, somehow, that they really *are* just colleagues like he said? I feel so overwhelmed and confused—and yet, full of want. I want this to be true. I want all of it to be true.

But his words also paint a different picture than the one I'd been remembering. In my mind, Jamie turning me down at the altar was him finally going with his gut and doing what he'd wanted to all along.

Now, however, it almost sounds like he let himself be convinced not to marry me. Like ending things between us was never what he wanted. And just the thought of that being possible nearly topples me out of my seat. I feel a mix of everything all at once. The grief and heartbreak of having lost him hits me like a wave, yet there's something else stirring within. This crazy spark of hope.

Another moment of silence as Jamie pulls an olive from its toothpick skewer. I give myself one breath to indulge in looking at him the way I used to. At the small scar over his left eyebrow he got from a friend's lacrosse stick in eighth grade, the single dimple on his right cheek, the faintest ring of green around the brown of his irises. I must look too long, because Jamie's smile tips down on one side. Then his eyes are sliding away from mine, down to my lips. The way the heat moves through my entire body just at his glance is out of control.

"Can you even imagine it?" I ask him. "Us, being married?"

"Oh, I *can* imagine it. And I have."

I swallow another sip of martini, feeling the burn not just in my throat but all the way down to my belly.

"If I'd listened to my instincts," he goes on, his voice growing huskier, quieter, so only I can hear, "we'd be here right now on our one-year anniversary, sharing memories of our romantic honeymoon at this very resort."

"Oh yeah? What kind of memories exactly?" I say, an eyebrow raised. "Us getting lost on a hike and arguing over which way to go?"

His lips tip up slightly at one side, and he blinks, as if trying to decide whether to go on. "I think we'd be laughing about how we very much got lost *on purpose.*"

"*Really*," I say with a smirk, playing along as I lean closer to him and drop my voice. "And what purpose would that have been?"

"Oh, you know, we'd heard of a particularly secluded vista—a spot where you can see the whole valley but no one can see *you.*"

I laugh. The martini glass is slick and cold under my fingers—I have to work to keep it steady. "Sounds dangerous."

"It was," he says, his voice still low and unwavering.

I clear my throat, trying not to break into a sweat from the rush of heat that has suddenly overtaken my body. I know we're just bantering but... "And what else would we be remembering? Did we check out the waterfalls?"

"You could say that. We were grateful to them, anyway."

"Grateful?" I set down the glass and brush a strand of hair out of my face.

"The roar of the current was loud enough to cover the sound of your voice as you—"

"Jamie!" I slap him lightly on the arm.

"Have I gone too far?" he asks quietly, his head dipped low, eyeing me from the side conspiratorially. It's almost like he's asking something else at the same time—like by saying yes, I'm confirming that I'm taken, and by saying no, I'm signaling the truth, which is that the "squid man" I claimed to have brought with me here was in fact a complete fiction.

I cross and uncross my legs, trying to figure out what to say. Because I *don't* want him to stop...but I don't want him to know that. "Well, it's *your* imagination," I finally respond, as diplomatically as possible. "I suppose you're just being honest."

"That's exactly how I feel," he says, and something in his eyes is communicating more than just that.

"Okay, so is that all we'd be remembering? It sounds like our honeymoon would have been very outdoorsy."

He laughs softly, the sound of it like a shiver against my skin. "Oh, no. We would have spent most of the time in our room."

By now, I can feel how hard I am blushing. "Doing what, exactly?"

Now it's his turn to blush. "I don't know if I can say what we were up to out loud, Sybil. I wouldn't want to offend anyone."

I take a shaky breath. The way he's talking, the tone of his voice, the intensity of his eyes, the closeness...It's almost too much. I feel heat forming between my thighs, coursing through me. I'm afraid if he keeps going, the need will become too strong. The need for him to touch me. To make good on these promises of things that never came to be. I might do something we both regret. I might—

"So as you can see, Sybil," he says, shattering the fantasy in an instant as he pulls back, "I very much did not listen to my gut. Like usual, I did what I thought was right..."

I swallow hard, struggling to find my voice. "Because of your family," I fill in.

"No! Because of *you*."

The shame that washes over me when he says this is almost unbearable. "Because of what I did, you mean? How much it hurt you . . ." And it's fair, even if that's the only reason, even if he didn't want to marry me just because of how I bolted on our wedding weekend. He's not wrong. It was hurtful and selfish of me. I had my reasons, but that doesn't make it right.

"No," he says again, looking distraught. He swipes his hair out of his eyes and squints at me. "Sybil, you have it all wrong."

"Then what—"

"I did the right thing that weekend because it was what *you* wanted," he says quietly, no longer looking at me but into his drink. "My family kept saying you weren't ready to settle down, but I didn't believe them. Because every time I looked at you . . . I just saw love." Jamie swallows, like he's trying to dislodge a lump in his throat. "But then you ran, and I thought, maybe they're right. That's what I meant when I said I'd been looking for a reason not to marry you. Not that I wanted an excuse to end things, but that I'd genuinely *been looking*. Trying to see what my family saw. Until that moment, I hadn't found anything. But suddenly, it was obvious. You wanted your freedom, Sybil, and when you love someone, you set them free. Right?"

I'm speechless, trying to figure out how to respond, when a new voice cuts through the heavy silence between us.

"Jamie! I've been looking all over for you." It's Genevieve, approaching us from around the bend in the bar.

I jerk back, sloshing the rest of my martini onto my bare legs.

"Oh shit." I reach for one of the cocktail napkins on the bar and start mopping the vodka off myself. My cheeks heat with embarrassment.

Genevieve looks at me. "Hey, Sybil. Boyfriend still busy with the squids?" The sunniness hasn't fully disappeared from her smile, but there's an undeniable edge to her words. She moves to stand beside Jamie, her hand resting on his upper arm in a way that reads as possessive. "J, we need to go over those financial reports tonight. Are you up for it?"

"Uh, sure. Let me just close out my tab."

"Oh no, you guys should stay!" I leap from my barstool and hold out an arm for Genevieve to take my spot. There's a gnawing feeling of guilt. I might be a bit of a flirt, but I draw the line at other people's boyfriends. With how he's been acting, I'm leaning toward believing Jamie when he says they aren't together. But that doesn't mean Genevieve isn't hoping this trip will change that.

And besides, what did I really think was going to happen here? That Jamie and I would both just suddenly forget all the reasons we were wrong for each other, all the ways we hurt each other, and have his way with me right here on the tiki bar?

"Oh, well, if you're sure..." Genevieve is already sliding between me and Jamie.

"Absolutely! I need to get cleaned up anyway." I gesture down at my vodka-soaked legs. "Y'all have a good night!"

As Jamie turns away from me and toward Genevieve, I finally admit something to myself.

I thought whatever was zinging between Jamie and me couldn't be more than residual lust. I thought that I'd swept up all the shards of my shattered dreams by now and pieced them back together into something new. But now I'm not so sure, because there's a sharp scrape against the inside of my chest, and it still feels like a broken heart.

10

For a trip that was supposed to be, at least partly, about rest and relaxation, I've been sleeping terribly. And it isn't Halia Falls's fault. The mattress is firm, the pillows are plush, and the sheets are soft. The problem, once again, is me.

I left Jamie at the tiki bar with Genevieve three hours ago and have been lying here ever since, unable to shut my brain off. In an attempt to exhaust myself into sleep, I try an old trick: coming up with an animal for every letter in the alphabet. *Aardvark. Beaver. Cat.* When I get to Zebra, I start over, this time coming up with Texas towns for every letter in the alphabet. I drift off somewhere between McKinney and Nacogdoches.

Except when I do get to sleep, I slide into one of those awful, lucid dreams, and I'm curled in a ball, crying uncontrollably, hardly able to breathe—like I'm drowning. One of those panic attacks I used to have a lot that first year of college, after the bad breakup with Liam. Full-body sobs wrack through me. From somewhere far away, I hear Nikki's voice, trying to soothe me. Telling me to sit up and wipe my eyes. When I finally do, I'm not in my USC dorm—I'm at my wedding venue in Malibu. And Jamie's there at the end of the aisle, telling me he has to do the right thing—which is to not marry me. And then I'm running away, but the aisle keeps growing longer with every step I take. I'll never make it to the end. I'll never escape the shame.

My eyes dart open for real this time, and I gulp in a breath, trying to calm myself. I'm here. In my hotel room in beautiful Hawaii. I sit up, trying to shake the dread and heartbreak from my dream. It's been a while since I've had one of those panic dreams.

I reach over for the glass of water on my bedside table and take a large gulp, letting the uncomfortable feelings pass through me instead of trying to fight them off.

My phone screen says it's a quarter past four—so just after eight a.m. back in Dallas. I go to my contacts and dial EMMA.

"Oh, thank god," she says immediately, "I've been trying to give you space, but I am dying to hear what the hell is going on with you and Jamie. Wait, why are you up right now?"

"Hello to you too," I say with a laugh. Emma's always been my fiercest protector, my mama bear. When we lived together in New York after college, she was the one keeping track of my insane schedule of side jobs, the one making sure I got home okay from a wild night out and didn't have toothpaste or vodka in my hair the next day. And I know she's always willing to go the extra mile, drive to the end of the road and back to help me mend any mess I'm in—in fact, she basically tried to last year when I briefly ditched my own wedding. The irony is, Emma found love along the way, and I was left with a shattered heart. It's been hard for us both since then; hard for her to watch me struggle when there's nothing she can do to fix it, and hard for me to watch her build the perfect relationship—like the one I *thought* I was going to have. But that doesn't mean that I don't still crave her advice—and her fiancé's—in pretty much every situation. "Is Finn home?" I ask her.

"Yeah, he's downstairs."

"Go put him on speaker, and I'll give you both the latest."

I fill them in on last night's conversation with Jamie—everything from the way my stomach swooped when he laid out the sexy vision of what our honeymoon at Halia Falls would have been like, to my shock at hearing his version of what happened on our wedding day. How he believed that the right thing to do was to set me free.

"It kills me to realize that we both misunderstood each other so badly," I say into the phone. "But maybe that's just further proof that we were never right for each other. I mean, you guys know me better than anybody. Tell me straight: was the idea of me and Jamie together just crazy from the start?"

"I don't think so," Finn says softly.

"Sybil," Emma says, her voice thick with sardonic amusement. "Finn and I literally drove across several state lines trying to find you and drag you back to the altar. Would we have bothered with that if we didn't believe your relationship with Jamie was worth saving?"

I suppose she has a point.

"It sounds like the problem wasn't incompatibility, it was communication," Finn says.

"When did you get to be so wise?" I say, half joking, half

not. Finn has definitely matured from the guy I knew in high school. But even back when we were crashing bonfires in the woods or cramming late at night for a chem test, he always did have that kind of clear-eyed way of looking at the world.

"Maybe when I realized my own communication issues were standing between me and the love of my life," he says. I can hear a faint ruffling of fabric and imagine Emma wrapping her arms around Finn for a hug.

"Ugh, stop. You guys are so cute, it's going to make me barf."

"Sorry, Sybs." Emma laughs, at the same time Finn says, "Not sorry!"

"Finn's right," I say, with a soft laugh. "Don't be sorry. I love you guys."

"We love you too," Emma says. "And you know what else I love?"

"What?"

"Those cute biker shorts I made you pack. Put them on and go for a run."

"I don't run," I remind her.

"You know what I mean. Move a little. Shake it off. I know how you get when you've been languishing."

I roll my eyes, even though they can't see my face. "Got it. Thanks, Mom."

"And don't forget your sunscree—" she says, but I'm already hanging up. Some things really never change.

And I wouldn't have it any other way.

★ ★ ★

BY THE TIME I'M actually out of bed, the first few rays of dawn are licking across the ocean and tropical birds are calling to one another from the thick foliage over my balcony. On this side of the island, the sunrise is slow and spectacular, revealing itself in one layer of silvery-gold light after another, lighting up the sea from a dark, undulating mass into something bright blue and alive.

It's early enough that when I get to the hotel gym, it's still totally empty. One side of the large room is entirely windows lined with treadmills that look out onto the ocean. The other side of the room is one long mirror. I check myself out as I grab a yoga mat. Emma's not wrong; the pink biker shorts are doing their job. With the vivid red cropped cut-off T-shirt I threw on, my hair back in a ponytail, and a slight sheen of humidity across my cheeks and brow, I look less like a sleep-deprived Millennial and more like a dewy, human lip gloss tube. A lip gloss I would buy.

When Gwendolyn suggested my mental health might benefit from getting more physical activity into my routine, I was skeptical, even though Emma had been telling me the same thing for years. While I do occasionally enjoy swimming, I've never been able to hold down a gym membership. I've never been a runner like Emma, either, or a booty boot camp aficionado like Nikki. But much to my couch-potato dismay, it turns out they're right.

I pull up a YouTube that walks me through a flow for "Inner Sanctuary," put in my noise-canceling earbuds, and prop my phone up against a kettlebell. Halfway through the video, I spot movement out of the corner of my eye but keep pushing myself. My thighs are shaking as I hold Warrior 2. Windmilling down into triangle pose, I finally see who's joined me in the gym and almost topple over.

Of course, I shouldn't be surprised. Jamie's regular early-morning exercise routine is something I used to find sickening but later came to appreciate as just another example of his discipline and dedication.

He's on the erg a few yards from me. His rowing form is still impeccable. He makes the worst exercise machine in the room look effortless. Straightening up, I pop my earbud out. "You weren't going to say 'hi'? I know you're not listening to anything."

Jamie doesn't listen to music or podcasts or audiobooks when he exercises because he is a masochist. One time he told me that he doesn't want to be distracted from the *feeling* of working out. He slows his strokes down at my words, the corner of his mouth tipping up in a smile. "I didn't want to interrupt your flow."

I return to my triangle pose, wincing briefly when my ankle buckles.

Concern clouds Jamie's face. "Should you be working out on that ankle?"

I attempt a shrug, but all it does is knock me off-balance. I catch myself, but Jamie stops mid-row, hooking the handle back on the machine before coming toward me. I let myself sprawl into a distinctly un-yoga-like pose. He squats down beside the mat, his elbows braced against his thighs. It's such a familiar pose it unlocks something in me, longing for a time when we were always this comfortable with each other. Reaching toward my ankle, he pauses, meeting my eyes. "May I?"

My pulse flutters against my throat, and instantly the memory of our flirty exchange from last night rushes back through my entire body. Not trusting myself to use words, I nod. Jamie gently presses his thumbs along the thin skin of my ankle. It is a little swollen, but it's been improving every day. "I should have taken you to the medic."

I clear my throat. "They wouldn't have done anything other than ice it. I just need a few days."

He reaches down to help me up but lets go of my hand as soon as he's sure I'm steady on my feet. For a moment, we just stand there, staring at each other, a swarm of unanswered questions filling the space between us. Then my stomach lets out the most obnoxious growl.

Jamie chuckles. "Hungry?"

"Maybe just a little," I admit.

"I have an idea." He grabs my yoga mat and wipes it down, returning it to the wall. "Come with me." He starts walking toward the gym door.

"But wait, what about your workout?" The Jamie I knew was always a man of routine.

But he just shrugs. "It can wait."

He takes my hand again, and something about the strength with which he grips it makes me feel like maybe he never wanted to drop it in the first place. We leave the gym and pad through the empty resort.

Jamie leads me past the concierge desk and around a large potted palm tree to an inconspicuous hallway toward an even more inconspicuous set of doors.

"Jamie!" I whisper-shout. "Where are we going?"

"You'll see."

Jamie's hand is warm in mine as he pushes through the doors. We've left the artfully curated halls of the hotel behind as we step into a dimly lit industrial kitchen.

"So, what are you in the mood for?" He plucks a fresh white towel from a stack and flings it over his shoulder. "You can have anything that doesn't involve the fryer."

I open my mouth, but no words come out. "I—you..." I start, before finally landing on, "I'm sorry—*what*?"

Jamie smirks at my disbelief. "I have my ways," he says enigmatically. Then he adds, a little more sheepish this time, "We should hurry, though; I bet the staff arrives soon to get brunch set up."

I burst out laughing, deciding I don't want to know how Jamie managed to gain access to the resort kitchen, instead preferring just to stay in this warm and cozy bubble where real-life things like logic don't apply.

"Well, well, well," I say. "Who's this new-and-improved Jamie? First you jump off a snorkel boat into the open ocean, then you forgo your sacred gym routine, now you're *trespassing*."

"Maybe you rubbed off on me." The look he gives me sends something sparkling through me from my face to my toes. "Anyway," he says, "what can I make you?"

"Surprise me."

Jamie narrows his eyes, studying me, then nods his head as if deciding something. He reaches for a skillet and slides it onto the stovetop. The burner beneath ignites with a soft whoosh. Then he disappears into a walk-in fridge, and I hop up onto the stainless-steel counter beside the stovetop. It's cool beneath my thighs. There are rustling noises for a few moments, and Jamie emerges with a carton of eggs, jugs of milk and cream, butter, and a couple of apples. He dumps the haul of food on the counter beside me.

Jamie is an incredibly competent person in general, but he especially shines in the kitchen. I remember watching him prepare an entire Friendsgiving dinner on a trip we took to Tahoe. It was the first trip we ever went on together, though back then, I wasn't sure if my crush was requited. By the end of the trip, however, Jamie had finally made his feelings known. My toes still curl remembering our first time together in the little twin bedroom of his friend's lake house. But leading up to that, I spent most of that weekend happy to just be in the same room with him as he diced potatoes and rubbed thyme leaves off the stem between his thumb and fingers. I was mesmerized then, as I am now, by the precision of his knife work—and by the sight of his sleeves pushed up, his lean forearms exposed. Jamie slices the apple into wedges and then into smaller cubes.

"Can you hand me those mixing bowls?"

"Let me help," I say, hopping off the counter. "Just tell me what to do."

"Okay. Slowly mix in the wet ingredients with these dry ones. Can you handle it?"

"Yes, chef." I don't mean it to sound suggestive, but I guess it kind of does because Jamie's face turns red. I clear my throat. "So, remind me again why you never pursued being a professional cook?"

"That was just a fantasy," he says, turning back to the ingredients. "I guess I wanted to be a cook in the way some kids want to be professional athletes. It was never a realistic thing." In a separate bowl, he whips cream until it's stiff.

I think about what he said last night at the tiki bar—about wishing he'd followed his instincts more. "Maybe being realistic is overrated," I say softly. "You shouldn't have to give up your childhood fantasies."

He turns and smiles at me. "Oh, I haven't given up on them, I just have new fantasies now." This time, it's my turn to blush, remembering the fantasies we shared last night over what our honeymoon might've been like. "Here," he says, spooning some of the whipped cream in his bowl. "Is it whipped enough?"

He almost feeds me a taste, but it's like he remembers we aren't actually together, and instead holds out the spoon for me to feed myself. It's sweet and effortless, and I nod, not trusting myself to say more without accidentally groaning in pleasure.

I feel my lips part, and as they do, Jamie's gaze dips to my mouth. He clears his throat and takes a step backward, placing the bowl of whipped cream on the counter and heating up a pan of butter.

The butter has taken on a slightly brown color, and a gentle nutty smell rises from the pan. There's a soft sizzle when he pours on perfect circles of batter. When we lived together, Jamie did most of the cooking. He enjoyed it and was much more skilled than me—plus, I find washing dishes soothing, so our division of labor worked out well. The meals he made were always delicious, but sometimes I felt like I was in a Noma incubator. There's only so much fermentation a girl can take. Once, we'd had rutabaga in every meal for a whole week until I finally revolted and ordered a meat-lovers pizza with extra jalapeños from Abbot's.

Jamie flips the pancakes, and the now-exposed sides are a

perfect golden brown. For a moment, neither of us says anything. The soft sizzling from the pan is the only sound. Staring at the strong curve of his shoulders and back, the way his hair curls up softly at the edges near the collar of his shirt. It's familiar and strange all at once. It's my Jamie, but it's not. He's the same, but different. On the snorkel boat, Jamie said that a lot can change in a year. But some things have only grown more apparent, like the way Jamie always seems to take care of me—in both the big ways, like following me into the ocean, and the quieter ones, like making me breakfast.

I think of what Emma and Finn said on the phone this morning. That compatibility was never our issue, it was communication. Maybe they're right.

I need to tell him the truth—I know I do.

But as I stare at the curve of his back while he works on our breakfast, it just feels so good to be in his presence, I find myself biting my tongue. Afraid to shatter the moment.

I just want to feel taken care of by him. Like I did from the very beginning.

IT HAD ONLY BEEN a few months of me and Jamie hanging out when he invited me out to Tahoe with his college buddies for a Friendsgiving dinner. He'd heard that I was staying in California for Thanksgiving, with no plans besides watching the Westminster dog show and eating a whole jar of cornichons by myself, and insisted I join him instead. I said yes, of course—I had a huge crush on him by that point, even though we weren't actually dating yet. And it seemed like he liked me.

I just couldn't tell in what way, yet. For years, I'd been so used to guys being nice to me because they wanted to sleep with me. But Jamie was nice to me because he was really nice to *everyone*.

When we arrived at the house, Jamie immediately began to prep the meal, shooing the rest of us out of the kitchen. Normally, I had no problem being around new people, but I felt a twinge of nervousness as I settled onto the couch in the living room with his friends. They passed around a bottle of wine from the Kauffmans' vineyard and told me how glad they were that I was here. Though I couldn't help but notice that no one was explicitly stating *in what capacity* I had been invited. Was I just the pathetic friend Jamie took pity on? Or someone with whom he hoped to become *more* than friends?

"You're good for him," Vittal said thoughtfully as we sat in front of the crackling fire he'd built in the lodge's massive stone fireplace.

"I am?" My face flushed with embarrassment, but I was also pleased. Vittal was one of Jamie's oldest friends, and I knew how much his good opinion mattered.

"When he's with you, he's ... lighter," Vittal said softly.

"You pull him out of his shell," Chris added.

"We all know our Jamie boy can be a little shy and awkward," Mike chimed in, and his wife, Shannon, elbowed his ribs. "What! He can! But he is also tall, handsome, and a scratch golfer. So of course Sybil likes him. What's not to like? To Jamie!"

It was their endorsement that made me confident enough to tell Jamie how I really felt. We were standing on the deck overlooking the lake, Jamie looking so handsome and earnest telling me about how he was on the crew team in high school, when suddenly something clicked in my chest. It was like the safety latch on our relationship had finally disengaged.

"Jamie, I have to be honest with you. This trip has been amazing, but it's also kind of been torture for me."

"What? Why?" he said, turning to me in concern.

A combination of lust, confusion, and exasperation threatened to overwhelm me. "Isn't it obvious? I *like* you! But I can't get a read on your feelings at all!"

A smile played slowly across his lips. "I'm sorry for not communicating how I felt sooner."

"Which is?" *Please don't be laughing at me*, I silently prayed.

"I knew you'd just gotten out of something serious. I had too. I just didn't want to move too fast."

"And now?" I asked.

"Now I definitely do," he said, his voice low and full. And then he pulled me toward him and kissed me.

FLASHES OF WHAT HAPPENED after that first kiss are making my whole body sweat with pleasurable memories, and I have to do something to refocus on the present or risk hyperventilating in the resort kitchen.

For his part, Jamie is fully focused on the pancakes, checking the doneness once again, thankfully oblivious to what I'm going through. But as I come back to the moment, all those butterfly feelings of when we first met start to flutter away, and I feel lost again, wondering what went so wrong—or if it had always been doomed from the start. Just another "fantasy."

But just like that night in Tahoe, I can't bear to not know anymore.

"Um, Jamie?" I take a breath. "There's something I have to tell you. About our wedding weekend..."

He stills, the hand holding the spatula freezing in midair. Then he turns away from the stove and folds his arms protectively across his chest.

"Okay." He says it like he's bracing himself.

Okay, I repeat internally, trying to figure out where to start.

"That day we all checked into the hotel in Malibu, I overheard a conversation between you and Amelia." Jamie's brow furrows, but he waits for me to continue. "I overheard her say I wasn't 'marriage material.'" I swallow, willing myself the strength to be vulnerable. "That really hurt, Jamie. It fed into all my worst insecurities about how I wasn't good enough for you."

"Sybil," Jamie says in a whisper, his hand coming to rest on top of mine. "I'm so sorry."

I suddenly feel hot—confessing to my deepest fears is, well, terrifying. Except I quickly realize that fear isn't the only thing making my face warm. A few curls of gray smoke are drifting up from the pan on the stove behind him. "Um, Jamie—"

"Please, Sybil. Let me say this. My sister has always been overprotective of me. But that doesn't excuse what she said. And I told her that. But I think I was worried too—"

"No, Jamie, the—"

"Because you weren't the only one who let their insecurities get the better of them, Sybil. I think I—"

"*Jamie!* The pancakes!"

He finally whips around to face the stove and lets out a swear when he sees the smoke billowing from the pan. I hop off the counter and hand him a dish cloth to use as an oven mitt. He wraps it around his hand before grabbing the pan and pulling it off the burner. I reach around him to turn off the stove.

Jamie uses the spatula to scrape the pancakes free of the pan and slide them onto the cutting board. From the top, you wouldn't know something was even wrong. Two perfectly golden pancakes smile up at us. I reach for the spatula that Jamie has discarded on the counter and flip them over. Sure enough: burned to a crisp. Jamie and I stand shoulder to shoulder, both staring at the blackcned circles.

"Damn it. I'm sorry, Sybs." His voice is grave.

"It's totally fine."

"Are you sure?"

"Yeah, I like stuff well-done anyway."

"Okay..." he says, unconvinced. "Well, bon appétit, I guess."

I glance over at him and see his brow furrowed in the way I remember—a little crease right between his eyes. He looks so disappointed with himself. But also, slightly like a puppy who's frustrated he can't catch his own tail.

So endearing, and yet so ridiculous. He looks like my Jamie.

I can't help it. A laugh bubbles up my throat.

I clap a hand to my mouth to smother it, but it's too late. Jamie's eyes fly to mine. I start to apologize, but before I can, he starts laughing too. It's the most beautiful sound. I start to laugh even harder, until both of us are giggling like children, tears spilling from the corners of my eyes. Tears of happiness, relief, and sadness at what could have been.

After we've collected ourselves, Jamie reaches across my body to grab the knife from where he left it on the counter. He uses the edge of the blade to scrape off the worst of the charred bits, then grabs a bottle of syrup. "We should really let them cool off a little," he says almost to himself before glancing over at me. But my desperation for carbs and sugar must be plastered across my face, because then he adds, "What the hell." There's no more hesitation when he forks a bite and this time, he does feed it to me.

"Oh my gawd," I say around a mouthful of sweet, melted-butter fluffiness. "This is the most amazing thing I've ever put in my mouth."

Jamie quirks an eyebrow at me. "You sure about that?"

For a second, I'm confused, but then I see a devilish glint in his eyes and realize that James Samuel Kauffman has just made a dirty joke.

"Jamie!" I can feel my cheeks redden as my mind is flooded with a few choice memories.

He just shoots me a devastating smile and bites into his own pancake.

Just then, the overhead lights snap on. I wince at the harshness of the industrial glare and turn toward the kitchen's double doors.

"What are you doing in here?" says the gruff voice of a man who is presumably one of Halia Falls's chefs arriving for his morning shift.

My eyes fly to Jamie's.

"What do we do?"

Jamie grabs my hand, and I know what he's about to say before he says it. Because I've felt this way a thousand times before. The racing heart, the wild eyes. Adrenaline surging through my veins. Only this time, I'm not bolting alone. Jamie is right here with me, gripping my hand in his like he never wants to let go.

"Run."

11

WE BURST OUT OF THE SWINGING DOORS AND PRACTICALLY CRASH INTO a startled bellhop, who eyes us with a mixture of amusement and suspicion. "Everything all right, folks?" he asks.

"Peachy!" I gasp, tugging Jamie's hand and pulling him toward the lobby. "Just...uh...testing the fire escape route."

The bellhop raises an eyebrow, but thankfully decides not to pursue it. When we reach the lobby lounge, we collapse onto a plush velvet sofa, the kind that practically swallows you whole. A light rain has started drumming against the massive windows overlooking the ocean, but the clouds are moving swiftly over the water, with breaks where sun leaks through. I think about what Ash said when I first arrived; the rain here is beautiful, and it always brings rainbows.

"Okay," I say, still a little breathless with laughter, "I think we officially owe that bellhop a fruit basket."

Jamie grins, his eyes sparkling with mischief. "Or maybe a lifetime supply of Kauffman Estates Cabernet?"

"Ooh, good call," I say, nudging him with my elbow. "Think your dad can up production by about 500 percent?"

He raises an eyebrow, looking amused but also a bit confused.

But before he can continue the bit, I spot a familiar-looking green cardboard box sitting on the coffee table among some other games. It's Monopoly Deal, a card game Jamie and I used to spend a shameful amount of time playing on random rainy Sundays or when we were stuck somewhere like an airport.

"Shall we?" I ask with a faux-formal gesture.

Jamie chuckles. "I thought you swore never to play against me again after what happened last time."

"I was petty furious Grandma G let you cheat," I say with a grin. "She always seemed like such an honest woman." I'm busy shuffling through the cards, so I don't notice the shadow that's crossed Jamie's face until I look up to ask, "How is she, by the way?"

"She...she passed away last year. Around Christmas."

The news hits me like a punch to the gut. "Oh, Jamie," I say, my voice thick with emotion. "I'm so sorry. I had no idea."

He shrugs, trying to appear nonchalant, but I can see the sadness in his eyes. "Thanks. It was pretty sudden. But we were all able to be there with her. And she lived a good, long life."

"That doesn't make it hurt any less." I reach over to take Jamie's hand. "She was an amazing woman," I say, my voice cracking. "She always treated me like family, even when..." I trail off, not wanting to dredge up old wounds.

Jamie squeezes my hand back. "She really liked you, Sybil. She always said you were a bright light in my life."

We sit in silence for a moment, the weight of the unspoken hanging between us. A year. A whole year we've been apart, missing out on each other's lives, unable to share the joys and sorrows.

Jamie clears his throat, breaking the spell. "What do you say? Care for a rematch? In Grandma G's honor, of course."

"Bring it on, Kauffman," I say, narrowing my eyes. "But don't expect any mercy this time."

We settle into a comfortable silence, the familiar drawing and flipping of cards.

After demanding one of my property cards, Jamie breaks the silence. "So," he says, his voice regaining its playful lilt, "tell me more about this marine biologist boyfriend of yours. What's his name again? He sounds..." I am certain he's going to say *fictional*, but instead he raises an eyebrow and says, "*fascinating.*"

I roll my eyes but can't help the smile that tugs at my lips. At this point, I think it's obvious we both know where this joke is headed. "Oh, he is. Absolutely fascinating. The total package. You might even call him a *fantasy* boyfriend."

"You know what else is fascinating," Jamie says, taking his turn to draw two cards, "is how I have yet to see him even once over these past three days." I can see the amusement in his eyes. We're only halfway through the game, but he looks like he's already won. "Tell me, does his research also include experiments on invisibility? Because that *would* be—"

"If you say 'fascinating' one more time..." I interrupt.

Jamie just smiles. He's clearly onto me, the little liar that I am. Would it be so bad if I were to fess up and admit to the whole charade? It would be mortifying, of course, to reveal how insecure and immature I still am. But it seems like Jamie already knows the truth anyway. And when I look at him, really look at him, his eyes are filled with a gentle warmth. A quiet understanding that makes my fears seem silly. He's not judging me; he's waiting, patiently, for me to open up.

Just then, his phone rings. He glances at the screen, and his smile falters. "It's Genevieve," he says, his voice laced with a hint of apology.

My stomach plummets. Of course. Genevieve.

"I should probably take this," he says, setting down his hand of cards and getting to his feet. "I'll be right back."

"Don't worry about it," I say, forcing a smile. "I think I'll head up to my room anyway. I should shower."

He hesitates, his eyes searching mine. "Are you sure?"

"Yeah, I'm sure," I say, trying to sound casual as I start gathering up all the cards and unceremoniously shoving them back into the box. "See you later."

He gives me a small smile and heads toward the front doors to take the call outside, where the rain has already stopped. I watch him go, my heart sinking.

With a sigh, I head toward the elevators. I'm so distracted by my own thoughts that I walk headlong into another person.

"Whoa, there." A man grabs my shoulders to steady me, and I look up into a pair of startlingly familiar blue eyes.

Oh. My. God.

"Seb—" The word comes out in a breathless exhale.

I can't believe it. Is it possible that somewhere between the couch and the elevator bank, I simply passed out and am now having some sort of ex-fiancé-related nightmare?

Sebastian Wallace-Conway. Broad chest, sandy-blond hair,

rucksack slung over his shoulder. The last time I saw his face was ... well, technically it was in his little profile picture on his Instagram account when we were messaging two days ago.

And now he is somehow here, in the flesh.

"What are you *doing* here?"

He flashes his trademark grin. "I told you I was coming." His blue eyes twinkle.

"What?" *Am I hallucinating this conversation?*

"I took a puddle jumper, like you said. Thought I'd come visit an old friend."

I'm still not really following ... "You what?"

"Besides, all that talk about being alone at the beach? I knew you wanted company."

Oh my god. He was serious about that?

I'm still barely comprehending the situation, but seeing him here now, in a rumpled linen shirt and khaki pants with his blond hair ruffled by the sea breeze and his blue eyes still as bright as sapphires, it all feels familiar. I remember the addictive rush of all the highs and lows with Sebastian. Grand romantic gestures to spackle over the disappointments.

I've lost myself in my thoughts again and don't notice Jamie and Genevieve walking toward us until they're almost upon us.

Genevieve has a huge smile on her face. "Sybil! This must be the boyfriend!" she exclaims, with something that, dare I say it, sounds a little like relief.

"The boy—" Jamie starts to repeat with a confused look on his face. But he stops mid-word when he recognizes the man I'm standing next to. Jamie looks from me to Sebastian and back again. They've never met, but Jamie obviously knows who Sebastian is. We did the whole "postmortem of exes" thing after two months of dating. When I showed Jamie Sebastian's picture, he gave a cocky little half smile and said, "This guy? He looks like an Indiana Jones wannabe." I'd giggled along with him, even though part of me had felt his assessment was a bit unfair.

But there's no confident smirk on Jamie's face right now. He looks completely blindsided. Not to mention, I'm sure he's wildly confused. He knows Seb is a photographer, not a marine biologist.

"We've heard all about you," Genevieve is saying to Seb. "Your research sounds really interesting."

"Hi," he says, gamely shaking their hands, because that's just what Seb does. Goes along to get along. It's always been his way; it's why he has friends all over the planet, in at least three dozen different countries. "My research?" he adds.

"He really is diversifying!" I say, brightly—almost hysterically— "We were just heading out, right, Seb?!" I'm basically shouting, though in the back of my throat I kind of feel like I'm about to cry or maybe even scream.

"But Syb, what's—" Seb starts.

Which is when I do the first stupid thing that comes to mind, and kiss him.

12

THE SECOND RING

SEBASTIAN WALLACE-CONWAY IS THE REASON WHY I NEVER LEAVE HOME without my passport. He blew into my life on a sultry summer night six years ago, cajoled me onto a flight to South Africa a week later, and hasn't ever fully exited my life since.

I was twenty-three years old and had arrived in New York about a year prior in a ball of ecstatic energy, certain I would land the job of my dreams and figure out all the grown-up things you were supposed to figure out about yourself out there in the world. But New York wasn't turning out to be the perfect place to find myself after all. There were too many options for someone like me—seventeen dive bars vying to be your favorite local spot, twenty-four "most stunning view" rooftops you had to hit up for happy hour, too many cute guys randomly lending you a dollar at the coffee cart on the corner of Madison and 24th (or standing in line behind you at the Strand, or kindly holding open the subway doors as you dashed down the stairs of the subway station in heeled boots). A zillion and one job postings that allowed you to imagine your life taking a fresh path. I was inside a pinball machine, pinging around with absolutely no direction whatsoever, and some little voice in my head was a tiny bit afraid I'd stay stuck that way forever.

Then, while waiting in line for some supposedly life-changing doughnut, I met a woman named Amity Floyd, who complimented my outfit (specifically, my turquoise feather-bottomed pajama pants). Turned out she was an ex–soap opera star, which of course I had a million questions about. We ended up talking and sharing doughnuts for over an hour and somehow it came up that she needed a house-sitter for a week while she was out of the country. She was worried about leaving her home unattended during high season, something about rowdy neighbors who wouldn't stay out of her pool. I jumped at the chance. Firstly, because who turns down a *paid* week in the Hamptons? And secondly, because my mom's words from a few days before were still ringing in my ear. *You lost another job? I'm giving you six more months in New York, then I'm pulling the plug.*

I had to make this work. I couldn't leave Emma on the hook for half the rent to our apartment. Even with a decent starting salary from the design firm she'd been working at since we graduated, there was no way she could swing the full $2,600 a month our little East Village two-bedroom was costing. But still, despite the long hours and demanding clients, I knew that Emma loved her job. I could feel the sense of purpose radiating off her each morning as she slipped on her sneakers, tucked her three-inch pumps into her tote bag, and headed for the subway. Everyone I knew in the city seemed to be flourishing. They loved going to their grown-up office jobs and staying until eight p.m. and talking about how busy they were when they went straight from work to cocktails. But I just wasn't any good at faking it. Leaving the office when it was dark outside was *terrible*. Being stuck in the same spot for hours on end was *horrible*. Eating a salad alone at your desk was *depressing*. Every time I'd gotten an entry-level job in *anything*, it had imploded in a cloud of "Can't you take our work seriously?" and "No, Mark. I don't give a shit about 'disrupting' the bodega industry."

But this job, house-sitting for Amity Floyd, was going to be a walk in the park. I was going to Eat, Pray, Love my way through the week and get back to the city fully refreshed. I was going to be a lady of leisure. If I ended up inviting a friend or twelve back to the house, I was sure I could have it cleaned up before I left. And if I ended up with someone else in my bed for a night or two, that wouldn't be the worst either. It'd been years since I'd been in a serious relationship, not since my high school boyfriend, Liam. I was enjoying being unattached in New York, letting myself fall into whatever romantic escapades the universe threw my way, but the truth was lately, nearly all the action in my love life came courtesy of the romance section at the Union Square Barnes & Noble and a vibrator Willow had mailed me because I "sounded stressed." Maybe I just needed some new scenery. To get away from the city and its teeming population of finance bros and skinny-mustached writers. This trip to the Hamptons, I'd decided, was going to be the best week of my life. Whatever troubles I had could wait until I was back in the city next Sunday.

I'd arrived at Penn Station with a whole three minutes to spare, and even managed to snag a seat on what I knew would be a full train. Sure enough, as we traveled east, more and more people crowded into the car. At Jamaica, the big transfer station in Queens, a gaggle of college girls clambered on, a cloud of spray-on sunscreen and Marc Jacobs Daisy in their wake. Then, just as the doors were about to close, a man shot through them, nearly losing his balance before grabbing onto one of the handrails. The commotion—along with the wave of giggles that spread through the girls—caught my attention.

The man who boarded the train was so gorgeous I had to blink twice to make sure I wasn't imagining him. Golden hair, a partially buttoned Oxford shirt, rumpled khaki shorts, and canvas shoes. Blue, blue eyes. They met mine, and my whole body felt electrified. More people crowded onto the train, and Hot Oxford kept getting pushed farther and farther away from me. Wedged in between the window and a girl in a crop top starting her second bottle of rosé, there was no way I could casually start up a conversation with him. He smiled at me, then motioned to the mob of people between us, shaking his head in regret.

For the rest of the ride, it was like my body was attuned to his, my eyes constantly drifting toward his end of the train car, watching as his hair ruffled under the AC vent, how the bright sun glinted off his blue eyes. Finally, the train pulled into the Bridgehampton stop, and about half the passengers began to clear the train car. This was my moment. He was walking my way. I was going to talk to him. But then he shot me a smirk and a small salute before pulling a beat-up leather bag from the overhead bins and exiting the train car. I seriously considered getting off too. But I had to make this job work. I couldn't jeopardize it for a pair of perfect blue eyes and tousled blond hair. I watched through the window as he stood for a moment on the platform, as if he, too, was mourning the loss of what could have been. And then, the train rumbled back to life, carrying me away with it.

Ten minutes later, I got off at the East Hampton stop, wrestling my luggage out of the train before calling a car to take me to the address Amity had sent last week. After so long in the city, I'd forgotten how good air could smell when it wasn't steeped in piles of garbage and pumped full of exhaust fumes. The Lyft passed between a towering privet hedge and crunched over pea gravel before pulling to a stop in front of an enormous shingle-style house. I couldn't believe I was going to spend the next week here. The inside was just as colorful and opulent as I would have expected of a former soap star. In the entryway, whose walls were adorned in a vivid chartreuse wall-paper, a massive, curved staircase rose up to the higher floors. I flicked on the modern chandeliers and passed poppy Ashley Longshore–esque paintings, as I walked from one vibrant yet tastefully decorated room to the next, finally ending up in a gigantic sitting room with floor-to-ceiling windows that looked out onto an immaculately manicured lawn bordered with fluffy white hydrangeas. Hanging above the massive fireplace was a portrait of Amity surrounded by four very short-legged corgis.

After settling into a black-and-white-film–inspired guest room with a view of the ocean, I took one of the bikes in the garage—which I could not picture Amity ever riding—to the closest grocery store and stocked up on cheese, crackers, spar-kling water, and Honey Nut Cheerios.

While I was loading up my bike basket, I spotted a flash of golden hair across the street. My heart started hammering wildly. It was the guy from the train. There he was, across the street, coming out of a liquor store straining under two large boxes. I threw my Brie into the basket and made to rush across the busy two-way road to—to what? To say hi? To introduce myself? To ask if he felt the same strange, cosmic pull between us? But by the time the light changed, he'd loaded the boxes into his car and merged into traffic. I considered flagging him down, but as the thought occurred to me, I suddenly realized how insane that would be. What if he didn't even remember me from earlier this afternoon? He was so gorgeous, I bet he made eyes at girls on every train ride. Deciding I also needed some wine to make it through the next week, I crossed the street safely and ducked into the liquor store that Hot Oxford had just left.

Back at the house, I sent texts to everyone I knew was out east this weekend, but didn't get any bites. It looked like I was going to be riding solo tonight. I poured myself another glass of wine and carefully made my way upstairs to watch the sunset from the terrace off the primary suite. *This is fine*, I told myself. I could handle seven days of a solitary existence. It might even be good for me. Zen, or something. A chance to figure out what the hell I was doing with my life. (And/or take a casual scroll through Hamptons Tinder.)

But as soon as I opened the balcony door, I was hit by the pounding thump of bass from what was apparently a pretty happening party next door. Looking down over the hedges separating the properties, I could see a DJ was set up at the far end of the neighbor's pool, and guests were moving between the cocktail tables set up outside and in the interior of a house even more enormous than Amity's. I leaned my arms over the railing, watching, feeling the energy, the *life* that was emanating from below.

Embrace the Zen, I told myself. *You don't need to go crash a party just because you're bored and lonely...*

Oh, who was I kidding? There's no amount of inner peace that beats good music and an open bar.

I hadn't brought anything cocktail attire–worthy, and I paused for a moment before remembering the huge walk-in closet in the primary suite. If I borrowed something, I could totally dry-clean it before I left, and she'd never know, right?

The closet was full of color and flamboyance, to be expected of someone like Amity. To be honest, it was the closet of my dreams, if I had a couple more zeros to my name. Skimming my hand along the dresses lining the far wall, my gaze caught on something sparkling in the far corner. I pulled the hanger from the closet rod to get a better look. It was a shell-pink slip with a shimmery mesh overlay. It felt like something a mermaid might choose if she came ashore. I slid on a pair of my own shoes since Amity's were all three sizes too small, swiped on a magenta lip, and slipped out the front door before I could change my mind.

I crunched down the crushed-shell driveway and onto the sidewalk. There was a line of cars waiting for the valet stand backed up all the way to Amity's house. A small group of arriving guests were walking toward an arched trellis that led around the house into the backyard, and I hustled up to walk close behind, like I belonged with them, then peeled off as soon as I was halfway across the lawn.

Plucking a glass of champagne from one of the servers passing by, I made a point to look like I knew where I was going. The first rule of being at a party alone is to never stay still, so I walked past the pool and the DJ booth and out to the edge of the lawn. The pounding bass quieted as I reached a set of wooden stairs that led down to the beach below. I took a moment to watch the edge of the sunset dipping below the horizon, willing some sense of the clarity I'd been hoping this trip would give me. *Come on, universe. Give me a sign.*

"Train Girl."

I whipped around to find him—Hot Oxford—somehow standing there, now dressed in a linen suit, his golden hair catching the ocean breeze.

"Train *Woman*," I corrected.

"Train Woman," he repeated with a smile. "I didn't expect to see you again. What brings you here?"

"Oh, I come to all of these parties." I motioned back toward the house with my champagne flute.

"All of Landon's parties?" He moved to stand beside me and look out toward the water.

"Yeah, Landon and I go way back."

"Do you?" he said as if he didn't really believe me, and I wondered if he was about to tell me to pack up my stolen outfit and go. "You do a lot of angel investing, do you?"

"Loads. Cherubim, seraphim, a cupid now and then. If an angel needs investing in, I'm the girl they turn to. Woman, I mean."

He let out a laugh, and I got the feeling like I'd surprised him. Up close, he was even more gorgeous than I could tell from the glimpses I'd gotten on the train and from across the street in town.

"I'm here with my boss. And you're here with...?" He let the question trail off and brought the beer he was holding to his lips.

"My friends left to go to another party." I had to stop myself from reaching toward him and pressing a finger to his dimples.

"And you didn't want to go with them?" he asked.

"I like the vibe here." I took another sip of my champagne and frowned when I realized it was finished.

"It's a good vibe." He took the glass from my hand. "Do you want to come inside with me to get another glass and say hi to Landon?"

I took a deep breath and let it out in one long exhale, hoping that whatever was buzzing between us would be enough for him to either keep quiet about my gate-crashing or come with me if I got kicked out. "Look, I'm not actually an angel investor. I'm house-sitting next door."

"You don't say." His eyes flicked to the hedge that separated Landon's property from Amity's.

"Ah yes, Amity Floyd. We met under"—he paused as if searching for the right words—"*interesting* circumstances." He gave me an appraising look as if deciding how to proceed. "One of her dogs escaped, and she came over here looking for it while I was in the pool with a friend." He gave a little cough into his beer. "Without any clothing on."

"A friend?" I asked.

"I'm very friendly." Sebastian's smile was a combination of pure, unadulterated confidence with a dollop of playfulness, and it was melt-your-clothes-off hot.

"I'm sure you are." A laugh bubbled out of me. "But why would you go skinny-dipping in a pool when the ocean is so close?"

He raised his eyebrows. "Is that a challenge?"

"It's an observation." His bright blue eyes met mine, and lust fizzed through me. He must have felt something, too, because his eyes dipped briefly to my lips.

"I'm Sebastian." His words were quiet, almost whispered, like he was telling me a secret.

My own name came out equally as soft. "Sybil. Sybil Rain."

"Come to the beach with me, Sybil Rain."

"Okay." At that moment, I would have followed him anywhere. He flagged down a server to take our glasses and pulled two more off a passing tray, handing one to me. We walked down the steps into the sand and Sebastian led us past a copse of trees away from the sight line of the party.

I wobbled as I bent down to unbuckle my shoe, and Sebastian's hands were around my waist in an instant steadying me. The shock of his touch sent something racing through me, and the crackle from earlier burst into a roar. The familiar centrifugal force of when I say "yes" to something began to pull at me, and I felt myself barreling toward something inevitable.

Somewhere in my chest, a cog that had been slightly off-kilter settled into place, and the mechanics of my heart that I'd thought rusted beyond repair after my terrible breakup with Liam in college began whirring back to life. I knew if I stood there, he'd kiss me. But I wasn't ready. I wanted to drag this moment out like saltwater taffy. Shooting him my most incandescent smile, I spun away and waded a few feet into the water, gathering up Amity's dress in my arms to keep it away from the waves. It was still pretty early in the summer—the water was bracingly cold but felt so good. I turned back to see Sebastian's blue eyes locked on me, bright with intensity. I was surprised to see he hadn't bothered to roll up the ankles of his pants. He was striding toward me in the water, waves lapping at his legs, drenching the linen suit, and in that moment, I was struck with the certainty that we were going to sleep together.

He reached for my hand as he got closer. "You're very interesting." His finger started tracing the veins up from my wrist to the crook of my elbow, and I shivered.

"Oh yeah? What's so interesting about me?" My words came out breathy.

"You just throw yourself into things, don't you? Consequences be damned."

I smiled. "These consequences don't seem too bad, so far. What's the worst that could happen right now?"

He smiled back. "We could both get our clothing very, very wet."

"A bit too late for you," I said.

"You're being very careful with that dress, though," he noticed. He traced his hand along the hem, along my thigh, which was now exposed. A thrill went through me, and I had half a mind to throw myself on him right then.

But I kept my cool—for the moment. "It's not mine," I said, as much to remind myself as anything else. I could not let my horny personality ruin someone else's dress that I had no means to replace! At least, not this early in the night...

"An imposter at the party, and not even wearing your own clothes? Who are you, Sybil Rain?"

I laughed. "To be honest, I think I'm still figuring that out."

It was hard to concentrate while Sebastian touched me. "My most promising job prospect right now is a canine-obsessed soap opera star."

His lips tipped up in a smile, but this time, it wasn't scorching. It was tentative, but the small break in his confidence made me want him even more. It was like seeing the slightest crack repaired with gold, and I wanted to drag my fingers along those sparkling seams. "We have that in common."

"We do?" The laughter was gone from my voice, replaced by breathy seriousness.

"I'm not interested in being Landon's assistant. I just took the job because of his connections." He paused, and his blue eyes met mine with an intensity that rooted me in place. "I want to travel the world. To work as a photographer. To cover important and beautiful things. Right as they're happening. I want to really see the world and be a part of it." He said the words quickly, almost like he was embarrassed by them, but each one surged through my body like an electric current. The whirring in my chest had gone into overdrive, and I worried I might spin apart. I placed a hand on his chest to keep myself upright, almost dropping the edge of the dress into the splashing waves. Everything Sebastian wanted was what I wanted: no desk job, no schedule, no limits. He wanted a life of adventure, and he had a plan. The one thing I lacked.

He pulled his fingers from my skin and curled them around my hands as if he knew the question would require my full attention. "Hey... Could I photograph you?"

"Right now?

"Right now."

"Okay." And with that answer, we crashed into inevitability.

In the few moments it took for Sebastian to retrieve his camera from the house, I pulled off the shimmering mesh overlay and threw it on the sand. I considered keeping the slip on. But I couldn't risk ruining something of Amity's so I pulled it over my head too. To this day, I don't know why I decided I wanted this near-stranger to photograph me naked, but I guess even then, something about Sebastian made me want to show him everything. He felt like someone who could handle all of me, just as I was.

"Wow, you look..." Sebastian's voice came from behind me. "Do you mind if I take a picture of you like this?"

I looked over my shoulder, unhooking my bra and letting it fall to the sand. "I don't mind." I shimmied out of my underwear, tossing them away. I could hear the soft click of Sebastian's camera as I waded back into the water. Being the full focus of someone's attention was exhilarating and intimate. It sent tingles across my entire body more intense than his fingers on my skin. Dipping my head beneath the waves, I didn't turn to face him until the water reached above my breasts. He followed me until the water lapped against his waist, taking one last photo.

I've seen the photo a hundred times: my hair plastered to my shoulders like a selkie rising from the sea, my eyes wide with lust. He splashed back to the beach to put his camera down, joined me in the water, and we had sex in the ocean.

I thought it was the most romantic night of my life. Even after Sebastian's boss, Landon, discovered us on the beach, in the middle of round two, and promptly fired Seb from his assistant duties.

With Sebastian, all the parts of me that had felt unacceptable before suddenly made sense. I'd finally found someone who fit even less into a mold than I did. He was the complete opposite of my first fiancé, Liam, the golden boy who'd wanted to wrap me up and put me in a box. *That* relationship had been all perfectly posed photos and stiff smiles hiding a silent scream. But with Seb, it was freedom and fun and anything goes. The constant self-doubt that had plagued me during my time with Liam finally began to fade. No more forced smiles or hiding the messy, complicated parts of myself. I started to embrace my quirks, my passions, the things that made me *me*. Suddenly, the world felt bigger, brighter, full of possibilities. I wasn't afraid to try new things, to speak my mind, to chase my dreams, even if they seemed a little crazy. Sebastian had given me back the courage to be myself, and that changed everything.

From that night on, we were together—even though we weren't always physically together. Seb became the photographer he dreamed about being, and his passion took him all over the world. But even through the tensions of long distance, through all the breakups and makeups, I allowed myself to begin to imagine a life where Seb and I were each other's forever.

THE PROPOSAL CAME TWO years after that first Hamptons meeting, when we were on a trip to Key West, a last little vacation before Seb started the new job in Tokyo. We stayed in a white Craftsman bungalow with acid-green shutters and spent the week drinking mojitos and eating fried conch.

On the last day, we decided to spend the afternoon on a boat, hopping from island to island. Sebastian had been blasting Jimmy Buffett from the speakers "ironically," but my father has always loved Jimmy Buffett completely unironically, so I did too.

Sebastian killed the engine on the boat, and we drifted for a few minutes until he dropped the anchor a few dozen yards off the coast of a small island. I climbed up onto the edge of the boat, about to jump into the water, my hand braced on the ladder that led to the platform above the helm.

The music cut off, and Sebastian asked, "Do you think you could live like this forever?"

I turned to face him but didn't leave my perch on the side of the boat. "Are you asking if I could drink rum and frolic on a beach for the rest of my life? Absolutely. Hard yes."

He left the steering wheel to stand behind me, putting both hands on my hips. I turned to face him. He was still on the deck, and I was on the ledge, so he had to tilt his head up at me, and his eyes, which were always spectacular, seemed even bluer after days in the sun had left his skin tanned and even more golden highlights in his hair.

"Seriously. Could you live like this? Moving from place to place without a home base?"

Without a home base. It sent a little shiver of uncertainty through me. I'd spent so much of my life feeling like that. Every time my emotions got too big as a kid or my passions too intense as a teenager, my parents looked at me like I was an alien. Of course, that house was home, technically, but I didn't always *feel* at home. Some part of me had been seeking that feeling ever since.

But as I looked at Seb, I thought, *maybe a person can be your home base.*

My hands came to his shoulders. "I could do anything as long as I was with you." I leaned forward and kissed him chastely on the lips. Then I spun around and leapt into the water.

When I returned to the surface, I turned back toward the boat, treading water. "Come catch me," I taunted and started kicking my way to shore.

Seconds later, there was a splash behind me, and Sebastian, with his strong arms and legs, reached me in moments. We clomped onto the beach, and he caught me around my waist again, pulling me to him. He kissed me, and this time, there was nothing chaste about the kiss. He lowered me to the sand and made love to me slowly, like I was something worth discovering.

Afterward, we lay there for a while, the surf lapping at our feet.

Sebastian reached for a strand of seaweed and pulled my hand to him. He started winding the seaweed around my ring finger, and I felt tears pricking my eyes. It was just so *us.* "Sybil, I can't imagine ever finding someone else as magnificent as you. You're a force of nature, and I love you." He tied the seaweed off and kissed my knuckle. Then his eyes held mine. "Would you stay? Forever?"

I pulled his face to mine and kissed him. I didn't ever say yes; we both knew my answer.

He hadn't been wrong—I was a force of nature. And so was he. It was what we loved about each other, but how could we have ever thought that was sustainable? Soon enough, the undertow of life got the best of us, pulled us out to sea, and what had seemed so spontaneous and free about our relationship turned to chaos, that almost-drowning feeling when you desperately want someone to be there for you, and they simply can't be.

But in that moment, all I could see was Sebastian. And the person I was when I was with him.

Someone wild, and precious, and alive.

13

"So let me see if I've got this straight—"

Seb is sprawled across my hotel bed, his golden-blond head propped up on one hand, blue eyes dancing with amusement.

"You're getting way too much enjoyment out of this," I tell him, pacing my room.

"—your ex-fiancé, the guy you left at the altar a year ago, randomly pops up at the same resort where you are covering a once-in-a-lifetime eclipse, and now you need me to pretend to be your fake boyfriend so you can save face in front of Jamie and his hot new girlfriend? Do I have that right?" Seb says, pushing himself into a sitting position, his back against the headboard, legs crossed at the ankle.

After our run-in with Jamie and Genevieve in the lobby, where I introduced Seb as my previously absent, Very Important Marine Biologist Who Used to Be a Photographer boyfriend, I dragged him into the elevator and up to my room to fill him in on the whole ridiculous story.

A move I am regretting more with each passing minute.

I've explained it all to him three times already. I am *not* humiliating myself for a fourth. I stop pacing and come to sit beside him on the bed. For a moment, we just sit like that in silence, both of us staring at the black TV screen on the wall opposite the bed.

"Go ahead," I finally say. "Let's hear it."

"Hear what?"

"That I'm a chaos bunny who creates her own disasters for reasons that surpass human, machine, or extraterrestrial understanding."

"I wouldn't say that."

"You wouldn't?" I turn to look at him, but Seb is still looking at the blank TV.

"No. Never thought you were a chaos bunny. Just a free spirit."

I snort and roll my eyes. "Same thing. Anyway, thank you for playing along in the lobby."

"No problem. It was kind of fun. I think I missed my calling as an actor."

"Well, you have always loved the spotlight," I say, rolling my eyes.

"Oh yes, and I know how much you *loathe* to be the center of attention." Seb nudges my shoulder with his own.

"'I swear I don't love the drama, it loves me,'" I quote, lifting my hands in a helpless gesture.

"Shakespeare?"

"Taylor Swift."

"Same difference."

My lips curve into a genuine smile. This part was always

easy with Seb. The back and forth, the banter. When things got real—that was the hard part. But I know I have to be real with him now.

"So...as grateful as I am that you played along with my stupid lie, I have to ask..."

"Yes?"

"Why are you really here?"

"I told you, had to check out these beaches."

"*Seb.*"

"I'm serious!" Seb twists his torso to look me in the eye. "Look, I was about to start making my way back to the States after the shoot, and I remembered you messaging me that you were going to be here, and I don't know..." He shrugs. "It just seemed like it'd be something fun to do, and it's pretty cheap to island hop once you're over here. So I caught the next flight to Maui." He says it so casually. Like he really just decided to come here on a whim, the way a person might decide last minute to take in a movie or a visitor to New York might hop the subway out to Coney Island.

"But don't you have..." I grasp around for the right words. "I don't know, plants that need to be watered? A cat that needs to be fed? A girlfriend that needs to be..." I trail off, realizing I kind of backed myself into a corner with that one.

"Oh please, finish that sentence." Seb's face is curled into a lascivious grin.

I swat at him. "But seriously."

"Seriously," he repeats. "No plants, no cat, no girlfriend— except a fake one, apparently." I swat him again, but this time, he grabs my hand, pressing a kiss to it before placing it back in my lap. It feels much the same as when his lips were against mine earlier today—soft, familiar, but devoid of the electricity that used to crackle between us. Back then, a kiss from Sebastian could set my whole body on fire. Now, it was just a pleasant warmth, a comfortable ember instead of a raging inferno.

"Honestly, Sybil," he continues, "I don't even really have an apartment right now. My place in Tokyo is on a long-term sublet, so I was planning to crash on my buddy's couch back in New York for a bit. But this"—he slides down the headboard, nestling into one of the fluffy down pillows—"this is much comfier."

I give his shoulder a hard shove. "Oh no. Don't even think about it."

He closes his eyes, a dreamy smile on his face. "Shh...it's sleepy time."

"It's barely eight a.m."

"Fine, fine." He pulls himself up and off the bed. "Guess I should go back down to the lobby and get myself a room of my own."

"You didn't even book a room?" I'm all for winging it, but even I draw the line at arriving at a destination without booking accommodations first.

Seb waves a dismissive hand, apparently completely unbothered that he hasn't secured a place to sleep tonight. "I'm sure they'll have something. If not, I'll figure it out."

Those four words are classic Seb. Classic me, too—especially back when we were together. Seb and I were always "figuring it out." Half the time, things worked out as perfectly as if we had planned them. The other half? Well, we came away with a great story to tell our friends.

Seb begins to walk toward the hotel room door, and I follow alongside to see him out.

"How long are you staying for?" I ask when we reach the threshold.

"I guess it depends." He pauses, leaning his back against the frame of the open door.

"Depends on what?"

"On how long my services are needed."

"Services?"

"As your fake boyfriend," Seb clarifies. His alley-cat grin is back.

"Oh." I laugh, looking away. "You don't have to—"

"Come on, let me have my fun. How long is what's-his-name going to be here?"

I roll my eyes. "I know you know his name. Jamie said he's leaving tomorrow."

"Great. I'll stay until then too."

"Are you sure?"

"Two days at one of Hawaii's top resorts, servicing a beautiful woman? Sounds like paradise."

I narrow my eyes at him. "There will be no servicing of any kind."

"Are you sure? Don't you want to make things convincing for Jimmy?"

"Jamie. And no. I mean, yes, I do. If you don't mind pretending—"

"I don't."

"—but just, like, holding hands and stuff. If we happen to run into them—"

"Sure."

"—which we probably won't, since it's a big resort—"

"Naturally."

"—although, I did run into them, like, an obscenely large number of times over the past forty-six hours, so—"

"Sybil?"

"Hmm?" I stop rambling and look up, suddenly realizing how close we are. Seb is now leaning forward on the door-frame, one hand gripping the molding along the top of the door, the other holding the strap of the duffel slung across his shoulder. Seb is not an especially tall man—he's probably only got a few inches on me—but there's something about the way he's standing now that makes him seem large. Mas-culine. I can smell his cologne, the same spicy one he used to wear.

Memories of a hundred moments just like this cloud my mind. Moments where we said we wouldn't but did anyway. Moments where we acted without thinking. Moments that, in the end, were only ever moments.

"I would be honored to play your fake-platonic-hand-holding boyfriend for the next two days," Seb says, drawing my attention back to the present.

"Thank you."

"Do you want to meet up later for brunch?"

Despite having already had a pancake breakfast with Jamie, I know I'll probably be hungry again later. Jamie used to call me a hobbit, given my affection for "second breakfast." "That'd be great," I tell Seb. "Meet in the lobby around ten?"

Seb nods, then pushes off the door.

"And you let me know if you change your mind about the servicing. We did always used to say, 'if you're single and I'm single, then—'"

"*Goodbye*, Sebastian."

He gives me a wink and heads down the hall to the elevator. But halfway there, he stops. Turns around.

"Forget something?" I call to him.

He walks halfway back down the hallway so we can speak at a normal volume and not risk waking anyone else on this floor. "Just—explain it to me one more time."

I let out a long groan and lean my head back against the wall. "Yes, okay—I panicked and made up a bald-faced lie about dating a fish scientist, are you happy?"

He smiles, but for once, it doesn't quite seem to reach his eyes. "Not that. What I can't understand is...why?" His voice is low now. I have to strain to hear him.

"Why what?"

"I mean, you left him at the altar, right?" Seb asks. "Shouldn't *he* be the one trying to save face around *you*? What are you trying to prove, Sybil?"

SEB'S WORDS HAUNT ME while I try to bang out a few work emails. After about forty minutes, I push away from my laptop and head into the bathroom to shower.

While I wait for the water to heat up, I survey my reflection in the driftwood-framed mirror. A messy pale blond topknot. I look chaotic, but nowhere near as bad as I looked running down the aisle last year. And I know *exactly* how awful I looked that day, thanks to some preteen cousin of Jamie's who had the audacity to film the whole thing and post it online. Emma tried to shield me, blocking terms like #runawaybride from my feed, but of course, the algorithm came for me anyway. That summer after the failed wedding, I used to lie in bed and watch the clip over and over, stuck in a self-pity doom spiral.

I wonder if Seb saw the video too. If that's why he believes *I'm* the one who left Jamie—even though that's not exactly what happened—I can see why Seb would think that. The video doesn't capture the heartbreaking words exchanged in harsh whispers under the flower arch. Just the moment where I took off down the aisle. Classic Sybil, doing a runner. Just like I'd broken my engagement to Seb two years prior.

Is that why I didn't correct him? Because on some level, it's easier to live with the story that I'm just not built for commitment instead of admitting that I'd run *back* to Jamie, only for him to call things off?

And now, after my talk with Jamie at the tiki bar, the story has a whole new layer to it. I'm still struggling to wrap my mind around the bittersweet reality—that Jamie hadn't rejected me because I'd disappointed him, but had set me free because he'd thought that was what I really wanted. It feels like we are finally starting to understand each other, and a part of me wants to throw caution to the wind, confess everything, and see if we can find a way forward. But I can't tell if that is just another wild Sybil instinct, destined to leave me hurt all over again. It's a tangled mess, and I'm not sure how to untangle it.

But I suppose I can start by untangling my hair.

The shower has filled the bathroom with steam, and I step inside the glass stall, letting the hot water wash away the remnants of sweat from this morning's workout and hoping it takes my anxiety down the drain with it.

I toss my still-wet hair with the tiniest bit of mousse so it will airdry looking beachy and effortless, then throw on an emerald-green one-piece with a low back and a pair of white linen pants. When I get to the lobby, I don't see any sign of Seb, so I make my way over to the concierge desk where Ash is wrapping up with another guest.

"Good morning, Sybil," she says once she's free.

"Hi! I'm wondering where you recommend for breakfast."

"Well, if you're looking for full-service, the Lotus Café has a wonderful brunch menu. And we also offer a poolside buffet breakfast until eleven."

"The buffet sounds great," I tell Ash, then fire off a text to Seb, telling him to meet me there.

When I get to the pool deck, I forgo the mimosa bar, though it is tempting, and instead, fix myself an iced coffee with sugar and almond milk. There's a tower of fresh fruit and a man making smoothies to order, so I get a green juice too.

I'm looking for an empty table when Dani waves me over to where she's standing by the omelet station.

"Double fisting this morning?" She gestures at my two beverages.

"I couldn't decide between the two." I shrug. "You're here early. Are you working brunch?"

Dani sighs. "No, I'm off today. Normally, Ash and I like to coordinate our days off, but—"

"Yeah." I incline my head back toward the lobby. "I saw her at the front desk. So what's your plan for the day? Besides lurking by the fresh eggs?"

"Probably read through this portfolio from a new winery the hotel is considering partnering with," Dani says with another sigh. "The Food and Beverage Director is trying to train me up to be his replacement when he retires, so he's been looping me in on all the boring business aspects of the job." She rolls her eyes fondly. "Hopefully, we'll at least get to do some taste testing. Anyway, I'll do that, and then I have to make a cake for Mason's birthday tonight—you know Mason, right? The snorkel instructor you completely bailed on." Dani arches an eyebrow at me and folds her arms.

"Shit, he told you about that?" I wince. "Not my finest moment. He didn't get in trouble or anything, did he?"

Dani waves a hand. "Nah, it was fine. He brought your tote bag back to the front desk himself. Made for a good story. We like to trade our most ridiculous guest anecdotes, and you spontaneously jumping ship definitely won that night."

"Well, happy I could help, I guess."

"You should come by the party tonight," Dani says.

"Are you sure?" I ask. "I wouldn't want to crash..."

"Totally." Dani nods. "Some of Mason's other friends are coming, too, so it won't just be staff."

"Okay, that sounds great. Thanks for the invite." We exchange numbers so Dani can text me the details.

"I'm so glad you're going to come! I'm dying to hear about the hot guy who was making eyes at you last night. Working behind the bar, I've seen dudes try a lot of things to get a woman into bed, but a shot of *ranch dressing*? That was a first."

"Oh," I blush. "Actually, that was my ex-fiancé. The one I told you about."

"*Really.* That's the soulless asshole who brought his new girlfriend on his ex-fiancée's honeymoon trip?"

"That's the one." I take a long drag from my iced coffee.

"*Damn...*" Dani says.

"My thoughts exactly. Though in his defense I may have

jumped the gun on the 'new girlfriend' thing. That said, there's clearly some kind of vibe going on between him and his coworker."

"It's so weird," Dani says, the tone of amazement still in her voice.

"What's weird?" There are so many things weird about this situation that I can't be sure which one she's referring to.

"Well, he doesn't *look* like evil incarnate. But I guess that sweet, lovesick-puppy thing I saw last night was just a mask to hide the horror within. I hate when that happens."

I laugh. Her description of Jamie as a supervillain is so over-the-top. It feels good to be able to see the comical side of this situation instead of wallowing in all the mixed-up feelings that seeing Jamie again has brought up.

Dani glances down at her phone. "Ugh, okay, I have to go home and get started reviewing those docs. Don't fall for any handsome devils while I'm gone."

"I'll do my best."

"And hey, have fun horseback riding! Unless..." she says, drawing out the word with relish, "you've already got something—or rather, some*one*—else to ride?"

She looks pointedly over my shoulder, and I turn around to follow her gaze. Seb is striding across the pool deck, looking like he just stepped off the cover of a surf magazine in board shorts and a pale blue polo tee that hugs his biceps and shows off his tan. I'm the only one who knows the truth: that he's a shit surfer—always jumping up too soon and wiping out before the wave's even crested.

When he makes it over to us, he grabs both my shoulders and places a kiss on the side of my head.

"Hey, sorry I'm late." He reaches a hand across to Dani. "Sebastian Wallace-Conway, pleasure to meet you."

"Dani Russo. And likewise." Then she turns to me and raises a studded eyebrow. "Well, I have to go. You enjoy yourself today, Sybil. Looks like you have two *delicious* options to choose from."

I choke a little on my iced coffee, but luckily, Seb is oblivious to Dani's double meaning. He just nods down earnestly at my two drinks and says, "Oh yeah, that green juice looks fire. Can I try some?"

I wordlessly hand him the glass as Dani heads out, throwing me a wink behind Seb's back as she goes.

14

It's a short walk to the stables, over a small stream, and down a tree-lined path. When I told Seb during brunch that I was going riding today, he quickly signed himself up as well, grabbing the last open spot for this morning's excursion. *After all,* he said with a grin, *it's the perfect opportunity to rehearse our fake relationship*—to which I rolled my eyes.

We reach the clearing where the rest of our horseback riding crew is gathered and introduce ourselves. There are two retired science teachers, Hank and Elliot, as well as an elaborately made-up woman named Harriet who is sporting not only glitter eyeshadow at eleven thirty in the morning but also a flowing caftan that looks like an accident waiting to happen. And there, in the back, petting a gray dappled mare with a lush black mane, is Genevieve. She waves hello, and I wave back—grateful that, for once, Jamie does not seem to be with her.

"Go ahead and pick a horse," Kaia, our leader for the morning's ride, tells the group. I walk toward a roan mare with a bright white star in the center of her forehead. The horse nuzzles my hand when I reach her, and I wish I'd thought to grab an apple or some sugar cubes from the breakfast buffet for her. After a few more sniffs, she gives up looking for food, and I'm able to stroke the soft white splash of color on her nose. One large brown eye looks at me, and I feel some of the nervous tension leak away. The mare's presence is calming. Her deep, glossy eyes stare at me knowingly, and I feel my breath slow down just a little.

Kaia comes up beside me and pats the horse on the neck. "This is Lo, she's a sweetheart." I scratch beneath her chin, and Lo snuffles into my hand.

Kaia gives her a couple firm pats on the neck and moves down the line of horses, double-checking all the tack and introducing the riders to their mounts.

"If you feel comfortable mounting the horse on your own, please do so," Kaia calls from the far end of the corral. "Otherwise, I'll come along to help you up."

"Oh, don't worry," Seb says casually from where he's standing beside his horse. "Sybil knows how to mount. Right, babe?"

Dear lord.

Sebastian takes a small hop to get up on the horse, and almost falls backward, but manages it. To his point, I *am* actually able to mount my horse without much incident.

"Everyone good?" Kaia asks. Then she mounts the horse next to Sebastian's and leads us out of the corral.

It's only a few minutes before the trail opens up, and we're out of the shady glade near the stable and onto the beach. Lo's steps are slow and sure, and I relax into the saddle, letting my body sway slightly with each step, listening to the horses splashing delicately through the surf. Kaia leads us to the trail that Jamie and I walked on Tuesday after we abandoned the snorkel boat, but where Jamie and I had kept closer to the beach, Kaia guides us away from the water and up the side of the mountain. The path narrows, and leaves brush against my calves.

We wind up a switchback, and Lo and I are forced into a single-file line behind the older woman, Harriet, and ahead of Seb. There's a dull roar ahead of us, and when the trail opens up into a clearing, it's obvious where the noise is coming from: at the far end of the clearing is a crystal pond fed by a fifty-foot waterfall.

"How gorgeous," I say softly, letting Lo come to a stop.

Kaia sees the expression on my face, too, and smiles. She brings her horse next to me and points up above the waterfall. There's another small clearing, but it doesn't look like we could get there on horseback. "This is my grandfather's favorite spot on the island. He always hikes up here when he has some problem to figure out." Kaia pats the neck of her horse. "He says if he hasn't solved it by the time he's reached the top of the waterfall, it's because he needs to get right with God. And if he hasn't solved it after a night under the stars, it's because he needs to get right with my grandmother."

"He sounds like a smart man." I laugh.

Kaia laughs, too, and steers her horse away. "Not as smart as my Tutu."

I spend a moment there, just listening to the roar of the waterfall, capturing a few videos standing almost underneath the spray, where you can see the rainbows the water droplets form.

But then there's another sound. A thundering growing louder and louder. I turn toward the noise, and in the distance, something catches my eye. It's a horse and rider, emerging from the dense foliage like a mirage. The wind picks up, tugging at my hair and carrying with it the pounding of hooves and a man's shout. Dust explodes around them for a moment, obscuring their details. But when it settles, I see him clearly— a grin splitting his face, hair whipping wildly in the breeze. This isn't the kind of controlled, follow-the-guide riding we've been doing; this is raw, untamed freedom. Him and his horse, one with the landscape, a picture straight out of an old Western movie.

When he reaches the clearing, Jamie pulls his horse to a stop, a cloud of dirt billowing behind him.

"Whoa there, Maverick," he calls out, his voice ragged from the exertion. He glances over at our group apologetically. "Sorry, I didn't realize there was a lesson out right now. I hope I didn't startle anyone."

So much for not startling anyone—my heart is pounding at the sight of him. Though less from being startled and more from being completely overwhelmed. Did I really think I could just relax with Sebastian and clear my head without having to face the conundrum of being on a beautiful island with not one but *two* ex-fiancés?

"That was quite an entrance, Mr. Kauffman," Kaia says with a smile. "Care to join us for lunch? We're just about to break."

Jamie hesitates for a moment, his gaze finally darting to mine but then quickly away again. "Yeah, sure. Thanks," he says to Kaia, dismounting with practiced ease.

Off to the side of the clearing are several employees from the resort and a spread of picnic blankets and overstuffed pillows. There's a grill set up, and the smell coming off it is amazing.

There's also a space to hitch our horses. Everyone begins to dismount, and Kaia comes by to gather our reins. I slide off of Lo and hand them to her.

"Feel free to swim, take photos, or just relax while we finish getting lunch set up," Kaia says with a smile. Everyone is headed toward the waterfall, but my eyes only catch on Jamie. He takes his shirt off and dives into the natural pool, resurfacing a few seconds later and shaking the water from his hair.

Jamie's movements are slow and languid as he pulls himself out of the water, and the flicker in my chest zips through the rest of my body, crackling along my skin. Water sluices across his chest and down his stomach. His shorts cling to his thighs, and when he reaches down to scoop his shirt from the ground, they stretch even tighter.

I clear my throat.

"Not going for a dip?" Seb appears at my side and is following my heated gaze.

"Nope," I say, my voice clipped. "How about you?"

"Darling, he can't swim right now," says Harriet, the woman in the glamorous caftan. "I need him to take my photo with that fancy camera of his." Her hand is suddenly wrapped possessively around Sebastian's arm, which makes me cock an eyebrow at Seb. He shrugs at me as if it's his lot in life to be accosted by ostentatious women at least two decades his senior. But at that moment, Kaia calls out that the food is ready.

The food is set out on a low table between the picnic blankets, and our small group convenes around it.

"Jamie, you looked excellent on that horse, man," Seb says, as we all start loading up our plates. His voice is warm, friendly. But still, I wish he wouldn't engage more than he has to. Jamie nods tightly, accepting the compliment. The two of them both being here feels like a weird rift in the time-space continuum. Like one wrong move could send us hurtling into a black hole.

"So," Elliot, one of the retired science teachers, says, once we're all settled. "Are the four of you here on a couples' trip?"

"No." The word comes out of Jamie's mouth like a bullet, and he doesn't elaborate.

Elliot's eyes go wide, but he's polite enough that he doesn't push further. "Oh, of course. My mistake." There's a moment of silence as everyone turns to their meal to escape the awkwardness, but it's broken almost immediately by Sebastian.

"Sybil and I are here celebrating," he says with a cheeky grin, reaching over to squeeze my hand.

"Actually, *babe*," I say with a tight smile, "we're here for work, remember?"

"Sure, sure," Seb says easily. "The squid and the moon and all that."

As an only child, I've never had the pleasure of dealing with an annoying little brother of my own. But I've heard Nikki talk about hers enough times to recognize the similarities in how I'm feeling toward Seb right now. I'm torn between wanting to sock him in the arm and bursting out laughing at his ridiculous attempt to play the besotted boyfriend. He's not even making an effort to be a convincing marine biologist. Though I'm glad that he at least seems to have retained the core details of our cover story.

"But still," Seb continues, "this is kind of a special trip for us, isn't it, Buttercup?"

"Oh?" Hank asks. "How come?"

I'm wondering the same thing. I narrow my eyes at Seb, silently warning him. But he ignores me, turning to Hank.

"Well, this is the first trip we've taken since we got back together."

"You two have a history?" Kaia asks.

"Oh yes." Seb's eyes are twinkling. He lets go of my hand to reach an arm around my shoulders. "Our love story is one for the ages."

There's a clatter near the end of the lunch table. Everyone turns to see Jamie picking up the serving spoon he just knocked over. "Sorry," he mutters.

"Well, I love a good romantic epic," Harriet says, drawing everyone's attention back to Seb. "Do tell."

"Sybil and I met back in New York—how long ago was it, Schmoopie?"

"Six years ago," I say through gritted teeth. "And I thought we agreed: no more pet names."

"She loves it," Seb says conspiratorially to Harriet.

"I really don't," I say to Harriet. I mean come on, *schmoopie?* Is he my fake boyfriend or my fake grandpa talking to his fake cat?

"Anyway," Seb continues, "we met and fell madly, deeply in love. I mean, honestly, can you blame me? Look at her." He casts me a look that's so genuinely affectionate that my cheeks turn pink despite my annoyance. "I was smitten. Even asked her to marry me. But tragically, fate intervened."

"What happened?" Elliot asks.

"We grew apart," "He moved to Tokyo," Seb and I say at the same time.

I look at him. *We grew apart?* Is that really why he thinks our relationship ended?

Hank and Elliot exchange glances.

"Well, yes," Seb says quickly, "I guess the breakup was kind of complicated. You see, I'm a photographer." He gestures down to his camera, still slung across his chest. Then panic paints his features. "Um, I mean, I sometimes take pictures in addition to being a, uh..." I mouth the words at him: *marine biologist.* "A marine biologist, right," he adds, and it's all I can do to not kick him. "Anyway," Seb continues, "I got this really amazing job opportunity in Tokyo. So I went, and that was the end of things."

"But you were engaged?" Genevieve says, looking at me curiously. "Why didn't you go with him?"

I hesitate. Seb's been mostly sticking to the real-life facts of our relationship so far, but I really don't want to get into everything that happened with Tokyo right now.

Luckily, Seb, who is clearly relishing holding the group's rapt attention, jumps in with the save. "Oh, we were young and stupid. Neither of us wanted to be tied down. It just wasn't meant to be."

Again, not quite how I remember things. But I try to keep a blissful smile on my face, pretending along with Seb that this is just a small blip in our past, a funny anecdote we can laugh about now and not one of the worst heartbreaks of my life.

"So how did you get back together?" Hank asks.

Seb's lips twist into a grin. He removes his arm from around my shoulder and leans his forearms on the table. Automatically,

Hank, Elliot, and Genevieve do the same. He's got them eating out of the palm of his hand. For a second, I worry Seb is going to tell them about all the times we "got back together" after the Tokyo breakup—aka all the ill-advised hookups we indulged in whenever he was passing through town, while I was still single and lost—before I met Jamie. But instead, he says, "About a year ago, I heard that Sybil was getting married."

Immediately, my spine tenses.

"I saw a social media post from one of her friends that she was at her bachelorette party, and I decided to give Sybil a call to wish her well—just as old friends, of course."

"Babe, I don't think anyone wants to hear this story," I say, the words tumbling out in a rush as I try to convey the urgency I feel without making it obvious. I was mildly annoyed and begrudgingly amused by Seb's antics before. But now he's verging toward dangerous territory.

"No, no! Keep going!" Harriet says, raising a heavily made-up brow, and I fight the impulse to fling a forkful of grilled steak salad at her.

"So I called, and we talked, and it was like no time had passed," Seb says. "We still knew each other so well. And I could tell that things weren't over between us—"

"Seb," I interject. He needs to stop this, right now. But he's either oblivious or getting some sick enjoyment out of this, because he keeps going.

"The next thing I knew, word came around that Sybil had decided not to get married after all. Guess he just wasn't the right guy."

His gaze drifts toward the other picnic blanket. It's subtle—I'm sure Hank and Elliot won't have even noticed—but Jamie has. He's gripping his fork with excessive strength, his knuckles white. Acid fills my throat. Jamie didn't know about Seb's phone call. There was no need for him to. It was irrelevant. Seb's making it out to be way more than it was. He's making it sound like I left Jamie *for him*.

I stare at Jamie, silently pleading with him to meet my eyes, but he refuses. Seb slings an arm around my shoulder again, tugging me close to his side.

"And the rest," he says, dropping a kiss to the crown of my head, "is history."

15

It was the Wednesday before my wedding, the night of my impromptu bachelorette party. The Core Four had enjoyed a beautiful ocean-side dinner at the Pelican Club, then Finn had arrived to join the party (much to Emma's annoyance—even though *I* had invited him, and the night was supposedly about celebrating me). After dinner, Emma and Willow wanted to go back to the hotel—Willow was very pregnant and wanted to get off her feet, and Emma, well, she just wanted to be wherever Finn wasn't. But I wanted to keep the night going. Jamie's sister, Amelia's, words from earlier that day were still ringing in my head. That I wasn't *marriage material*. I knew if I went back to the hotel, I'd just continue to stew, wondering if Jamie felt the same way. So when Finn suggested we check out a nearby tequila bar, I immediately said yes.

A couple of karaoke-fueled hours later, I was feeling better. Finn and I were dueting loudly (I was Dolly, he was Kenny) while Nikki recorded us on her phone. Finn was like the big brother I never had. He and Emma had been on debate team together, so I always kind of knew him, but he and I became close friends senior year of high school. He rescued me from a tight spot my then-boyfriend, Liam, had left me in, and from that day on, it was like Finn and I had an unspoken understanding that we had each other's backs. When his dad was dying of cancer and Finn just wanted to get away from it all, I was there with *Dawn of the Planet of the Apes* ready to stream. And when I needed someone to remind me that I deserved better than the crap Liam was sending my way, I knew I could count on Finn to set me straight.

After the final lines of our silly, off-key duet of "Islands in the Stream" faded out, I waved off doing a shot with Nikki and excused myself to the bathroom. In fact, I'd been waving off shots or tossing them behind me into the bushes all night and had been a little crampy, but still, I was that wistful kind of high-on-life where everything was soft around the edges, and I was feeling sappy about how lucky I was to have such good friends. When I got to the ladies' room, all the stalls were full, so I leaned against the sink to wait my turn. It was crowded, with people coming in and out, laughing and singing. A cluster of girls who made me nostalgic for my USC sorority sisters tumbled into the bathroom just as my phone started to buzz in my pocket. I answered, pressing the phone to my ear.

"Sybil? You there?" someone said, but the voice on the phone was all but drowned out by the whoosh of the hand dryer.

"Whoops! My bad!" One of the girls had accidentally leaned against the motion sensor and was now giggling with her friends like this was the funniest thing to ever happen. I smiled at them and nodded for them to go ahead of me in line so I could take the call.

"Hi, hi—sorry, who is this?"

There was an amused chuckle on the other end of the line. "It's Sebastian."

I really do think he meant well, that he did just want to send me off with his good wishes. I just think Seb couldn't help being Seb.

We traded small talk for a bit, then Seb got to the real reason why he was calling.

"So tell me about The Banker." His voice was tinny over the cell connection. He hadn't told me where he was in the world, only that he'd just had breakfast, so it must have been somewhere far away. It was nearing one a.m. in California.

"He's not a banker," I said, leaning over the bathroom sink to reapply lip gloss.

"Oh," Sebastian said. "He gives off banker vibes in your photos."

"What's a 'banker vibe'?" I asked, bypassing the other question that sprang to mind: *You still look at my social media pics?*

"Clean cut. Predictable. Good at math." The adjective that Sebastian implied, but didn't say, hung between us: *boring*.

"There's nothing wrong with being any of those things." The buzz of the bar, the thumping bass line bleeding through the bathroom walls, made all my thoughts feel like they were pulled through taffy.

"I didn't say there was." There was a beat of silence on the other end of the line. "Just not the type of guy I pictured you ending up with."

A swooping feeling I couldn't quite identify shot through my lower belly. "What kind of person did you think I'd end up with?"

"I don't know. Someone who matched your"—another beat as he seemed to search for the right word—"energy."

Shakily, I met my own gaze in the mirror. "That sounds dangerous."

"What's life without a little danger?"

Raw, unfiltered panic ripped through me. Were things with Jamie too safe? Could a relationship be too easy? I thought back to the dumb newlywed game Emma had organized for us to play at dinner. She had prerecorded a video, asking Jamie questions to see how well he knew me, and Jamie had nailed nearly every single one. Even though we were literally getting married in three days, it still got to me—that sense of being known so fully by another person. It was thrilling, but also terrifying. I was self-aware enough to know that I thrived on being a little enigmatic. A colorful kaleidoscope that everyone agreed was striking to look at, but that no one could really see the full picture of. What would it be like, to spend forever with someone who knew me so fully? Who saw beyond the Sybil Sparkle?

And what about the most secret parts of myself that even Jamie didn't know about yet—the fragile pieces I kept hidden in the darkest corners of my heart? What would happen to our relationship when he finally came to know those too?

"I don't know." It was more an answer to my own internal questions than Sebastian's. "I don't know," I repeated softly. Suddenly, the bathroom mirror looked like a fun-house glass. My reflection oscillating, morphing into someone I didn't recognize. The heat in the crowded bar must have gone straight to my head.

"So, he's not a banker. What is he then? A lion tamer? Rodeo cowboy? Astronaut?" Sebastian teased.

"Private equity," I said through the rising nausea in my abdomen. "He works at his family's office."

Sebastian let out a small whistle. "A rich guy, huh?"

My words came out softly. "I don't care about that." And I didn't. That was never what drew me to Jamie. If anything, I found all that wealth intimidating. Especially given his family's obvious disdain for me. The Kauffmans had softened a little toward me since that painfully awkward first meeting at their house in Napa, but they still held me at arm's length. I suspected they still thought I wasn't good enough for Jamie. Truth be told, what hurt in overhearing that comment from Amelia earlier had been that it didn't surprise me.

"I know you don't," Seb said, his voice uncharacteristically serious. Just then, the door to the bathroom opened as another gaggle of laughing college girls poured in. The noise must have traveled through the phone, because Seb said, "Anyway, I don't want to keep you during your party. Just wanted to say..." He paused. "I just wanted to say good luck."

The words felt ominous. He didn't say "congratulations," or "I'm so happy for you." And his tone. It was like he was sending me off to battle, praying against the odds that I'd make it out alive.

Sebastian hung up without having any idea how his words had affected me. The cramps had intensified while we were talking—was it nerves or something else? Finally, a stall opened up and I sat down on the toilet gingerly. My head was pounding and my stomach felt unsettled, almost as if I were hungover, even though I hadn't had anything to drink all night. I hadn't had any alcohol in several weeks, in fact.

Not since the positive test.

It had been tricky, hiding my lack of drinking from my friends—especially in the lead-up to the wedding when it felt like there was a champagne toast happening every five minutes. But I knew it would be worth it when I could finally tell them the news. Of course, I'd have to tell Jamie first. I'd been waiting to make sure it was really real before I did. I had visions of telling him as we lay tangled up in bed together at Halia Falls, the stunning resort where we'd be honeymooning in just over a week.

But as I went to toss the toilet paper into the bowl after I peed, something stopped me cold.

Blood.

The toilet bowl was full of it.

Tears formed in my eyes, but I angrily wiped them away. I was mad at myself for being so stupid. For thinking it would suddenly be this easy. That my body would cooperate with me, despite what the doctors had warned me about back when I was seventeen and scared, and Finn was offering me a ride home from the hospital because my boyfriend had abandoned me there.

Maybe because of the bond we formed that day, Finn could see distress written all over my face when I emerged from the bathroom.

"Hey, there you are!" Nikki said with a bright smile. "We were wondering where you got to."

"Sybil, what's wrong?" Finn asked, a gentle hand at my elbow.

"I just—" I swallowed. The anxiety that had been pooling

in my gut began creeping its way up my throat. "I don't know if I can do this."

"Do what?" Finn asked.

"Get married."

And then, I ran back to the bathroom and emptied the contents of my stomach.

SEB'S ARM IS STILL slung casually around my shoulders as he wraps up his tale of the phone call that allegedly rekindled our romance. When in fact, that couldn't be further from the truth. It was the phone call that preceded one of the more awful nights of my life.

The horseback riding group all has blissful smiles on their faces, basking in fake story of true love reunited.

All except one.

"Jamie—" I start, not caring who is listening, not even knowing what I'm going to say, exactly. Just knowing I need to set the record straight.

But Jamie ignores me. He stands and turns toward Kaia. "I'll put the tack away and rub him down." His face is placid, except for a telltale twitch in his jaw muscle.

Kaia nods, though she's clearly taken aback, and I realize Jamie is leaving. He walks over to his horse, unties it, and a few seconds later, he's disappeared back down the trail.

Everyone else at the table goes back to their meal, chatting happily about how beautiful the resort is and how today's weather couldn't be more perfect and how they can't wait for Friday's lunar eclipse. But I'm boiling with rage.

"What the *frick*, Seb?" I hiss.

"What?" He's looking at me wide-eyed, the picture of innocence. But after a few moments on the receiving end of my most withering glare, he acquiesces. "Okay, fine. I'm sorry. I know that was kind of a dick move. I just got carried away. You know, remembering..." He lets his gaze drift toward the waterfall, his expression uncharacteristically contemplative. The corners of his mouth, which are usually poised to tip up into a smile at any moment, are cast downward. He looks almost melancholy.

It's such a strange, unsettling sight that something inside me softens. How is he supposed to know why I'm so upset, when I've been lying to everyone, him included?

"Seb..." He's still watching the waterfall and doesn't turn when I say his name, so I speak to his profile—boyish nose and golden stubble on his chin. "That story you told. About that phone call..." A wild thought has come over me as I watch this subdued version of Seb, and suddenly, I have to know. "Was that really how you felt?"

"About what?" His eyes flash back to mine.

"You know, about thinking that call meant things weren't over between us or whatever."

There's a half-second pause, then Seb shrugs, a nonchalant smile forming on his lips. "Nah. Of course not. That was just for the performance. And okay, I did want to rile Jimmy up a bit."

"*Jamie*," I correct, automatically.

"He just looked so smug, didn't you think? Pulling up on his literal steed? I mean, come on." Sebastian rolls his eyes, but there's no real malice in it.

"Okay, good," I say. "I just wanted to make sure. I didn't want you thinking that I walked out on my wedding because of you or anything."

"Didn't think you did." His eyes are back on the waterfall. The rest of our group has finished their lunch and are now walking toward the natural pool, Hank and Elliot rolling up their pants to wade into the cool water, Harriet whipping off her caftan to reveal a spangled bathing suit underneath while Genevieve and Kaia look on, amused. "If it's any consolation," Seb adds, without meeting my eyes, "Mr. Tall, Dark, and Stick-Up-His-Ass is clearly not over you."

I snort out a derisive laugh, but inside my chest, my heart has started pounding ferociously. "I don't think that's true," I say quietly. Because as much as I wish it were, the fact is, Jamie is here with someone else. And besides, too much time has gone by. Too much hurt and miscommunication. Jamie made that quite clear when he stormed off just now instead of letting me explain. It would be foolish to think we could just wipe the slate clean and pick up where we left off before everything went wrong. "Jamie's moved on," I tell Seb. "And so have I."

"Come on, Sybil." Seb's giving me that look again that's half pitying, half annoyed. "I know you're not stupid. The guy's clearly jealous. Even *Lo* could see it, couldn't you, girl?" he calls toward my tied-up horse.

I let the word sit in the air for a moment. *Jealous.* I think of Jamie's heated glare that first day at the pool when he learned I was supposedly vacationing with a boyfriend. Of the harsh words he spit out about my "squid man" on our hike. His clenched jaw meeting Sebastian in the lobby this morning. If he wasn't jealous, he sure was pulling off a very convincing performance of the emotion.

"Maybe so," I admit to Seb, "but it doesn't mean anything. That's just, like, classic macho guy stuff."

"'Guy stuff'?" Seb asks.

"Yeah, you know, 'Grog want girl,'" I say, adopting a gruff caveman voice. "Actually, Grog do not want girl, but do not want any other Grogs to have girl."

Seb lets out an easy laugh, then rolls his eyes at me affectionately. "Please tell me we men don't sound like that."

"Well, *you* don't," I say with a friendly smile. "Only the jealous Neanderthal assholes do."

"And you really think that's Jamie in this scenario?" Seb raises an eyebrow at me. "That his storming off just now was nothing deeper than a base, primal instinct?"

"Seb..." I draw out his name, pleading with my eyes for him to drop it. "Look, I really don't need someone to psycho-analyze the situation right now. What I need is a drinking buddy. Okay?"

"Whatever you say, Sybil." Seb's arm comes around my shoulder again, and I let myself lean into the crook of his neck. "Whatever you say."

16

I DON'T SAY MUCH ON THE WAY BACK TO THE RESORT, BUT AS WE NEAR the hotel pool, Sebastian nudges my shoulder. "You up for going into town? The guy who dropped me off from the airport told me there's an aloha festival this afternoon. I thought I'd go and get some shots."

"Rum?"

"Photography."

"Ah, right. That too." I give Seb a small grin. "Sounds good." I'm too spun out to get any real work done this afternoon, so I might as well enjoy what the island has to offer.

"Perfect." Seb grins down at me. "You know, you're my favorite person to photograph."

"Really?" I always loved being photographed by Sebastian. It was the only time I could be certain that he was fully in the moment with me. I knew I had his unwavering attention, and he wasn't planning his next trip or looking for his next adventure.

"Really. The camera loves you."

I'm about to respond with something teasing, like, *are you sure it's just the camera?* but the words get stuck in my mouth when I spot a sweet little scene playing out across the pool.

An older man is helping his wife down the small set of stairs from the garden that leads from the bar to the pool area, his hands on her elbow. Once they both reach the bottom, she turns to cup his face with one hand, and he bends down to drop a kiss on her cheek before whispering something in her ear. She swats at his arm but lets out a short bark of laughter. They're both grinning as they settle into a pair of lounge chairs. My heart clenches.

Sebastian follows my gaze.

I swallow the lump in my throat and try to smile. "The festival thing sounds great. Let me just change again." I'm still wearing a bathing suit and linen pants from the ride and picnic. "Meet back down in the lobby at four?"

"Perfect," he says with a grin, and I start to make my way toward the elevator bank. "And hey, Sybil," he says quietly. I turn to face him. "I'm sorry again about before."

I nod, not trusting my voice to respond. "I'll see you in a bit."

AT FOUR P.M., I go to meet Sebastian in the hotel lobby as planned. I'm feeling rejuvenated in a fitted coral-red maxi-dress with halter-style straps that tie behind my neck, hair loose and just a little wavy, the tiniest bit of blush. I managed to create a really good Flowies reel with all my waterfall footage from earlier. I'm determined to put the horseback riding incident out of my mind. To not let myself get hung up on the past—both what happened this afternoon, *and* what happened a year ago. *In order to move forward, we need to unburden ourselves from what's come before,* Gwendolyn always tells me.

I've always kind of believed in fate, and maybe I'm here not just for work but for a reason: for the actual transformation the blood moon eclipse promises.

Maybe what feels like chaos is just attempting to swim against the current; maybe what I really need to do is actually *go with the flow.*

Sebastian's waiting for me. He's changed into an ostentatious Hawaiian shirt with the top two buttons undone, but somehow, he's pulling it off. He steers me through the lobby and out to the front of the hotel, where he hops into the driver's seat of a gold cart emblazoned with Halia Falls's logo.

"How'd you convince them to give you a golf cart?" I take the seat beside him.

"I'm very persuasive." He gives me a conspiratorial wink, and I'm surprised by the laugh that escapes me. We crest a small hill and head the short distance to town. Sebastian has always been a skilled driver; I watch him maneuver around a small sedan and a couple of cyclists. The breeze ruffles his blond hair, and *something* flickers in my chest.

The road is blocked off for the festival, so when we get close to the center of town, we park the golf cart and start walking. The streets are strung with bright streamers and lined with huge, car-sized arrangements of plumeria, pink hibiscus, and other bright-green native foliage. There are stalls selling leis, ti leaf wreaths, goddess sculptures, authentic food, and all sorts of hand-crafted souvenirs. On the other side of the street, a stage has been set up, where hula dancers perform to guitarists singing soothing Hawaiian music that instantly relaxes me. A few stalls in, a man flips sticky Portuguese sausages and Hawaiian pork, the edges slightly charred. Its sweet barbeque smoke billows off the grill, and my mouth waters.

We continue to wander, passing a cart selling bright-purple ube ice cream. Next to that is someone frying malasadas, which I learn are a Portuguese tradition and basically the most delicious doughnut holes on the planet. Seb swings his arms around my shoulder, pulling me deeper into the crowd. The familiar, spicy scent of him surrounds me, and I let my arm come around his waist.

What am I doing, exactly—trying to convince myself of the boyfriend charade too? But I shoo away those thoughts. *Go with the flow*, I tell myself. I deserve to feel good, and right now, leaning into Sebastian feels a hell of a lot better than darting around the resort dodging Jamie.

We pass a stall filled with racks of brightly colored sarongs that flap in the afternoon breeze and another piled high with koa wood that seems to glow from within. While Sebastian buys us a couple of beers, I stop at a jewelry stall. The pieces are all handmade, the vendor tells me as I trail a hand along the display tables, and I recognize her name as the shop owner Ash told me about, the one who made Ash's green beaded earrings. A milky, pearlescent stone winks up at me from its setting in a delicate gold band. It's unique. Almost otherworldly. "That's moonstone," the vendor says.

"It's beautiful," I tell her, captivated by the way the light plays across its surface. My fingers trace the smooth face of the stone, and I imagine it catching the moonlight, its iridescent glow shimmering against my skin. It's stunning, but probably way out of my budget. I thank the woman and move on to browse some other pieces in her shop while I wait for Seb.

At one point, I slip a woven bracelet over my wrist. I'm admiring it when Sebastian returns.

"It suits you." He takes my hand and twists the bracelet around to get a better look. "I've always thought you looked good in organic jewelry," he says with a wink, and the flakes of seaweed in my jewelry box flash across my mind.

"What do you say?" He squeezes my hand and nods down at the bracelet. "Want to make a run for it?"

I roll my eyes and drop his hand. "After the dine-and-dash disaster of 2019, I'm going to say no."

Seb had forgotten his wallet when we were out to dinner one night at a little hole-in-the-wall on St. Mark's Place not far from my apartment, and I hadn't brought anything, assuming he was going to pick up the check (I'd gotten the last one). He convinced me to dash after we'd finished our entrees, but predictably, the restaurant caught us. If I hadn't convinced the owner to take Seb's watch as collateral while we waited for Emma to come down to the restaurant with my purse, we'd probably have found ourselves sitting in some Manhattan precinct office, awaiting sentencing for Grand Theft Dumplings.

"Guess I've got to pay for it, then," Sebastian says, his eyes sparkling.

He gives the crafter some money for the bracelet, and we maneuver through the crowd that seems to have grown even denser since we got here.

We find an empty picnic table on a lawn near the bandstand, and Seb takes a seat beside me, his hand coming up to my back. Resting beneath my shoulder blades, his thumb rubs up and down along the bare skin of my spine, exposed from the open back of the coral dress, and even though the weather is mild, I swallow and suppress a shiver. I'm not sure if I should lean away, but before I can decide, Sebastian's hand drops to the bench, as if he's not sure either.

Sebastian lifts his beer bottle in a toast, his eyes sparkling down at me. "To losing sight of the shore."

Smiling at the familiar words, I lift the cool glass bottle to my lips. The quote has always been one of Sebastian's favorites. *Man cannot discover new oceans unless he has the courage to lose sight of the shore.* That's how it's always been with Sebastian. Like we were throwing ourselves into the unknown with the hope that we'd land somewhere new and dazzling.

"This might sound corny to say." Sebastian doesn't look at me as he sets his beer gently on the table. "But this feels like fate." His bright blue eyes come to mine, and I'm struck by the sincerity in them. They're totally serious, free of the mirth that usually sparks in them. "It feels like fate," he repeats, "that we were both in the Pacific Islands at the same time. That we got to reconnect."

"Would it still be fate if it had been one of your other exes in Hawaii this week?" I tease.

"If you must know," he says, almost primly, "I don't keep tabs on any of my other exes."

That surprises me. "Really?"

"Really. You're special, Sybil Rain. It's like..." He trails a hand through his hair. "I never felt like the door was fully closed with us, you know?"

I swallow and nod. "I felt that way for a long time too. Until..."

"Until you met him."

"Yeah." I begin to peel the label off my beer bottle.

He presses his lips together and looks away, toward the hula dancers.

"You were really right for me, for a certain time in my life, Seb," I say, willing him to believe me. "But I don't think we ever would have been right forever. We just didn't want the same things."

"Is this about Tokyo?" Seb asks, a slight edge of defensiveness creeping into his voice. "Because I did apologize for that, Sybil. I thought you *wanted* to come with me."

"And *I* thought you were going to pick me up. Like you said you would."

The debacle was classic Sebastian. He always means what he says when he says it, but somehow, something always seems to come up. An opportunity he can't say no to. A freak traffic delay that maybe could have been avoided if he hadn't waited to leave until the last minute. A misunderstanding because he was only half listening when making plans...

I remember sitting at the arrivals gate at Tokyo-Haneda International Airport, waiting for Seb to pick me up. Waiting hours, with no international cell phone plan, in a foreign country where I didn't speak a word of the language, didn't know the address of the place I was going to be staying at. Finally, after I'd cried myself to sleep on a bench near baggage claim, Sebastian came and found me. He'd gotten the times wrong. He was wrapped up in a shoot. He was sorry. I accepted his apology and went to stay with him in his new Tokyo apartment for the week like we'd planned, but the sour, stilted feeling between us lasted the whole trip. We were planning to get married; I still had that strand of kelp wrapped around my finger. But I couldn't stop thinking that while I had been willing to drop everything and join him on the other side of the world, he hadn't been willing to drop his photo shoot to meet me halfway across the city. When the trip was over, I returned home, and he stayed. That was that. I think the trip had simply confirmed what I'd always suspected. That some part of me was always going to be left disappointed and heartbroken by Sebastian.

"I don't want to talk about Tokyo," I say. "That's water under the bridge. Besides, that's not even what I meant, about wanting different things."

A squeal of microphone feedback makes us both wince. On the stage, the hula dancers have been replaced by a new band. They have just finished setting up, and the lead singer steps up to the mic as the musicians start playing a sweet folk song.

Seb and I watch a father pull his young daughter onto the street in front of the bandstand. She places her little feet on top of his, and they start dancing—really just swaying in place—her crooked smile beaming up at him.

"Did you ever want kids?" The words tumble out of me. I can't look at Seb while I wait for his answer, so I start picking at the label on my beer again.

After a moment, I hear Seb say, "Not really, no." He says it simply, not apologetic or defiant. Just a statement of fact. "I mean, I love my nephews like crazy, but...I never wanted that life for myself. I value my spontaneity too much." He chuckles. "I don't know if you know this about me, but I kiiiind of like winging it."

This gets a laugh from me. "You don't say?"

"I do, in fact."

For a moment, we just grin at each other.

"I think...I think I knew that," I say, putting my beer bottle down on the table and stilling my fidgeting hands. "I mean, we never really talked about it, but I knew that's how you felt. And I think I found that comforting."

"Comforting?" Seb wrinkles his brow.

"Yeah." I nod at him, realizing the truth of what I'm saying as I say it. "Because I wasn't sure if kids were in my future. And being with you, it was like the decision was made for me. It was the safe choice."

"But..." Seb prompts me, and I both hate and love that he knows me so well. That I can't get away with anything when I'm with him.

"But as I got older, my feelings changed. I knew I wanted a family, but I was afraid to say it."

"I hate that you felt like you couldn't tell me," Seb says. "I'm not sure if I would have changed my mind, but we could have at least talked about it."

I shake my head. "It wasn't you. I was afraid to say it because...I wasn't sure if I *could* have children. Like, physically."

"Sybil," Seb says, his spine tensing. "Are you okay? I mean, are you sick or—"

"I'm fine, I'm fine," I assure him. "Just some stuff with my ovaries that doesn't quite work right. It's called PCOS. I've known about it since I was in high school." I remember sitting on that cold exam table, doctors saying words I could barely define, like "polycystic" and "mild adrenal hyperplasia." All I remember understanding was that my own anatomy had betrayed me. And it likely would again. I was lucky—and still am—that my symptoms mostly took the form of irregular periods, but the doctors said it could affect my fertility. They just couldn't be sure to what extent.

"Anyway," I say to Seb, swallowing down the memory, "I think I was afraid to voice what I truly wanted, because I was afraid I'd never get to have it. And being with you, I could sometimes let myself forget that I even wanted it. But then a few weeks before my wedding, I found out I was pregnant."

Seb looks at me in surprise, reaching a hand across the table to hold mine. I see confusion across his face as he pieces together the inevitable. Because clearly, there is no baby here today with us.

"Sybil," he says, his voice low. "Does Jamie know?"

"Obviously I'd been planning to tell him. I wanted it to be a surprise. Once I was confident that it would, you know... last."

Seb nods.

"Only," my throat feels like it's closing up, "it didn't. I miscarried Wednesday night before our wedding."

Now he looks pale, shaking his head. "Sybil, I just... I can't believe you went through that. And that you didn't *say* anything."

"I was such a mess. I think I was kind of in denial," I admit.

He's quiet for a minute, digesting all of this. "Look, it's not really my business, but if that's why you didn't marry him— because you were afraid you couldn't give him children—I think the guy at least deserves to know the truth."

It sounds absurd—that *isn't* why Jamie and I ended things. At least not on the surface. But I guess deep down, maybe I *did* think that if, on top of all my other failures, it turned out that kids also weren't in the cards, it would just be one more strike against me. I had never said it out loud because I didn't rationally think Jamie would break up with me over it. But was it there in the background, a part of the larger puzzle?

Or was it never really about Jamie at all? Maybe, just as I'd told Seb, I was simply afraid of saying what *I* really wanted. Because then I'd have to face the heartbreak that I might not be able to have it. Maybe what I was running away from was the fear deep down that I'd never have a true sense of home and family.

Just then the band strikes up "Come Monday," and the familiar chords cause Sebastian's expression to soften. He'd never admit, but he's a secret Parrothead. This very song was playing on the boat in Key West the day Sebastian proposed. As if remembering the same thing, Seb extends his hand, and I reach for it. His hands curl around mine, and he pulls us both to our feet. I let him guide me over to an empty patch of grass near the side of the stage.

My right hand remains clasped in Sebastian's while my left comes to rest on his shoulder, a healthy distance between our bodies as we start to sway to the music. At one point, he tries to twirl me around, but my feet get tangled in each other. I land hard on Sebastian's toes, and we both wince, laughing.

"Sorry. Some things never change, I guess." I've never been the most elegant dancer. Enthusiastic, sure. But graceful, not so much.

"We really had our moments though, didn't we?"

It feels like we're having another moment now. The warm sun and the distant roar of the ocean, not fully drowned out by the music. "We really did."

I've always tried to hold our best moments at the forefront of my memory. Maybe that's why it was so easy for us to keep getting back together, even after Tokyo. The good memories crowded out the bad, making me forget why we ever broke up in the first place.

Seb spins me out and reels me back in, and I try to lose myself in the feeling, my body flush with his, the warm breeze tickling my skin. The familiar last lines of the song float up around us, *I just want you back by my side.* A lump forms in my throat. Because even though I'm here with Sebastian, dancing to a song that's always been ours, I still can't get *Jamie* out of my mind. Questions stirring. Wondering when it all went wrong—not with Jamie, but with *me.*

What was the point in my life where I lost some key ingredient to myself that I've been trying, ever since, to find again?

17

THE FIRST RING

LIAM FOUND THE POSITIVE PREGNANCY TEST IN MY BATHROOM TRASH CAN in May of our junior year, and a week later he proposed.

"No one will love you like I do," he told me, looking up from one knee. He was holding a ring: a simple gold band with a tiny setting containing an amber-hued stone that I realized was a citrine. "I know all your flaws, all your sins, all your brokenness, and I still love you, Sybil."

His happiness about the pregnancy was directly inverse to my terror about it. It would mean a total recalibration of my life's trajectory. But Liam had a plan: we would get married. We would live with his parents until we had enough money for an apartment. He'd picked out the citrine ring specifically because he thought if I was 12 weeks pregnant, the baby would be born in November, and citrine would be his or her birthstone. This was exactly the kind of thing Liam loved to do; on the surface it seemed so thoughtful, but in reality, it felt like *too* much thought, too much anticipation, too much control. But his plan went on: when we graduated from high school, he would go to school a few blocks away at SMU while I would stay home with the baby. All the things I wanted to do and places I wanted to visit would be closed to me.

It was overwhelming, but our relationship had evolved so fast, I felt powerless to it, like a tide had overtaken me. When we'd first started dating, it had been such a high. Before then, I'd seen myself as a square-shaped peg trying to fit into a round hole all the time; a free spirit with weird ideas and big, spontaneous outbursts of emotion, who everyone liked enough, yet no one really understood. But when Liam started paying attention to me, everything changed. He was a pastor's son and the hot guy that all the other girls in our school had crushes on. When I was with him, everyone saw me in a whole new light—including my family, who just *adored* him. It felt like *I* finally made sense, like I finally fit somewhere.

But over the months we dated, something turned. I couldn't put my finger on when I'd started feeling so claustrophobic, but soon, I found myself constantly on eggshells with Liam. In groups, he was charismatic, always remembering people's birthdays and high-fiving them after a football win, but when it was just us, he would go from hot to cold in a second. He'd praise me and then throw hurtful barbs with a casual laugh. I was too young and inexperienced to realize this was toxic; I thought I was doing something to make him mad, and that if I could just figure out what that was and stop it, things would go back to being perfect.

But it had only gotten worse; he'd taken to coming into my room even when I wasn't home and finding "evidence" of ways I had betrayed him or kept secrets from him. That was how he'd found the pregnancy test. I had always wanted to get married and start a family, but not at seventeen!

Then, three days after Liam proposed, I started bleeding. Heavily. It was the day of junior prom, and I was supposed to be getting ready then heading to Liam's for pre-prom photos with some of his church friends. Instead, I hid my physical pain and picked a fight with my parents, saying it would be lame for them to come to the Russells' house for pictures and that I was getting a ride with a friend anyway. They were clearly hurt, but didn't want to deal with another Sybil meltdown. They let me walk out of the house with a garment bag over my arm and a sweatshirt tied around my waist to hide any possible bloodstains.

I couldn't tell my parents what I suspected was happening to me, because that would mean I'd have to admit I'd been having sex with Liam, much less that I'd gotten pregnant.

And when I thought about calling Liam himself, all I could hear were his usual complaints about how this would ruin his prom night, how I was always causing drama and making things about me.

Of course, I know now that if I had dialed Willow or Emma, they would have been there in a heartbeat. But my all-consuming relationship with Liam had chipped away at those friendships. They didn't know how bad things really were with him, and the thought of reaching out to them in that moment, when I was at my lowest, filled me with shame.

So when I got a few blocks away from my house, I called a cab to take me to the emergency room.

At the hospital, I took another pregnancy test, but this time it came back negative. "It might have been a chemical pregnancy, or it might have been a false positive," the resident said. "It's rare, but certain medications can impact an at-home-test's accuracy. Are you taking any antianxiety meds, or an antihistamine?" I nodded. I had terrible spring allergies. "Well, that could be it. What about your periods. Are they generally regular?"

I told her that no, my periods were actually pretty erratic. Some months it didn't come at all, and then would be super heavy when it finally arrived. I saw her make a note about that. Then she looked me in the eye and said calmly, "It's possible you miscarried. It's also possible you were never pregnant. But I can confirm either way that you are not pregnant now. Here, take some pads. You might have heavier bleeding for a few more days."

Despite a few cramps roiling in my abdomen, the sweet and cool relief that I hadn't dared to hope for rushed through me, and I felt my life open back up before me. In the waiting room, I called Liam to tell him the news.

"Thank god, right?"

And I genuinely meant it.

"How can you say that?" Liam said in horror. "How can you be happy our child died?"

"We don't even know if there ever was a baby," I pleaded. "We have our whole lives now." But Liam hung up on me. I tried to call him back. And tried and tried. But it was clear that Liam was furious with me.

"Miss Rain, could you come back here for a minute, please?"

Numbly, I walked back to the receptionist's desk, where she told me that the doctor had just finished looking at my results more fully and wanted to talk to me again. That's when they explained that they wanted to run an ultrasound on my ovaries. Before the results even came in, the doctor told me that they were looking for signs of PCOS. It would explain my frequently late periods... But there was something else. PCOS could also mean I might have trouble getting pregnant—or at least staying pregnant—down the road.

I felt the crush of conflicting emotions. While I didn't want to be pregnant *now*, the thought that I might not be able to have a baby *ever* was devastating.

When the doctor released me, I tried Liam one last time, but got voicemail again. I was just about to redial the cab company when I heard someone calling my name.

"Sybil, is that you?"

I turned to find Finn Hughes, Emma's debate team friend. They were supposed to be having their first date that very night at junior prom. Finn told me he was here at the hospital with his dad, who had been going through cancer treatments. He looked like a wreck, and it seemed like prom was far from his mind.

"What are you doing here?" he asked me.

I didn't mean to, but in a jumble of raw emotions, I broke down right there in the hospital lobby and told everything to Finn, who'd pressed his car keys into my hand and told me it was all going to be okay.

When I got home from the hospital, my parents had gone out. Their absence felt like a blessing. Like a chance for me to truly pretend this day had never happened. So I finished my hair and makeup, put on my dress, and changed my pad. The bleeding began to taper off, and I folded up all my thoughts and tucked them into a box in the back of my mind.

For a while after prom, Liam completely froze me out. I think he was trying to punish me. But eventually, he must have felt me starting to slip away.

One day early in the fall of senior year, he let himself into my house, and I found him in my room. "I know I've been distant lately. I've had a lot to work through. It's been a hard couple of months for me. Really hard."

"I'm sorry," I heard myself apologize.

"We're still getting married, Sybil. Just because you lost the baby doesn't mean I don't love you anymore. I forgive you. I want to spend forever with you."

Forever.

I felt the walls of inevitability rise up around me, closing in brick by brick.

"I'm going to school in California," I said, as if that was some get-out-of-jail-free card. "I just got into USC."

"I know." Liam's face darkened, but he reached out and grabbed my hand. "We'll make it work." But it didn't feel like a promise. It felt like a sentence.

"Don't tell my parents," I said. I didn't want them—or anyone else—to know about our engagement. That would make it real. "Let me tell them when I'm ready, okay?" Liam must have feared that my parents would try to talk us out of getting married so young, because he agreed.

When the summer came to an end, we loaded up the car to

drive to California. The citrine ring was tucked in my jewelry box, my clothes and books all carefully packed by my mom.

I kissed Liam goodbye and felt the lightest I had in months.

It was easy to fall into a new life with new patterns at school, but still, I *had* tried to make things work with Liam. Kind of. But the distance between us meant he had to resort to more and more elaborate ploys to keep me leashed to him. He demanded that any night I was out past midnight, I had to call him every fifteen minutes. *I need to make sure you're safe,* he insisted. He wanted to know everyone I talked to. Everywhere I went. What I was drinking. What I was wearing.

Things finally came to a head on video chat when he threatened to hurt himself if I didn't transfer to SMU. I slammed my laptop shut, knowing that Liam was bluffing, but terrified all the same. A week later, I awoke to angry banging on my door. It was Liam. He'd flown all the way to California to force *me* to apologize for abandoning him. When I refused and mustered the courage to tell him it was over between us, he said: "It doesn't matter. You're damaged goods anyway. I could never marry someone who didn't respect themselves enough to wait for marriage."

The hypocrisy of it rolled over me—after all, the only person I'd ever slept with was Liam himself—but I didn't try to contradict him. I just sat on my extra-long dorm bed in stony silence until Liam left the dorm, slamming the door behind him.

I was depressed for weeks after that, but eventually, Nikki coaxed me out of our room to a party, and that night I decided to be the exact opposite of the person that Liam wanted.

I let myself be wild and carefree.

And yet, it was always there, lingering somewhere in the recesses of my mind: the fear that I'd never *really* be free, because the brokenness was in me. The fear that Liam, for all his toxic traits, might have been right about this one thing. Even now, all these years later, I can still feel it. The fear that my past would always be waiting, like a dark tide, to swallow me under.

18

THE DRIVE BACK TO THE HOTEL FROM THE FESTIVAL IS MORE LEISURELY, the lush rainforest to our left and the ocean to our right. The wind tugs strands of my hair loose, and they flutter around my face as we round the curve that leads to the hotel entrance. The golf cart rolls to a stop as the fountain bubbles quietly and the scent of plumeria rises up around me. Sebastian hops out of the golf cart, then turns to wait for me. He doesn't hold out a hand to help me down, and I wonder why I should care. It's an old-fashioned gesture, something Jamie would do.

"I guess this is good night." Something in Seb's tone catches my attention. He stuffs his hands in his pockets and looks at me with a half grin, and I realize he looks *nervous*. Or as nervous as Seb gets. Uncertain might be a better word. He looks *uncertain*. And it's something I've never seen from him. I always admired how clear-eyed he was with his future. He stepped, sure-footed, out of his front door into the wide, wide world, with a camera slung across his chest, staring straight ahead. He never looked back to see if I was behind him. I would either follow or I wouldn't.

But right now, he doesn't look so sure. I shiver at the cool breeze, and without a word, Seb takes off his button-down shirt and slips it over my shoulders. The movement seems to loosen something within, and his lips turn up in a conspiratorial smile.

"Would you want to go for a late-night boat ride with me? I know where they keep all the keys." He loops his arms through mine, pulling me into the lobby. "We can swipe a bottle of rum from the bar. Really make a night of it."

I laugh, but then notice Seb's not laughing with me. "Oh wait—you're serious? Seb, we can't."

"Why not?"

"Um, because it would be super dangerous?"

Something flickers across Sebastian's face, as if he's recalibrating his memory of me to match the person I am now. There's something about his expression that makes me want to throw him a bone. If only to prove to him that I'm not, despite the way he's looking at me, some body-snatching alien inhabiting the corporeal form of one Sybil Rain.

"Besides," I say with a shrug, "I'm already on thin ice with the resort's boat people. I *maaaay* have jumped off the side of the snorkel catamaran before we were officially instructed to do so."

"I knew it," Seb says with a grin. He starts walking backward, toward the east end elevator banks. "Haven't changed a bit."

"Still the same old me," I reply with an eye roll.

He raises his hand in a quick salute before he turns to walk away. As I watch him leave, I realize how much Seb still wants to see me as the old, carefree Sybil. The person I always tried to be when I was with him. After Liam, he was the antidote I needed. A breath of fresh air. The perfect twin flame who never judged me for my wild ways, who encouraged every questionable impulse I had and made me feel like I just might be okay, if only I could keep the party going long enough.

I'm about to head to the west end elevators and my own room when I remember: Mason's birthday party. If I head there now, I should be right on time to be fashionably late.

THERE ARE PROBABLY TWO dozen people scattered along the beach and mingling around a bonfire piled high with driftwood and palm tree bark. Dani had texted me directions to this little cove that's separate from the resort's main beachfront. There's a low one-story building, which must be the staff housing. The sun is just setting, and the sky is a dazzling rainbow of yellows and pinks doubled in the sea's reflection.

Ash greets me with a Solo cup filled with something fruity. I was expecting a full-on luau, but this is giving more USC beach party energy. I notice Ash has traded the crisp suits I'm used to seeing her wear for a vibrant yellow silk mini-dress, but she still has a flower tucked into her long brown hair. I tilt the cup back, hoping that whatever's inside will quiet the confusion ricocheting through my brain and bring out Fun Sybil, in all her glory.

There's the sharp taste of rum and the sweetness of pineapple. The drink goes down easily. "This is amazing."

"And potent. It pays to marry a bartender." As Ash says this, Dani comes up behind her and loops an arm around her waist before dropping a kiss on her cheek.

"Hey, Sybil, so glad you made it!" Dani says. "Also—why the hell didn't you tell me your evil ex-fiancé was the wine guy!"

"What are you talking about?"

"I'm talking about this." She hands me a shiny brochure with a familiar-looking vineyard on the cover. The heading reads: *Kauffman Estates & Winery.*

What in the world... I start flipping through the pages of marketing materials. There's a photo of Jamie, looking impossibly handsome in a crisp white shirt, his sleeves rolled up as he inspects a cluster of grapes. Beneath it, a quote: "Our family has always believed in investing in what matters most. With Kauffman Estates & Winery, we're investing in passion, in heritage, and in the future of fine winemaking."

My heart swells with a ridiculous amount of pride. He did it. He actually did it. He defied his father, he chased his dream, and he finally expanded on the vineyard's potential. And suddenly, the memory of that first conversation at the pool comes flooding back. Something about diversifying the portfolio. I had been so blinded by the shock of seeing him that I hadn't truly listened, hadn't grasped the significance of what Jamie was telling me.

I'm struck by a burning impulse to find Jamie and tell him how impressed I am by all of this—and more importantly, to clear the air about Sebastian's story about how we rekindled. It might be too late for me and Jamie to rebuild what we lost, but I can't let him go on thinking that I left him for Seb.

But before I can make a move, Dani grabs my arm and starts leading me toward the party. "Come meet the rest of the gang!"

I desperately want to abandon the party and go find Jamie *right now*, but I know it would be rude to ditch Dani when she was gracious enough to invite me. Besides, the memory of his furious expression as he stormed off on horseback earlier today still stings. What if he's still angry and refuses to listen? It's been such a long day already, and the truth is, I'm exhausted. Maybe tonight what I need is to let loose, have some fun, and pretend, for a few blissful hours, that my life isn't a complete and utter disaster.

"Lead the way," I say to Dani.

"THE REST OF THE gang" turns out to be an international crew of young people. A found family made up of bartenders, bell-hops, servers, housekeeping staff, and grounds crew. They rib each other and tell funny stories about past seasons at the resort. The energy is infectious and exactly what I needed. It feels like being with friends from college or summer camp—a feeling that only grows when someone suggests a round of Kings, followed by a drinking game called Legends that I struggle to understand the rules of, and then a girl with box braids suggests the old standby: Truth or Dare, and everyone cheers.

Which is how I end up wading out into the moonlit ocean until I'm deep enough to attempt an underwater handstand.

After, I run back to the group, shivering. When I get closer, I hear a guy named Kostas, who I'm pretty sure is the resort medic, chanting, "Sy-bil! Sy-bil!"

"I can't believe you just did that!" Ash squeals with a slight hiccup.

"Rules are rules," I shrug, yanking a sandy blanket out from under Dani's butt and wrapping it around myself like a towel.

"Okay, okay, my turn," Dani says. "I pick truth."

"What's one thing I do that *really* annoys you?" Ash asks, devilishly.

I let myself tune out a little as they playfully start arguing back and forth, and the game moves on to daring one of the housekeepers to make out sensually with a snorkel mask. It feels good to be among a group of new friends, here in this beautiful place. To just be Fun Sybil and not think about any of the things that have been weighing me down since I landed in Hawaii. And yet, the minute that thought strikes me, reality starts creeping back in, and I find myself wondering where Jamie is right now, what he's doing. Is he alone in his hotel room? Is he with Genevieve? The thought makes my stomach squirm. Is he—

"Sybil." Dani nudges me. "It's your turn."

I swallow the lump that has unexpectedly formed in my throat. "Truth."

"Hmmm..." Dani gives me a wicked grin. "What's your most embarrassing moment from high school?"

It should be an easy one—I could rattle off the funny story about the time my sweatpants fell down, causing me to trip over my own legs during my ill-fated tryouts for cheerleading, or how I was so pumped about going out with my freshman year crush and possibly getting my first kiss that I drank two jumbo Diet Cokes beforehand, and the kiss was thwarted by an uncontrollable and mortifying case of violent hiccups.

But for some reason—maybe because of the conversation Seb and I had earlier tonight at the street fair—my mind skips past the silly stuff and flashes to prom night. The smell of the antiseptic soap still clinging to my hands. Sitting next to Finn in the waiting room and spiraling out while he holds my now-raw hand and rubs my back. Finn's keys cool in my palm as he says, *You deserve better than this.* There's the slick stab of shame and the physical pain in my abdomen as I lie to Emma on the dance floor about why I was late, Rihanna singing in the background. Even now, I can feel the bass pumping in my skull. I realize it's the sound of my own heartbeat, and I take in a breath that only dips into the tops of my lungs.

"Sybil?" Ash's voice drifts through the haze of my anxiety and anchors me back to the present moment.

"You gotta answer or drink," Dani says.

"I'll pass," I say, prompting cheers of "Drink! Drink!" to go up from the group. I force a grin, salute the crew with what's left of my beverage, and finish in one long pull.

EVENTUALLY, EVERYONE STARTS PAIRING off, the cloud of phero-mones working its particular brand of magic. Ash and Dani say good night and walk back toward their room, arms slung around each other, heads bent together, the picture of easy intimacy.

I slip away from the dwindling crowd and wander alone down the beach, the sand cool and soft beneath my feet. As I walk, the music and laughter fade behind me, replaced by the rhythmic roar of the waves crashing against the shore. I round a bend in the coastline, and the lights of the main resort come into view, twinkling like a constellation against the velvet night sky. Reaching the stone steps that lead up to the main lawn, I pause, pull out my phone. Willow picks up on the second ring.

"Hey, Bill," I say, cradling the phone between my ear and shoulder.

"Hey, Bill," she echoes back. Over the years, Willow got shortened to Wills which morphed into Bill, which is also the last syllable of *my* name. Since at least middle school, maybe earlier, it's been what we've called each other. Our mothers, who both gave us the wispy, feminine names of romance novel heroines, *hated* it. One time, when I called the landline at Willow's house and asked for "Bill," her mother hung up on me three times until I finally caved and asked for "Willow." But I think the nickname suits her. Unconventional, but still, in its own way, classic.

"What's up?" Willow asks through a yawn.

"Did I wake you up?"

"No, no. Don't worry—Nora's teething, so I just got up for the fifth time tonight to settle her." And I feel a warm sensation skate over me, like slipping into a hot bath with a glass of red wine. It's the way Willow makes everyone feel. And it's exactly why she was the one I needed to call right now. I try to picture her calm face, framed by soft bangs—effortless, like a brunette Brigitte Bardot—her warm brown eyes and gentle smile. "So what's up? Talk to me."

"I just... This trip was supposed to be this refreshing, cleansing vacation, but I've been thinking a lot about the past."

"About Jamie?"

"Well, yeah, but also..." I don't even know what I'm trying to say, exactly. But I try to let the words pour out of me anyway. "Like, the deep past. The Liam days. And you know, the whole PCOS thing. Aside from irregular periods, I've been super lucky so far when it comes to symptoms. And because of that, I haven't really had to worry about it. I could kind of put the whole thing in the past. Try to pretend it didn't exist, you know?"

Willow hums encouragingly on the other end of the line. She was one of the first people I told about the diagnosis, and ever since, I've always known I could count on her—whether for an emergency tampon or a hook-up to French pharmacy skincare to combat the occasional acne flare-ups, or most importantly, for an ear to listen.

"But I guess what I'm saying is, the miscarriage last year messed me up more than I thought it did." I feel my throat closing up, and I'm trying not to cry.

Willow lets out a deep sigh. "Oh, honey. Of course it did. And that's okay. That's totally normal. When I had mine before Nora, it was scary and devastating, and the worst thing is how life just seems to go on around you, no one having any idea what you're going through. And what you've lost."

I take a shaky breath. "Exactly." I hate that this is something Willow and I have both suffered, but I'm grateful that our shared experience makes us both feel less alone. "The thing is, with Jamie, I thought the miscarriage and the breakup were kind of two separate things, you know? It was just bad timing mixed with the inevitable. Jamie had been waiting for the other shoe to drop for probably the entire length of our relationship anyway. Or that's what I believed. But now..."

"Now?"

"Well, I just wonder if I was the one putting up the walls, afraid of not being..."

"Not being what, Sybil?"

"The wife he wanted." Now I'm crying despite my best efforts, and thankful for the cloak of darkness, the moon and stars obscured by thick clouds. "Am I really the person he thought he was marrying? How do you even know if you are who people think you are? Am I even making sense?"

"Wow." Willow's deadpan voice in my ear brings me back to our phone call. "You go for the big existential questions, huh?"

I huff out a laugh. "Sorry."

"Nah, it's okay. I get it. I always start questioning my life path around the full moon. That shit brings up all kinds of big feelings."

"Tell me about it."

I hear Nora start to cry again through the phone and try to imagine the four of us bouncing from small Mediterranean town to small Mediterranean town, like we did when the Core Four took our first trip abroad. Eating bread and cheese until we pass out somewhere in a patch of sunlight. Nothing different from that first trip except Willow's baby strapped to her chest.

Of course, it couldn't really be that simple. There would be nap times to plan around; international phone calls to husbands and fiancés back home. Probably some camera crew trailing Nikki for a *LovedBy* featurette about finding love abroad. People change. Lives change. Maybe that's okay.

Even if it sometimes still feels like a kind of loss.

After a few minutes of silence on the line, Willow speaks. "Can I ask you something, Sybil?"

"Of course!"

"Why do you think it's been so hard for you to just say all this to Jamie?"

I blink back the fresh tears that threaten, and swallow through the lump in my throat. "Because he'll feel so guilty. And—I *couldn't* tell him that weekend. I didn't want him to marry me out of guilt. I couldn't do that, Bill. I couldn't let that happen."

"But you're not together anymore. Don't you think he'd appreciate getting the full story?"

"Well, it's a bit more complicated than that."

"How so?"

"I know it's going to sound crazy, but since seeing him again, there's this... spark between us. Like whatever was there before... it's still alive. Bill, if I'm being honest, I don't think I ever got over Jamie," I blurt out. It's shocking to hear myself say it out loud, and yet it feels so completely obvious as soon as I do. "Not really, anyway. Sometimes, it feels like I never will."

"Maybe you won't have to," Willow says, and my breath hitches with hope. After we ended our marriage in front of all our friends and loved ones, my crew was quick to swoop in and tell me that I deserved better. But secretly, I just want to deserve *him*. "I have a good feeling about this, Bill," she says. "The fact that he's there with you. It means something. Just be open to whatever the universe sends your way. Maybe it's Jamie, maybe it's not. Maybe it's just about finally making some peace with yourself." Willow's words are a balm, and exactly what I need to hear. Stop thinking about the past and start living in the present.

I let out a deep breath. "Thanks, Bill."

"Anytime, Bill," she says, and I can hear the smile in her voice.

We say our goodbyes, and there's a scuffle over my shoulder as I pull the phone from my ear. I turn and follow the sound.

It's Jamie.

THE SOFT GLOW OF moonlight settles on Jamie's skin, highlighting the sharp angles of his jaw and the tousled mess of his dark hair. My breath catches in my throat. He lifts his hand in a small wave. He's wearing a faded T-shirt and shorts, and I notice his feet are clad in a pair of old hiking boots. I wonder if he's been out on one of those evening cultural walking tours he was so excited about back when we were planning our honeymoon last year. The thought brings a bittersweet ache to my chest, a reminder of all the shared dreams we once had. But then I see the expression on his face—curious, and even a little hopeful. And that flicker of hope in his eyes is enough to rekindle my own.

Did he overhear my words to Willow? *I don't think I ever got over Jamie.*

Is it possible he feels the same way?

I give a gentle wave back, and Jamie's lips quirk up in a small smile.

A gust of wind lifts his hair, and the hem of my dress is also sent fluttering. The wind has steadily been picking up over the course of the evening. What was just a light breeze earlier this afternoon has turned into the start of a full-blown storm.

Without saying a word, Jamie starts to walk down the stone steps that lead from the main lawn down to the sand. Even in the dark, I can see a slight sparkle in his warm brown eyes. With each step he takes, my heart starts to beat faster.

Maybe this is our moment. The universe, the approaching full moon, the melodic sounds of some new pop band blaring through someone's portable speakers farther down the beach— all of them guiding Jamie to me so we can finally make things right between us. Maybe this is the second chance we both deserve.

And then—the moment is broken by someone shouting from the distance. "Sybil!"

19

I TURN AT THE SOUND OF MY NAME AND SEE ONE OF THE HALIA FALLS Polaris ATVs rumbling along the edge of the beach, through the darkness. *What the...*

Then the ATV passes one of the ground lights along the path from the resort to the beach, and I see that it's Sebastian at the wheel. He parks and hops out.

I wave to Seb, confused as to what the hell he's doing here, then look back to Jamie, who has frozen on the last step. But he hasn't walked away, which is something. At least, that's what I'm willing myself to believe.

"Sybil, I'm so glad you're still up!" Seb is now standing at my elbow, a little out of breath. "You gotta come see these waves. This storm's supposed to be a good one. Passing offshore, but the photos will be incredible."

"What?" I stare at his happy, smiling face, trying to figure out what he's talking about. "You're taking photos in the middle of the night?"

"No, silly!" he says, giving me a nudge. "I'm going to get some shots at sunrise. The waves are going to be even better at this place called the Secret Cove a couple hours south, and I gotta get there before dawn to set up. It's going to be absolutely stunning."

"Secret Cove? Wait, you're planning to drive to a different beach *a couple hours away* in a—is that a *stolen* Polaris from the resort?"

"Borrowed," Seb answers with an easy shrug. "And it's not two hours if I off-road it. Literally only an hour, if I'm reading the map right," he answers, like this is perfectly sane logic. "You wanna come? A little less reckless than borrowing a boat, right? What do you think?"

"I think it's an incredibly stupid idea."

Seb and I both whip our heads over to the stone staircase. Jamie's arms are folded across his chest, the muscle in his jaw twitching.

"Oh, hey, man." Seb says. "Didn't realize you were standing there." There's nothing outright hostile in Seb's tone, but I can feel the tension radiating off his body.

"The resort won't allow that. And I wouldn't recommend it anyway in a vehicle like that, in bad weather," Jamie says stiffly.

"Well, that's why we won't tell them." Seb gives an exaggerated wink but it's not playful—it's annoyed. "No one likes a narc, Jamie." He turns back to me, with the eagerness of a child who can't wait to open his Christmas presents. "So, what do you say, Sybs?"

"Oh, well..." I look out to the water, and then along the narrow strip of beach, worrying my bottom lip between my teeth. The waves are picking up, crashing against the shore with more force than I've seen so far this trip. This supposed storm hasn't hit yet, but I can feel the uptick in the wind, and a heavy moisture in the air. I'm sure Seb could get some really amazing shots of these waves from right where we're standing if he just waits a few hours, and the idea of taking a little unprotected ATV out over the dunes in this weather seems like a very bad idea. Even as I think it, a light drizzle is starting to frizz my hair, and there's a charged energy in the air that suggests an oncoming thunderstorm.

Or maybe that's just the crackling animosity between the two men standing before me.

"She's not taking off with you in this weather," Jamie says through gritted teeth.

"Um, I think she can decide for herself what she wants, buddy," Seb snaps back.

"Of course she can," Jamie says, like it's the most obvious thing in the world. "And she *doesn't* want to—it's written all over her face. If you knew her at all, you'd realize that. You're pressuring her—"

"Bullshit."

"—and," Jamie continues, raising his voice over a loud whoosh of wind, "because she doesn't want to disappoint you, she's considering doing it anyway. Even if it means she might get hurt."

"Oh yeah?" Seb says, slinging an arm around my shoulder. His lips twist in a cruel grin. "Is that what she was doing when she almost married you?"

Jamie flinches almost imperceptibly. A brief fluttering of one eyelid. But I know him well enough to tell the blow has landed.

"Jamie," I start.

"Forget it." He takes a deep breath, looking off to the side where a crop of palm trees is swaying aggressively. "I just wanted to come say goodbye. Gen and I are flying back home tomorrow."

"Jamie, wait, please. Can we talk? Things with Seb aren't what you think—"

"It's none of my business."

"It *is* your business," I insist. "I'm sorry I didn't tell you that he called me that night during my bachelorette party. He was just wishing me good luck, I swear. That conversation is not why I ran off to Vegas. Or why you and I didn't..." I can't say the words: *get married. Spend the rest of our lives together. Come to this very resort on our honeymoon like we were supposed to.*

I can feel Seb stiffen beside me. "She's telling the truth, dude," he mutters.

"So you're not—" Jamie cuts himself off with a swallow. He rubs his nose. "You guys haven't been dating since then?"

"No! God, no." I shake my head emphatically. "This thing with Seb is..." *Completely fake. A stupid ruse to save face in front of you.* "...very new," I say, chickening out.

"Very, *very* new," Seb says sardonically.

"What are you—" Jamie starts to say, but Seb cuts him off before he can form the question.

"She's saying this whole thing is bullshit." He removes his arm from my shoulders. "We're not dating. I just happened to be in town at the same time, and we thought it would be fun to pretend."

"Fun," Jamie repeats flatly.

"Yeah, and let me tell you, it's been a real barrel of laughs." There's an edge of bitterness in Seb's voice. He turns and walks a few paces up the beach toward his "borrowed" Polaris, leaving me and Jamie staring at each other.

"So..." I start, a little sheepishly, looking down at my feet. This isn't how I wanted the truth to come out, but maybe now that all the cards are on the table, Jamie and I can have a real conversation about what we're both feeling. About this undeniable tug that's been drawing us together for the past few days. He must feel it too, right?

Except, when I look up, I see that the confusion on Jamie's face has been replaced with an icy stillness. "What else have you lied to me about, Sybil?"

"What? Nothing!" I blurt out, suddenly feeling caught like a deer in headlights. Guilt pummels my stomach, making me feel like I'm going to throw up.

But Jamie ignores me, methodically counting off all the times I've lied to him on his fingers. "Your college degree, your fake boyfriend, where you went on our *wedding* weekend." What grates the most is how *calm* he is as he lists my mistakes. "I really thought you'd changed."

"You said you didn't care about the college thing!" I hate that my voice rises. I hate the emotion that breaks through when Jamie's able to stand there like he's made of stone.

"I don't care about the college thing. I care that you *lied* to me about it." He says it matter-of-factly. As if that one lie disqualifies me from being worthy of a place in his life. Any deviation from perfection is enough to get me ejected from Jamie's meticulously curated, pristinely unspoiled life. I thought maybe I was ready to open up to him but instead, his words unleash something in me.

"Have you ever spent any time thinking about *why* it's so hard to be honest with you?" I shout, taking a step toward him.

A crackle of fire breaks through the ice of Jamie's expression.

"Don't put your bad decisions on me, Sybil." Jamie's voice has dropped dangerously low, and he takes a step toward me too.

"You put everyone you love up on some pedestal and then turn your back when we can't live up to your insane standards."

"What are you talking about?" Jamie says, looking genuinely nonplussed now. "You know, sometimes you say things, and it's like..." He runs an exasperated hand through his hair. "Like you don't even know me at all. Like you're describing a totally different person." He stalks a few paces down the beach before turning back to me. "I never expected you to be perfect."

"Your family sure did," I scoff. "They never liked me. They thought I wasn't good enough for you, not smart enough, not sophisticated enough."

"Sybil, we've had this conversation." Jamie puts his hands on his hips. "They aren't outgoing like you. They don't express themselves well."

"So, it's okay to be aloof and judgmental because you're not 'good at expressing yourself'?" I ask, unable to keep the bite out of my voice.

He winces. "That's not what I meant. Look, I'm sorry. I should have done more to make you feel comfortable, to bridge the gap between you and them. But Sybs," he says, his voice strained, "you lying to me is not okay. If we can't be honest with each other, then how are we supposed to—"

"Oh, like you've been so honest with me?" I interrupt. Because some part of me knows he's right, and yet, I can't let him have it. I'm still too hurt, too angry. It's as if all the wounds and feelings of rejection and abandonment from our wedding weekend have taken over my body and I can't control what spews out of me.

"I have!" Indignation is creeping back into Jamie's voice. "What haven't I been truthful about?"

"How about Genevieve being just your 'colleague,' for starts."

"She *is* just my colleague."

"Jamie, she's always around. Always calling you—"

"Because we're here for work!"

"Always looking at you like you hung the damn moon."

Jamie's affronted expression falters slightly, as if he's realizing something for the first time. But I just barrel right on.

"It's more than just that," I tell him. "You've been lying to me since the day you proposed. You said you loved me because I brought color to your life. Because I felt things more strongly than anyone you'd ever known." Hot, angry tears are forming in the corners of my eyes, but I wipe them away. "But you didn't want the reality that came with that, did you? When things weren't all sparkly and fun. When shit got real. You just pulled the plug. All that bullshit about wanting to 'set me free'...that was just an excuse to make yourself feel better, wasn't it? So yes, I made up a story about a fake boyfriend. But you lied to me too, Jamie. And yours was worse."

I turn on my heel and start heading for the path where Sebastian stands waiting, fearing that if I stay here one second longer, I will only do more damage, or have to admit that I'm doing it again.

That I'm ruining everything.

"Sybil, come on. Don't do this," Jamie says. "Stay here and fight with me."

I ignore his pleas and continue down the beach.

"Where are you going?" Jamie calls sharply.

I whip around to face him. "To the beach cove. With some-one who never expects me to be someone other than who I am."

"Of course," Jamie says, the muscle in his jaw jumping. "There you go. Running away...again."

"Yes, I am. And you can't stop me," I add, even though there's a huge part of me that's praying he will do exactly that.

Instead, all he says is, "If that's what you want."

Then he turns and walks back up the stone steps to the hotel at the top of the ridge.

And I feel whatever delicate threads were keeping my heart together snap.

I march across the beach to Sebastian. As I get closer, I can see the back of the ATV is loaded with supplies—some sort of tarp, and what looks like his tripod and expensive camera gear.

"Sybil, I'm sorry about—"

"That way." I point to a dirt road that departs from the edge of the beach, away from the resort and to the south.

Seb just raises an eyebrow at me, swallowing whatever he'd been about to say. "Well, hop in, then. No time like the present."

I jump onto the seat beside him.

He starts the weak engine. "You sure you want to do this?"

"I'm sure."

Seb turns the stolen key and pushes the pedal, and off we go, bumping up and down over the sand, under a heavy black sky, now entirely devoid of stars.

20

SEB STEERS US THROUGH BUMPY TERRAIN FOR THE BETTER PART OF A HALF an hour, and then, harrowingly, he finds the southern road that loops us toward the eastern coast, driving along the shoulder as the rain and wind grow ever fiercer, pummeling us from the open sides of the vehicle. I'm convinced we're going to tip over, run out of gas, get hit by passing traffic, or get arrested, but somehow, none of the above occurs. The entire way, I'm fighting myself not to insist we turn right back around, but what would be the point? We've already gone this far, and it feels like there really is no going back. We'll just have to face the consequences of this terrible idea, and if I'm being honest, I don't want to give Jamie the satisfaction of being right.

Sebastian, meanwhile, talks the whole way—loudly, over the sounds of the growing squall—and seems electrified by all the elements of danger that have me regretting saying yes to this.

By the time he pulls down an entirely-too-steep narrow dirt road toward a secluded beach lord-knows-where, I'm soaked to the bone and freezing. For the first time, as he turns off the engine, Seb seems to notice that I'm a wreck.

"Wait just a second," he says, hopping off the driver's seat. I'm sitting there, rain still hitting my legs from the open air at the side of the ATV when he comes back around with a rain slicker. "Only brought one, but you can take it." It looks altogether too little too late, but I appreciate the gesture. I shiver, slipping it on over my wet clothes.

The wind kicks up as I hop from the vehicle onto the beach. Sticky windblown sand and sprays of water plaster my hair to my face, but I take a deep breath, determined to embrace the excitement—this is what I used to love about Seb, and not just about him, but about him and me together. There was always something new and thrilling around the corner for us. The feeling of discovering something that only the two of us shared—that was a high unlike anything else. Maybe this is what I need, after all. A jolt to the system.

Around us, the night is still dark, but either my hope is getting the best of me, or I detect a faint line of silver at the very base of the horizon.

Seb wasn't wrong: it *is* beautiful. Despite the wind and rain on shore, the real storm is at sea, and you actually *watch* the way the dark clouds and torrents pass over the ocean in the distance.

He grabs something else from the back of the ATV, and I swallow down my nervousness and follow Sebastian to a small clearing between rocks and a cliffside, forming a little cove. "Here, this is protected enough from the wind that I think we can get away with setting up a tent. Can you help?"

I dig into the bag he's holding out to me—which is also

soaked through with rain—and extract some flimsy-looking plastic poles, realizing what this is. "Seb, this is just a beach tent. Like, for shade from the sun. There's no way it'll hold up in this weather!"

He shrugs. "It was the best I could find on short notice."

I try not to grumble or snap back. Best he could find on short notice—that's one I've heard before. Because everything with him is short notice.

"Can you help me tie this down?" Seb shouts over the rain, motioning to one corner of the tent while he heads to the other. I reach for the end of the rope, but the wind snaps it from my hand. It takes three more tries before I close my fist around the damp cord. I try to channel my Girl Scout days and dig the tent's plastic stakes into the sand, but the poles keep popping back out. Holding on with both hands, I watch as in seconds, Sebastian ties off his corner to a palm tree. He returns, taking my end of the rope. "Here," Seb shouts. "Give that to me." The wind only seems to be getting louder and louder. "Why don't you get *in* the tent. To help hold it in place. And then I'll finish securing the corners!"

"Okay!" I shout back, grateful for the break—from the effort, from the weather, and frankly, from having to pretend I'm not a devastated mess of a human on the inside. The fight with Jamie is still coursing through my blood, making me feel at turns angry, mournful, and humiliated. I hate how he can see right through me. I hate that he was right.

I hate that I ran off—and that he let me go. Again. But can I blame him? Who would want to be with a lunatic who thought (or even pretended to think) that *this* last-minute wave-catching scheme was a good idea?

The rain is loud against the top of the tent as I sit inside it, my arms wrapped around my knees, and every now and then, a gust of wind threatens to rip it totally free.

"Sybil..." Seb's voice surprises me. He tucks into the tiny tent beside me with new items: his camera bag and a backpack, out of which he pulls a blanket and...a bottle of champagne.

"Ah, thank you."

He arranges the blanket over our wet legs and then pops the cork, and I huddle closer to him with a shiver. I've never been more grateful for warmth, or alcohol, though I'm not exactly in a celebratory mood.

"Didn't bring any cups because I wasn't planning on company," Seb says sheepishly.

"I don't mind drinking from the bottle." At this point I'd be happy to drink out of a conch shell that still had a live conch in it.

He hands me the bottle, a light vapor rising from the lip, and I take a sip, my mouth filling with the cool froth of champagne.

"Hey, Sybil? I'm sorry." Seb's eyes are downcast as I hand the bottle back to him. I'm assuming he means for dragging me all the way out here to this remote, isolated beach cove in the dead of night, straight into the mouth of a storm—even though I agreed to come. But he takes a swig before speaking again, and then goes on, "I shouldn't have spilled the truth to Jamie. That wasn't my place."

"I don't want to talk about it." I grab the bottle back and take another sip.

"Well, maybe I do." There's a rare earnestness in Sebastian's voice. "Maybe I got sick of just pretending." He reaches for the bottle and our fingers graze as he takes it from my hands and places it on the floor between us. "Seeing you again...it's been intense, Sybil. I didn't realize that so many of my old feelings were still there." His eyes meet mine.

My breath hitches, and I catch my lip with my teeth. I feel my expression mirroring Jamie's from earlier on the beach. *Surprised*, I realize. Jamie was surprised when I said Genevieve looks at him like he hung the moon. It had seemed inconceivable to me that Jamie hadn't noticed her obvious feelings for him. But now, I think maybe I should have given Jamie the benefit of the doubt. Because I'm genuinely floored by Seb's confession. All day, I thought he was just goofing around, playing the flirt. But the look on his face is honest, vulnerable.

"Oh, Seb..."

Three years ago, I would've given anything for Sebastian to say these words to me. I chased after him for years, but the moments when he admitted to *really* feeling something for me were so few and far between that eventually, I stopped waiting for them.

"I'm not expecting anything." Sebastian turns away from me and shrugs as if slightly embarrassed at the outpouring of feelings. "I just wanted to be honest with you. I've always wanted to be honest." And he was. I knew when we were dating that I would always come second to his career, and for a while, it was enough. Until one day, it wasn't. Seb clears his throat. "Also...I've got a new gig in Thailand. The *Times* one."

"Seb, that's so great!" The news pulls me out of my thoughts. "You've wanted that job for forever."

"I have," he agrees. He pauses for a moment, then seems to

decide something. "You could come with me? Let me make up for Japan."

I don't know what to say to that, so I swallow down another sip of champagne.

When he asked me to go to Tokyo with him all those years ago, I agreed instantly, like there was no other option. I can feel that same impulsive tingle in my chest now. It sounds insane and appealing all at the same time—the idea of just moving on and leaving the latest shitstorm behind. And maybe without a romantic relationship to complicate things, Seb and I could thrive as friends. Travel buddies. Fellow ex-pats. Maybe Thailand would be the escape I'd hoped Hawaii would be. A restorative reset.

And yet...

"I have a job—a legit one," I tell Seb. "I'm actually doing some work for them while I'm here."

"Oh." Seb looks surprised, and I realize that in the two days he's been here, he hasn't once asked what's new with me, or what I have going on in my life. "Um, what's the gig?"

"I run the social media accounts for a women's underwear brand called Flowies. I create marketing campaigns and do a lot of content creation."

"Huh," Seb says reaching for the bottle. "Sounds cool." Though the look on his face is only mildly interested.

Could I keep working for Flowies from Thailand? I could see Meredith *maybe* letting me work remotely full-time, but what's the time difference between LA and Thailand? Would I really be up for four a.m. calls? And what about all the things I love about LA? Could I really leave them all behind? After Jamie and I broke up last year, I worried the city might never feel like home again. But little by little, I found things that didn't remind me of him. People who made me feel whole again. The smoothie shop where the owner knows I really want two scoops of blueberries when I say I only want one. My favorite romance bookstore, tucked between the hair salon and the Indian restaurant.

But beyond all that, there's a deeper question holding me back from the idea of going to Thailand.

Would I really be moving on? Or running away?

"You know," Seb says, drawing my attention back to him, "you shouldn't feel like you have to have some big corporate job or whatever. I've never cared whether you have a career." The unspoken words are obvious: *unlike Jamie and his family.*

And while I appreciate the sentiment, Sebastian is missing the point. This isn't something I'm doing to prove Jamie or the Kauffmans wrong about me. It's something I'm finally doing for myself.

"I like my job," I tell him. "And I'm good at it."

"Totally. I'm sure you are. I just thought..."

"Seb?"

"Yeah?" He looks at me, and I swear it's hope I see flickering in his eyes. "You broke my heart in Tokyo. But I loved you," I say simply.

He holds my gaze. "I know."

"I don't anymore though." I choke the words out. If Sebastian is being honest with me, then I need to be honest with him.

He nods, his voice soft. "I know." Sebastian's face is half in shadow. He's so beautiful. It would be so easy to lean toward him to lose myself in his touch, like I've done many times before. But this time, I know I won't.

My feelings for Sebastian are still there in my memory,

suspended in amber, and with enough time and heat, I might be able to chip away at them. But my feelings for Jamie are molten lava right now, roaring out of my heart, billowing steam as it pours into the ocean. And I can't bring myself to settle when I know that kind of love is out there.

Seb pats me twice on the knee and stands. "I'm going to head out there to get some shots. You're welcome to come with me."

"I think I'll enjoy being just damp instead of sopping wet for a few more minutes."

Seb smiles and grabs his tripod, then extracts his camera from his pack, carefully wrapping it in its protective covering before stepping into the storm.

I try to get a signal on my phone, but the weather has completely knocked out any hope of reception. The strength of the storm seems to have picked up. The percussion against the roof of the tent is more insistent and the flutterings at the edges of the opening have reached a frenetic tempo. A strain of worry courses through me again. We should go back.

I peek out of the flap and see Seb in the distance. The sky is beginning to lighten ever so slightly in the distance, but the weather is holding darkness over the length of the beach. Still, I can see him, his shirt and hair going crazy in the wind as he struggles to right the tripod, which keeps collapsing. The storm is much too chaotic, surely he can see that. But I watch as he tries again and again, finally managing to wedge it around one of the shiny, slippery rocks at the end of the outcropping. And he's right on time, because silvery-gold light starts to thread across the water from the east, lighting up the chaos of the wave, and I know this moment is one Seb couldn't miss. Even if I wish I hadn't gone along for the ride, I can feel how power-ful these pictures will be. I know how talented he is, and how obsessive he'll be, taking shot after shot until he feels he's got-ten the right ones. And I envy him that clarity—that passion. That ability to throw himself into something headlong, even if that thing isn't a relationship.

Still, despite the stunning view that's emerging, it's freez-ing and wet, and the rain is still coming down. I tuck back inside the tent again. I can't leave anyway—if I step outside of it, the wind will almost definitely pick up the whole thing and send it flying off down the beach.

So I sit there amid the beating and the roaring of the storm, stuck. For once, I can't run from my problems.

As a kid, I would run away from my parents and climb into my tree house, a place that felt like it could hold my big, con-fusing feelings when there was nowhere else safe to put them. But my dad would eventually come find me. He'd poke his head through the small hatch that functioned as the door and say, *You know, baby, you can hoof it as far and as fast as you want, but you can't outrun a problem if it's between your ears.*

Turns out Dad was right.

I take another swig of the bottle, feeling tired and freezing and lonely.

I squeeze my own eyes shut, dropping my head onto my knees.

Then my fight with Jamie. Him telling me I don't know him. That sometimes I'm looking at him, but not actually seeing him.

Is that true?

Have I really just been projecting old traumas from Liam onto everything that came after?

Willow was so right. I need to talk to Jamie. For real this time. He deserves to know everything. But he said he was leaving tomorrow, and I don't know what time his flight is. Tonight might've been my last chance.

I step out of the tent, my gaze drawn to the stormy horizon. The rain is still falling, but there's a lull in the wind—I'm hoping it's enough to let me leave the tent without it blowing away. I call out to Seb, but I don't see him. Where the tripod had been propped, I now see it at a jagged angle, tossed half-upside-down against the rocks.

Oh god. Where is he?

"*Seb!*" I scream, running in the direction of the rocky outcropping.

The wind begins howling again, drowning out my voice and increasing my panic. I swivel around and see the tent shaking, one of the poles popping up out of the sand. In moments, it's loose and tumbling away, but I can't deal with that now. I turn back toward the rocks, running faster. Sand and plant debris hurtle across my path, and a piece of palm frond slaps my leg hard. I scan the shoreline for Seb but still don't see him. If he went back to the ATV or is simply somewhere on the other side of the rocks where I can't see, I'm going to kill him with my bare hands. But until I know that for sure, I'm filled with dread.

And that dread only increases when I see something that looks like the cuff of his jeans in between two rocks, not far from the toppled tripod.

I let out a scream that's muffled by another roar of wind, and sprint toward him.

"Sebastian!" He's sprawled in between the rocks and a

patch of sand. Blood pooling in the sand beneath him is already pockmarked by rain. *Oh my god, oh my god.*

I grab his shoulders and shake him, hoping his eyes will flutter open, but his head just lolls to the side. I have to get him away from the water, and I have to get someone out here to help him.

I scramble for my phone in my pocket, but there are still no bars of service.

"Fuck!"

"Sybil?" Seb's voice is faint, his eyes still mostly closed.

"I'm here, Seb! I think you—you hit your head on the rocks. It's going to be okay." But nothing has ever felt less okay. I have to drag him to the Polaris. Maybe if I get us back on the road, we'll get a signal there.

"Seb? I'm going to try to carry you back to the ATV, okay?"

He doesn't say anything in response. His eyes have fluttered shut again, and his body is basically deadweight against mine. His camera has fallen into the sand, and I know he won't forgive me if I save him but let his film get destroyed. I loop the camera over my neck, tuck my hands beneath his armpits, and try to pull him back up over the rocks and toward the smoother part of the beach. But I can barely lift him, and the water keeps rising. I try to pull from a different direction, hoping it's just a problem with the angle, but I've always had pathetic noodle arms, especially for a swimmer. The howling of the wind takes on a pulsing, chopping energy, and terror rips through me. Is it possible that the storm is about to get *worse*?

But when I look toward the sky, I let out a sob of relief, not fear. Because it's not the wind, it's a helicopter. A rescue helicopter. I send a silent prayer of thanks to God and the resort staff, who must have noticed the Polaris was gone and sent a team out to save us.

A basket lowers from the chopper, swinging in the wind.

"We're over here!" I shout, waving my arms. The dawn has broken enough that even with the rain, they can see us easily now.

When the basket reaches the sand, a man hops out, and I sag in relief. "He hit his head," I start to say, but it's hard to have any kind of conversation with the blades still whirring above us. The medic motions that he's going to get Seb up into the basket first, and then come back for me. I force myself to take deep breaths as I watch the medic transport Seb up to the helicopter.

It's okay. You're okay.

I close my eyes, trying to focus on my breathing, and when I open them again, the basket has returned.

But it's not a medic who reaches for my hand.

It's Jamie.

21

THANKFULLY, AND BY SOME MIRACLE, SEB IS ALREADY BLINKING AWAKE by the time the helicopter sets down on the tennis courts at the hotel. I watch in a daze as a medic patches up the cut on the back of his head before they load him onto a stretcher to transfer him to a local hospital on the island to monitor his concussion. I automatically go to climb in the ambulance with him, but Seb waves me away, saying he'll be fine. I try to insist—he shouldn't go alone, but they tell me I can't get in the ambulance with him if I'm not a relative or spouse.

"Relax, Sybil. The docs will take care of me," Seb says. "Besides, they're probably going to put me in one of those ridiculous hospital johnnies..." He winces, and I'm not sure if it's from actual, physical pain, or just the idea of being forced into sad hospital garb. "You stay here, and spare me my dignity, okay?"

He weakly smiles at me as they close the van door and I'm reminded of many times when things got tough during our relationship and Seb had refused to let me in. Like when his grandfather died, and he wouldn't talk about it, instead going silent on me for two weeks. *He's so much like me*, I realize. He only wants people around for the good times, the fun Seb. But you can't build a relationship that way. *We* certainly failed to.

I feel Jamie gently pulling me back, muttering reassurances I can barely hear. The rain is still pounding down, and I haven't slept—the trash-can punch from the party last night, the fight, the champagne, the surprising conversation with Seb and seeing him injured like that—it's taken out almost all of my energy, and I feel myself starting to sway.

Jamie is there, steadying me. I feel his chest against my back, his arms holding me up, and that's when I realize I'm crying. I don't even know when the tears started falling, but I'm shaking, a full-body tremble that's part from cold and part from complete emotional overwhelm.

"Come on, Sybs," he says softly. "We need to get you warmed up."

He steers me back toward the hotel, through the lobby, and into the elevator bank. When it arrives, we step into the elevator together, him still supporting my body with one arm.

"Hey, Sybil, can you look at me," he asks, wiping a tear from my cheeks with his thumb. "Are you injured? Should we get you to the hospital too?" His face is contorted with concern.

"No, no," I manage to get out, "It's not that, I'm okay, it's just—" my voice chokes off with another sob.

"I know." Jamie rubs my back. The soothing motion grounds me, so calming and so familiar, reminding me of all the times in our past when Jamie has helped me through a panic episode. "Shh," he whispers, "It's okay. It was a lot, getting trapped out there in the storm, then the helicopter. It's scary, but you're safe now, Sybil. You're safe," he says, placing a gentle kiss on top of my head.

By the time the elevator reaches my floor, my body-shaking sobs have subsided. I'm still feeling fragile, but beneath it I can feel the faintest flicker of strength. We walk down the hall, and Jamie helps when I fumble with my key card. When we get inside the room, I turn, my back against the closed door, and finally look up at him, straight into his eyes. I don't know if I've ever let someone really look at me like this, up close, while I'm broken down with tears. It's scary to be so exposed, but I don't look away. Inside me, the flicker of strength grows. "Jamie," I tell him, my voice wavering. "You were right. When you said I was lying, holding back from you. I was. I still am," I say.

"Shh, it's okay," he says, wiping more tears from my face with his fingers. "You don't have to tell me anything right now. Just take your time and make sure you're feeling better. It's okay, Sybil. It's okay. I love you."

I glance up at him, startled, and the look on his face is just as surprised. It's clear he didn't mean to say it, it just slipped out.

"I—I—" I almost tell him I love him too. But instead, other words flow out of me. Words that desperately needed to find their way out, find their way to a safe place. Find their way to *him*.

JAMIE LISTENS, WRAPPING HIS arms around me in a huge hug, holding me steady, crying along with me through some of the details.

He knew already about my PCOS and what happened with Liam, but never realized the extent to which it still had been hanging over me—which, to be fair, I clearly didn't realize either. And of course, he had no idea that I was pregnant in the weeks leading up to our wedding.

I tell him how I chased down Gwendolyn Green in Vegas, and how she helped me realize that what I really needed in that moment was medical attention. I tell him how my frazzled brain latched onto that idea with a perverse, single-minded focus—deciding, against all logic, that the best thing for me to do would be to fly home to Dallas to see my regular OB. I knew everyone was waiting for me back in Malibu, but how could I walk down the aisle before I knew if I was actually going to be okay? No one was there when I arrived home to my parents' house that Thursday night, of course. They were all at the ranch, wondering where the hell I'd gone. So I didn't even bother to go into the house; I went straight to the old tree house in our backyard and climbed up to the little fort, collapsed beneath my now-crumbling alien photographs and homemade space mobiles, curled into a ball, and fell asleep.

I wrap up my story, accounting for every minute of my disappearance that wedding weekend, then take a deep breath and wait for Jamie's response.

I've been so worried that he'd feel guilty for choosing to cancel our wedding after hearing this—or worse, that he'd be furious and hurt that I hadn't let him in. Or devastated with a sense of loss over what could have been, grieving the unborn child in the cold accusing way Liam had.

Instead, I can feel a different emotion wafting off him. Incredulity, and . . . sorrow. For *me*.

THE FOUR ENGAGEMENT RINGS OF SYBIL RAIN

"Sybil," he whispers, wrapping his arms around me. "I'm so sorry." He's quiet for a minute, then he adds, "I just can't imagine how you felt, and it kills me that you thought you had to keep it all in, deal with it yourself."

He speaks the words with such gentleness, I feel a relief I haven't known in a long time. The relief of a veil being lifted, of being seen and understood.

"Just know that you're safe now. And you're not alone." Jamie sits me down at the desk chair and then goes into the bathroom and turns the shower on. He delivers me into the bathroom.

"You should get in there and warm up. Your body has been through a lot, and you're still shaking," he says quietly. "I can come back a little later to make sure you're okay," he adds, about to shut the door and leave me to my privacy, but I glance over my shoulder.

"Stay?" It's all I can manage, but he nods, then gently closes the bathroom door.

THE WARMTH OF THE shower begins to seep through my skin, and my teeth finally stop their rattling. My tears are gentler now, mixing with the shower water. Tears of humiliation at the stupidity of racing off in a storm, and of sadness for Seb, injured and alone in the hospital. But mostly, they are tears of relief. I turn off the water, wrap myself in a towel, and dry the foggy mirror enough to see if my eyes are puffy. I put on a little lotion and brush my wet hair, my arms feeling heavy—but a good tired. A cozy, cared-for kind of tired.

I crack open the bathroom door, letting out a cloud of steam.

"Hey," I say softly into the room.

Jamie is sitting at the desk by the window, in the dim glow of a small desk lamp, reading some of the moon and fertility articles I'd printed out to read by the pool. Beyond the parted curtains of the balcony doors, I can see the storm still raging outside, hard rain pummeling down onto the patio tiles, palm trees swaying in the gray. I look at the clock. It's barely past six a.m., but I feel like I've been awake for three straight days.

"Hi," he says, looking up. For all his competence on the helicopter, he looks unsure of himself now. "Here." He comes up to me and wraps a fluffy hotel robe around me.

"Thank you," I say, hoping I don't cry again—to see the care with which Jamie is handling first the crisis of rescuing us, and then everything I told him.

"Sybil, I—"

I hold my breath, waiting for him to say more.

But all he says is, "You're welcome."

He stands up and starts to walk toward the door to the hall, and I panic and grab his arm softly. Immediately he stops and turns back to me.

"So um, are you moonlighting as a member of the coast guard these days?" I ask, trying to seem more casual than I feel.

He rubs the back of his neck. "I made them take me with them."

"Made them?"

"There may have been some shouting." He cracks a small grin at himself. "I told Ash that you guys had taken an ATV out, and she got the rescue team on it right away."

"I'm sorry you guys had to go through all that trouble."

Jamie shrugs, like it's nothing. Like saving my life is just something he does. And then it hits me. I poured my heart out to him earlier, confessed everything, but there was one thing I somehow forgot to say.

"I'm so sorry, Jamie," I blurt out. "For... for *everything*."

Jamie hitches a breath, then swallows, but he doesn't say anything.

So I continue. I know there's more I need to say, to fully take accountability for what happened between us. "I'm sorry that I wasn't ready, that I was scared, that I couldn't open up about what I was going through. I wanted to be perfect for you. Ever since I was a kid, I've been like this. I've always tried so hard to be sparkly and special and at the same time be exactly what my partner wants, and I was doing that with you, too, but I didn't realize it. I should have just been me. The real me."

"You *were* the real you, Sybil," he says quietly. "You know I didn't fall in love with you just for your sparkles and sunshine, right?"

I stare at him. Because no. I truly did not know that.

"I loved every part of you. I loved that I got to be the one you came home to, the one who saw you without all the party jokes and the charm that everyone loves. I got to be the one you truly let your hair down with, the one to rub your sore feet and see your bad moods and try to cheer you up. I wanted to be that person."

I catch a sob as it rises in my throat. "And I ruined everything. Both then and now—"

Jamie interrupts before I can finish. "That's not true." His focus is totally on me. His words are low, but they ring through my body like church bells. He gives his head a little shake, like he's laughing at himself, or me, I'm not sure which. "I hated myself the minute I let you drive off into the night. I was pissed you lied about Seb being your boyfriend, but—"

"I know. It was so stupid. I was just embarrassed. And jealous of you and Genevieve. But it was so petty and immature—"

"No," Jamie interrupts, putting a hand on my shoulder. "I mean, yes, it was, kind of." One side of his mouth quirks up into an affectionate grin. "But that's not why I was so mad. I was mad because I'd been killing myself all day, ever since Sebastian got here, holding myself back from you because of him. Because I thought you were happy with someone else."

Holding myself back from you. The words send a shiver of electricity through me. My mouth has gone dry, and I have to lick my lips before I can continue. Jamie's eyes follow the path of my tongue.

I'm frozen in place as he looks at me, almost pleadingly. I can see the apology, and the hurt, and the longing, all clearly etched on his handsome face. The smell of him surrounds me. The damp of his shirt clings to his shoulders and biceps and to the muscles along his back.

"I should go and let you sleep," he says, and starts to pull his hand away.

"Don't go," I whisper.

For a moment, it's silent between us, everything concentrated in the place where his fingers are touching my shoulder through the robe. I feel them twitch, and he pushes some of my still-wet hair away from my neck.

"Are you sure?"

A shiver runs through my entire body and I can barely speak, so I simply nod.

"Come here," he says, pulling me close. Then he lifts me gently, carrying me to the bed, and lying down beside me, covering us both with the duvet. I roll onto my side, and he spoons me, putting his arms gently around me. Wrapped in the safety of him, the smell of him, I feel like I'm finally home.

I begin to relax to the quiet beating of his heart, and eventually, we both drift off to sleep.

22

I WAKE TO THE SOUND OF RAIN. QUIETER NOW, A GENTLE TAP.

I close my eyes again, unwilling to shake the heady warmth of this moment. Jamie is still here in the bed beside me, breathing softly into the back of my neck, and I'm afraid that if I wake him, this comfort and closeness I'm feeling will vanish with the night.

"Mmm," he moans into my neck, beginning to stir. And then, as if realizing for the first time the intimacy of the moment, he pulls away a little, removing his arm. "Morning," he whispers.

"Morning," I say, rolling over to face him. "Thank you."

"For what?" he asks.

"For all of this," I say. "For taking care of me. For being here. Even after everything I told you."

"Sybil," he whispers, his eyes scanning my face.

"Yeah?"

"You need to stop feeling guilty, okay? I know I shouted at

you for lying to me, for keeping things from me, but the truth is, you were right too. I was keeping things from you as well."

"You were?"

"Of course. I mean, look," he says, taking a breath, as if readying himself for something. "I think it's obvious."

"Obvious? What is?"

"That I'm still in love with you, Sybil." His voice is low and raw, his face flushed with emotion. "That I never got over you. I don't think I ever will."

"Jamie, I—"

"Wait, let me finish. You don't have to say anything," he says quietly. "But I would be a fool not to tell you now. Not to just leave it all on the table. I have no expectations. I just need you to know that I am fully and completely in love with you. And if you want me to leave now and give you your space, I totally get that. I just want us both, finally, to be as honest as we can. And that is the honest truth."

"Jamie," I say, my chest racing with a strange mix of euphoria and fear and hope. "You idiot. I love you, too. Obviously."

His face breaks into an uncontrollable grin. "Really? And you're not just saying that because I saved you on a dumb helicopter?"

I laugh. "The helicopter has very little to do with it. Though it was a nice, dramatic touch, I will admit."

He laughs quietly, and then we're both silent, staring into each other's eyes.

And then, slowly, he closes the small distance between us.

He whispers my name one last time. And then his lips find mine.

★ ★ ★

JAMIE KISSES WITH HIS whole body. As his tongue softly pushes apart my lips, the energy of his body changes. I feel him tensing against me, his breath hitching in his chest.

He pulls back slightly. "God, I've missed you."

"I know," I whisper, reaching up to touch the collar on his shirt. He slept in it last night, and most of the dampness has dried off, but it can't have been very comfortable. Maybe I should help him out of it...

To say that our movements are hasty, like desperate teenagers, is an understatement. It's like I've never met a button before, the way I tear at his shirt, even as his lips trail my neck and behind my ear. There's a gentle tug on the knot in the bathrobe I slept in, and then, it comes undone.

He pushes the robe apart as I pull him even closer, feeling alive and focused in a way I haven't felt in a long time.

His hands run through my hair, drawing another gasp from me as he moves his mouth along my jaw, licking and kissing my neck, my collarbones, my shoulders, his mouth finding my breast and sucking. A tiny bite makes me catch my breath and writhe, but he doesn't slow down, trailing his hands along the sides of my stomach, toward my hips as his head slips beneath the sheets. He kisses my belly button, then moves lower, until I find I can hardly breathe. His mouth comes to the place between my thighs, and my hands clench the sheets as he spends what feels like forever relearning which spots make me gasp and which spots make my muscles quiver.

Outside, rain is still tapping gently at the windows. I hear

the wind, and the shuddering of his breath against my skin...
And then—

He pulls himself back. I feel cool air race across my bare
skin, making me shiver. He's on his knees, staring up at me,
his hand at his belt, as if deciding whether to go through with
this.

"Sybil..." he whispers, looking at me as if seeking an
answer.

I search his eyes. "You don't have to hold back," I tell him.
I feel like I'm going to completely come apart.

He turns to me, ready. Leans over me, and whispers,
"You're everything to me." I gasp as he presses inside of me.
He takes my arms and places them up above my head, and I
surrender to him, to this.

To us.

WE SPEND A COUPLE more hours tangled up together. Kissing,
laughing, clearly both of us in a little bit of shock that this is
happening. I rest with my head on his chest, and we talk about
all of it a million times. Then we let our conversations wander
to silly, irrelevant things—funny memories from the past, our
favorite foods on the hotel menu. And it's surreal, like we are
on the honeymoon we never had.

By now, streaks of midday light are dancing through the
curtains when I feel Jamie's lips on my neck. His hands roam
down the length of my side, sending tingles all along my skin.

And then we're kissing again, and unstoppable.

The second time is slower. He pulls me to him, my back to

his chest, pressing hot lips to my shoulder and across the back of my neck. His hands sliding down the length of my torso to circle my waist. We rock together, as his hands reach around my hips, pulling me gently into him, and I feel fully in the moment as we connect, moving as one, until all of a sudden I'm gasping and laughing a little at the same time, my whole body trembling.

Then we lay together for a little longer, before Jamie clears his throat. "My flight is in a few hours," he whispers. "I have to pack up and head out to the airport soon."

"Cutting it close then." My smile is watery. This morning was so special I let myself forget that Jamie is supposed to be leaving this afternoon.

But before I can let myself spiral too far, Jamie says, "Come with me," his lips ghosting against my back.

I roll over to face him, curling my lips into a bigger grin. "I believe I already did. Twice."

"*Sybil.*" His cheeks turn pink, and I love that I can make him blush with a dirty joke, even after everything we just did.

"I can't come with you," I say, letting regret creep into my voice. "I have the—"

"Oh!" He cuts me off with his little gasp of realization. "Your eclipse event. That's tonight, right?"

I nod, a little shocked myself to find that the day is already here.

"You could..." I pause to swallow down any insecurities, trying to just trust myself, trust Jamie and this fragile moment between us. "You could stay?"

Jamie's eyes turn down in the corners as he looks at me. I can't read all the emotions reflecting off his beautiful face, but

I think he's maybe considering it. God knows Jamie's financially secure enough to eat whatever change fee the airline would impose on him for pushing his travel back a couple of days. Something ripples like a cloud across his forehead, wrinkled for a moment in thought, and then it clears. He reaches out to take my left hand in his, pulling it to his face and pressing a kiss against the back of my fingers.

"I wish I could, Sybs," he says, after placing my hand on his chest. "But I really do have to get home. I'm supposed to give my dad and the rest of the board a full report on Halia Falls this evening."

"Oh!" I trail my hand over to his bicep and give it a squeeze, excitement bubbling up inside me. "That's right! Kauffman Estates & Winery. I can't believe I didn't tell you before how proud I am!" I explain to him about my misunderstanding, how I only realized the true purpose of his business trip when Dani showed me the brochure. "Jamie, it's incredible what you've done."

He shrugs, trying to downplay it, but I can see the pride shining in his eyes. "It's been a lot of work, but it's been worth it. I really believe in this, Sybs."

"And I believe in you," I say, bringing my hand up to cradle his cheek. "You're incredible, you know that?"

He chuckles, a blush creeping up his neck. "I think you might be a little biased."

"Maybe," I concede, "but I'm also right. You've followed your passion, built something meaningful, and you're making your dreams a reality. What's not to admire?"

He looks at me for a moment, his gaze intense. "You have no idea how much it means to me to hear you say that."

"Well, then get used to it," I say, leaning in to kiss him softly. "Because I'm going to be saying it a lot."

"Is that a promise, Sybil Rain?"

I nod, and he leans in to meet me in another kiss.

"Honestly," Jamie says after we pull away, "after we . . . after you left, working on building out the winery was the only thing that kept me going. I felt so lost, so directionless. But at least I had something to focus my energy on so I wouldn't go crazy without you."

I nod, smiling sadly. "It was the same for me," I admit. "Flowies became my whole world. I poured everything I had into it, just to keep myself from falling apart. You should have seen the color-coded calendars I devised. I'm, like, super organized now. At least, I am when it comes to social media post planning."

Jamie chuckles. "You'll have to show me later."

"And you'll have to take me on a world tour of all the places that are now proudly carrying Kauffman wines."

Jamie nuzzles his face into my neck, eliciting a tickled shriek from me.

I put my hands on his shoulders, pushing him back a few inches so I can look into his eyes. "It's kind of funny, isn't it?"

"What is?"

"How the things we clung to for distraction during our heartbreak ended up shaping us, changing us, and brought us back . . . *here*." I meet his gaze, a warmth spreading through me. "Maybe we needed that time apart, that time to grow and heal, so that we could find our way back to each other, stronger and more ready than before."

Jamie nods. "I think you might be right."

"So what happens now?" It comes out in a whisper.

"I don't know." Jamie swallows. "What do you want to happen?"

And maybe for the first time ever, in all my relationships, I know exactly what I want, and I'm willing to ask for it. Even though it's terrifying.

"I want to try again," I say. "I still love you, and I want to be with you. We're different now, Jamie. We're the same in all the good ways, but we've grown. Both of us. I think maybe this time would be better."

"God, I was hoping you were going to say that." Jamie leans in and captures my lips in a kiss. We lose ourselves in it for a moment before Jamie pulls back just a fraction, our foreheads still nearly touching. I give myself the luxury of drinking him in. The day's growth of stubble along his jaw, the gold and green flecked among the warm brown in his eyes, the full curve of his lower lip. "I believe in us, Sybil," he says.

I blink rapidly, trying to stay the swell of emotion I feel building inside me.

"I do too," I agree. And I mean it.

"And there's one more thing I want to be sure you understand. The two of us—we'll be family regardless of whether kids come into the picture. I meant it when I said I love all of you."

"I know that now," I say, tears falling down my cheeks in earnest now. "I knew it then, too, but I was such a mess, reliving my past...I wasn't thinking clearly. I was just scared."

"And it didn't help that I was so focused on my own paranoia. I was the biggest jerk in the world," he admits, his voice laced with regret. "Sybil, I am so sorry. I should have listened to you, given you a chance to explain. Instead, I let my own fears get the better of me." He reaches for my hand, his thumb gently stroking my knuckles.

"We were idiots," I say softly, another watery smile gracing my lips.

He chuckles, a low rumble in his chest. "Yeah, I guess we were. Ah, so young and lost back then," he says, and I laugh too.

We stay like that for a long moment, wrapped in each other's arms, the silence filled with a comfortable understanding. The past, with all its hurt and confusion, finally feels settled, replaced by a sense of peace and possibility.

Reluctantly, I glance at the clock on the nightstand. It's past noon. Jamie's flight leaves in less than two hours.

"You should probably get going," I say, even though it's the last thing I want. "You have to change, get your suitcase..."

He sighs. "Yeah, you're right."

We untangle ourselves from the sheets, the cool morning air a stark contrast to the warmth we shared under the covers. As Jamie throws on his clothes from last night, I can't help but admire the way his muscles flex with each movement, the way his hair falls carelessly across his forehead. He's even more handsome now than he was a year ago, more mature, more confident. And the realization that he's mine, that we have a second chance, fills me with a joy that borders on disbelief.

"Good luck with the eclipse event," Jamie says, standing in my doorway. "I wish I could be here for it, but I'll be sure to watch the Instagram live."

I give a little laugh and come to give him a hug in the doorway. "Jamie, it'll be, like, two in the morning LA time."

"I don't care; I'll stay up." The look on his face is so open and affectionate that I lean up to kiss him again. The kiss grows, Jamie's hand coming up to grip the back of my neck, and I can feel myself starting to be pressed back into the doorframe before Jamie wrenches himself away with a groan. "Ugh. I really do have to go."

This is really it. Jamie's heading back to the real world, and I'm not far behind.

What will happen when we leave paradise and get back home?

"I fly back tomorrow afternoon, so maybe you could come over tomorrow night?" I hate the uncertainty that's crept into my voice. It's like this perfect bubble Jamie and I have been floating in since last night is now drifting toward a field of pushpins. At any second, we could pop.

"Count on it," Jamie says, squeezing my hand.

"Well, um...Safe travels." *Safe travels?* Am I signing off a business email? Jamie presses a kiss to my forehead. I watch him make his way down the hall. I blink, trying to hold back the tears. When he gets to the elevator, he turns back and offers me a half-hearted wave. I wave back, and once he disappears, let myself sink to the floor.

23

I THINK ABOUT CRAWLING RIGHT BACK INTO BED AND SPENDING THE REST of the day replaying the last few hours between me and Jamie, but I've got too much to do. First, I manage to reach the local hospital by phone and learn that Seb is recovering fine and will be discharged back to the hotel shortly. Another huge weight lifts off me. In the meantime, I throw on a simple black bikini and return to the beach. By now it is mostly cleaned of debris from the storm but it's still a little quieter than usual, the sand cold and compact beneath my feet. Behind me, a couple hotel employees are opening sun umbrellas over the white-and-green–striped chairs where guests are having lunch. I pull out my phone and think about gathering more content for Flowies, but after everything that's happened, I feel a stronger urge to just stay in the present. So instead of shooting a quick video, I FaceTime Willow.

"Bill!" she answers, and Nora's chubby face pops into view beneath her chin. Nora lets out a delighted gurgle and reaches

269

for the phone, but I get a glimpse of the ceiling fan as Willow maneuvers to keep the phone out of her grip. Her face fills the screen again. "I'm back."

"I slept with Jamie," I say without preamble.

Willow freezes. "Let me patch in Emma and Nikki, okay?"

I should have known Willow would send for reinforcements. There are a few moments while I wait for everyone's face to appear on the screen, and then Willow says, "Start over."

I tell them everything while pacing the beach—the fake boyfriend, Seb's shocking arrival, the chaotic storm, Jamie's unexpected rescue—and laugh as the girls gasp at various twists in the tale.

"We left things on good terms," I conclude. "We're going to try again. And I'm... happy. But also, if I'm being honest, I feel kind of terrified?"

"You'd be crazy if you *weren't* scared," Emma says. "Trust me on this, I know."

I smile a little, thinking of Emma and Finn and how they found their way back to each other after years of false starts. If they can have a second chance at love, maybe Jamie and I can too.

"Yeah, it's just..." My voice catches in my throat as I try to explain to them. "We talked about finally leaving the past behind us. But... have I really changed enough to deserve his love this time?"

Emma sucks in a breath, and when she finally speaks, it's so intense, she sounds almost like a stern teacher telling me I'm in trouble. "Sybil Rain. I need you to hear me on this. He did not decide to get back together with you because he thinks you're some new Sybil 2.0 who is suddenly responsible and stable enough to earn his love. Besides, that's not how love works anyway."

I know she's right. Jamie said as much last night—that he was never looking for me to change or be someone I'm not. But some uncertainty must still register on my face because Willow jumps in.

"Emma's right," she says. "I know you've both had issues with trust in the past, but it sounds like you're working through that—being more open with each other so there are no more doubts. But *love*? Jamie's mind never had to be changed about that. The only person who needs to be convinced that you are worthy of a great love, Sybil, is you."

Well, crap. I hadn't meant to start crying, but here we are. But still, I press on. "But...he's headed straight from the airport to a Kauffman Group board meeting, and we all know how much they love me. What if his family talks him out of it again?" I try not to let my voice tremble, to betray how much this fear still has a grip on me.

Nikki clears her throat, and I realize that up until now, she's been uncharacteristically quiet through this call. "Sybil. I have to tell you something."

If I didn't know better, I'd say she sounds...guilty. "Okay."

"I knew that Jamie was going to be at Halia Falls this week."

"Wait—what?"

"His sister told me about how he was going to be taking a trip down for his new wine business." Emma's mouth has dropped open, but Nikki keeps going. "Which is why when your ticket vouchers were running out...I pushed you to stay at Halia Falls too."

"Nikki!" I almost trip on a piece of driftwood.

"You've been doing so well, but you haven't been with any-one since the wedding. Jamie's also been in a huge rut, appar-ently. Amelia said he's been miserable. 'Like a shell of a person,' she said. And I guess I thought there might still be something there between y'all. It always seemed like y'all were endgame." Nikki's accent has begun to deepen, as it does whenever she's under pressure.

Emma's voice is soft with awe. "Nikki, you're a master-mind."

"What the hell were you doing talking to Amelia?" I ask, still trying to process this. The whole thing was . . . a setup? I'm not sure whether to be amused or humiliated.

"She's a big *LovedBy* fan. We met at the wedding, and she's been DMing me," Nikki says, and in any other scenario this would be a golden nugget of information I would cherish for-ever: Miss Hoity-Toity District Court Judge loves reality TV just like the rest of us. "I'm sorry, Sybs. I shouldn't have played matchmaker behind your back like that."

"Well, I guess I can't hate you for wanting what's best for me," I admit, my initial shock giving way to something more tender. The idea not just that my friends were concerned about me after the breakup, but that Amelia could see what a toll it had taken on Jamie. That's what really gets me.

"I just hope it all works out," Nikki says, chewing on her lip. "Can you blame me for wanting a happy ending for you?"

"Of course not," I say, swallowing down a lump in my throat. "I want that for you too." In that moment, it's like the clouds in my mind have parted, and I see with perfect clar-ity how, beyond all the troubles in my own life, Nikki has had a crazy time of her own, ever since her public breakup on

LovedBy, and I've barely had the bandwidth to be there for *her.* Yet despite that, she's gone out of her way to try and save *my* love story.

Suddenly, it hits me: maybe I *am* worthy of great love. Maybe I'm lucky enough to already have it. Because the bond I share with these three girls is fierce and unbreakable. And strangely, I've never once questioned whether I deserve it—because they've never made me feel less than wholly and unconditionally loved. I'm so overwhelmed by it that I want to cry all over again. But now is not the time for more tears.

"Listen, girls, I've gotta get ready for the eclipse event," I tell them. "I'll call you all when I get home."

There's an echo of "Love you"s from everyone as we sign off. I turn to face the ocean—those beautiful waves Seb had been so determined to photograph. It was only last night, but it feels like a lifetime ago that I was shivering alone on the beach in the darkness and the cold while Seb was out there with his camera, chasing the thing that mattered most to him—which wasn't me, and never had been.

As the storm has left the island, the waves have gentled somewhat; the sun sparkles off the blue, and I take a deep breath, ready to let go of the fear.

Ready to believe that I can accept a great love—because, in fact, I have.

I SPEND THE NEXT hour prepping some Flowies merch bags I plan to hand out at tonight's eclipse watch party, filling the bright purple totes with rose quartz crystals, night-blooming jasmine bath salts, and a set of celestial-themed tarot cards along with a discount coupon for our most popular panties set.

I text back and forth with Seb, who seems to have mostly recovered from his one-sided fight with the camera tripod. He tells me he's spending the day resting up in his room, but promises to make an appearance tonight at the viewing party.

I'm desperate to text Jamie, and almost type out some needy messages: *Hey just checking real quick do you still love all of me?* But there's no point, since Jamie's surely in the air by now anyway, with his phone dutifully set to airplane mode. Besides, if this is going to work, I have to trust him. I have to trust us.

I have a couple of hours left in the day before I need to get ready for tonight, so I leave the room determined to just hang at the hotel without the angst of worrying about who I'll run into or what I have to hide. Another dip in the pool (and a quick horoscope exchange with Derek, my favorite poolside waiter), a wander through those sculpture gardens (finally). An iced tea at the tiki bar with Dani, whose eyes pop out of her skull when I tell her everything she's missed out on (though Ash had obviously filled her in on the whole helicopter rescue mission).

Finally, I go back to my room and put some finishing touches on the little speech that I'm going to give during the Instagram live tonight. I don't want it to feel too scripted, but I also don't want to stream out to thousands of people with nothing to say. So I jot down some notes about wellness, sustainability, and empowering people with uteruses.

Around six, I shut my laptop and start to get ready for the event. I pull on a dark blue low-cut maxi dress with a slit nearly all the way up the thigh—it's ethereal, like something Willow would wear. When I picked it out, I thought it was the perfect dress for a once-in-a-lifetime cosmic event: the same color as the night sky. But now I'm realizing how tricky this outfit is to accessorize. Any earrings I try on seem to overly dominate the ease of the dress, and the neckline doesn't really work for a necklace. Ultimately, I decide to keep it simple, letting the dress speak for itself, and going full beach waves with my hair instead of trying to fight the humidity.

Once I'm dressed and ready, I call down to the front desk to have someone help transfer the merch bags to the event space. My mind is still reeling with everything that's happened since last night, plus the revelation about how Nikki—and, more shockingly, *Amelia*—had a hand in orchestrating this whole trip. But I try to psych myself up for tonight. This was my pitch. Meredith took a chance on me, and I can't let her down.

And through all the other things I'm feeling today, I am proud of myself for spearheading this campaign. Maybe prouder than I've felt since I walked across the stage at USC this May with all those twenty-two-year-olds, having finally gone back and completed the last few credits I needed to graduate.

I didn't tell anyone I was taking online courses until a few days before the ceremony. I think a part of me was afraid to tell my friends and family what I was doing until I had actually done it. That way if I failed, I'd only be letting myself down. The person I most wanted to tell was Jamie, of course. But by then, he and I weren't speaking. So it was the Core Four who cheered me on from the stands. Nikki holding a handmade sign with my name on it, Emma giving a two-finger whistle, Willow stamping her feet. My parents were there as well. I remember looking out to the audience and seeing my mom dabbing her eyes as I was handed my diploma. Period underwear and social media and the sheer concept of Los Angeles, they didn't understand. But a healthier, happier version of their daughter completing her undergraduate degree? That, they got.

And while I wish Liam hadn't come to campus my senior year and sent me into a tailspin, maybe the fact that it took me an extra seven years to officially graduate made the whole thing that much more meaningful. I wonder if I'll feel that way if Jamie and I ever make it back to the aisle. If the joy I'll feel looking down at that future ring on my left hand will be that much stronger because of all the rings that came before.

I pull out the little velvet sack from the bottom of my suitcase and pour the three rings into my hand.

The citrine. The seaweed. The diamond.

Liam. Sebastian. Jamie.

Part of me is tempted to pull a *Titanic* and hurl them off the balcony into the ocean below. To completely wipe the slate clean and release myself from the burden of this history. To really start fresh with Jamie, pretending our past never happened. But I know chucking my engagement rings into the sea wouldn't actually free me.

And besides, I've decided I like having them around. They're not talismans of failure. I can keep them safe in my heart without being weighed down by them. I can let them go, and still be grateful for what those relationships taught me about love—and about myself.

I don't know if my relationship with Jamie will work out this time. Even now that we've been fully honest with each other, there are no guarantees. The only thing I know for sure is that

I'm not going to run away. Not just because Jamie deserves better. But because *I* do.

And just as I think those last two words, I realize exactly what my outfit is missing.

IT'S A SHORT RIDE on a Halia Falls golf cart (borrowed with permission this time) back to the small market town. I find the jewelry seller's stall, and the same woman I remember from yesterday is working again today.

"Hi," I say. "I was here the other day. You had this ring—"

"The moonstone." The woman nods slowly. "I knew you'd be back." She leads me toward a shelf in the back of the booth and pulls the ring down from its velvet display. "Here. Try it on," she encourages.

I slip on the ring and hold my right hand up to the sun. The light reveals swirls of blue and purple, green and gold. It's unlike any ring I've ever owned. It's unique. Almost otherworldly. Something about it speaks to me. It's a ring that can symbolize this commitment I'm making to myself.

"They say moonstones are supposed to support healing," the woman says. "I've always felt like they signal new beginnings."

"I'll take it."

24

MUSIC DRIFTS TOWARD ME AS I PASS THROUGH THE POOL AREA TOWARD the deck overlooking the ocean. The sun hangs low over the water, and the sky is streaked with bright pinks, poppy reds, and melon oranges, the mountains and trees in the distance taking on a deep, almost purple tinge in silhouette.

The resort staff has hung iridescent glass orbs in place of the paper lanterns that usually adorn the pool area. I think they're supposed to be full moons, but it gives the sensation of being a very small person in a very large bubble bath.

A woman sets a flower crown onto my head, and I'm engulfed by the fragrant scent of plumeria as a waiter passes by with a tray of champagne. I take one and wander around the edge of the party. Dani and Ash are there, holding hands. I recognize some of the guests from seeing them around the hotel this week too. There's that extravagant woman Harriet, who wanted Sebastian to become her personal photographer for a minute there, as well as Elliot and Hank, the middle-aged couple from horseback riding whom Seb regaled with the false stories of our romance. There's a group of women I recognize from the swimming pool. And the mother with her two teenage daughters from the snorkel boat. I look at them and feel a pang of inspiration; one day, I want to be able to travel with my daughters like that, if I have any. That *if* no longer seems like a heavy one either. I feel a sense of lightness, a sense of trust that whatever is meant to be for me will come.

The band is already in full swing, and something twangs in my heart when I realize the song they're playing—Sinatra's "Fly Me to the Moon"—would've been on the set list for cocktail hour at my wedding.

I wonder where Jamie is now. He would have landed at LAX earlier this evening, so he's probably already at his dad's office, walking the board through a carefully curated pitch deck. I wonder if he's told his family about *us*. If Amelia is there and can tell her little plot worked.

I'm shaken from these musings when, across the dancefloor, I spot a familiar face. He has on a cream linen suit and looks just as gorgeous cleaned up as he does with windblown hair on a beach. He maneuvers through the crowd easily, but his steps slow as he nears me.

I rush to hug him. "Seb! You're healed!"

He winces, but there's a smile on his face as he pulls back from me, his hands still on my shoulders. "Mostly healed." He pauses, and I take a sip of champagne. "I'm sorry," he says, "for dragging you along. I got too carried away, and you got pulled into my mess."

The sparkling wine stills on my tongue. "I went on my own volition," I say.

Seb grins. "I'm just glad it wasn't you that got hurt."

"And I'm glad I went," I say. "What would have happened to you if you'd been out there alone?"

"That's true." Seb seems to realize something. There's a roughness to his voice as he says, "You might have saved my life, Sybil Rain."

"Wrong place, right time, I guess." Offering him a small smile, I take another sip of champagne to steady my nerves.

"I'll be thinking about you in Thailand," he says. "You'd like the waves there even more."

I bark out a laugh. "I bet it will be incredible. In fact, I know it will." Truth be told, so much has happened since last night, I'd almost forgotten about his offer to join him on the next leg of his journey. But I think it's pretty clear to both of us where I stand on that.

His blue eyes bore into my own, then he gives me a small but genuine smile, the corners of his eyes crinkling. "I just want you to be happy, Sybil."

I feel like I'm seeing him all over again for the first time, but at a distance now. "I want you to be happy too." I mean it more than I can even express in words. Seb deserves someone who's as over the moon about him as I am about Jamie.

But then I look at the camera that is, even now, dangling from his neck, and I realize—he'll never be alone, and that's okay too.

"And by the way, I suppose I should also be thanking you," I say. "For being the best fake boyfriend a girl could ask for." We both laugh, and it's weird. For years, I struggled with him not being the boyfriend I needed him to be. And yet, for this brief window of time, he became *exactly* what

I needed. "Really, though. For being here for me this week. For understanding."

He shrugs, sheepish now. "Eh. I owed you," he says.

My lips turn up in a small smile. "Well, call us even then." We toast.

Sebastian doesn't sip from his glass, though. Instead, he just takes my hand and presses a kiss to my fingers before turning to disappear into the crowd.

WHEN I GET BACK to the pool area, I see the staff have started to herd guests onto golf carts that will take us up the path into the mountains where we'll have the best view of the eclipse without the light pollution from the resort. I clamber onto one of the last ones leaving, finding myself squashed beside a pair of honeymooners making out.

As we wind up the trail, I can hear the chirps of unknown creatures—crickets? cicadas? frogs?—and the soft patter of falling water somewhere in the distance. It's fully dark now, and the little headlights on the front of the golf cart and the full moon above us are the only things illuminating our path. Despite the similarities to last night's journey across the island with Seb, this ride is decidedly more peaceful. For one, it's not pouring rain, and the driver knows where they're going. But also, everyone on the cart is speaking in hushed tones, as if they recognize the weight of this moment. An eclipse like this doesn't come around often, and everyone's treating it with the reverence it deserves.

We come to a stop in a clearing, different than the one we'd picnicked in during the horseback riding lesson. There's no waterfall here, just a soft expanse of grass surrounded by natural vegetation. Blankets have been laid out for people to sit on. There's a little pop-up tent adorned with twinkle lights where some staff members are pouring champagne.

My phone buzzes, and my heart leaps with both hope and anxiety that it might be Jamie. But it's just my calendar reminder that the Flowies live stream is scheduled to start in five minutes. I pull out my tripod and pivot so that the full moon is in the background of my shot and the soft glow from the twinkle-lit tent casts just enough light on my face. Perfect.

I start the live feed, letting a few seconds tick by as more and more followers join the stream. Once there are a couple hundred people watching, I start to speak. "Hey, y'all, Sybil Rain here from Flowies. I'm in Hawaii, where we're going to be lucky enough to witness the path of totality for tonight's lunar eclipse. But first, I just want to thank you all for sticking by me. Your stories about womanhood, dealing with periods, and all the ways that our brand has helped you in your own lives have been so inspiring. I hope that wherever you are watching this from, whether you can see the eclipse out your window or just through your phone screen, that you take this opportunity to launch a new phase of your life and break patterns that no longer serve you. And I hope you remember that your shadowy parts are beautiful too."

I settle back on the blanket, laying my back against the ground and bending my knees up toward the sky. About half the moon is now covered in its rosy glow and I can hear people around me oohing and ahhing.

I think about the whole idea of a full moon or a new moon.

Of course, the moon is never not whole, and it's never *really* new either. It's always there, unwavering. It's just a matter of how much of it is shining down on us, reflecting back the sun's light. And I guess that's true of people too. We never really start over, we just find new ways to light up again, even if, for a time, we've been cloaked in darkness.

THE NEXT MORNING, I wake up early, feeling at ease, proud of the event last night, at peace. The sun is bright through the billowing curtains, and I swing open the balcony doors. It's my last day here, and I want to get out of my head and enjoy it. Throwing on my favorite bright-pink triangle top bikini with a playful peach and turquoise mini-dress over it and some sunscreen, I pad out of the resort in my flip-flops, past the breakfast setup and the pool, and head down to the beach one last time, realizing that aside from my ill-advised leap off of Mason's snorkel boat excursion, I haven't actually had a nice, relaxing swim the entire time I've been here. I peel off my cover-up, leaving it on the sand with my pool towel, and splash into the waves, feeling their cold spray. I squeal a little to myself, hesitating for a second, before taking a huge breath and diving in.

The water surrounds and holds me, and for a few moments, I swim under the waves, my hair billowing around me like a mermaid's, feeling light and free. Surrounded by a huge, unending love, an ocean-sized love. It encompasses all of me: my childhood days of feeling like I didn't fit people's expectations, and all of my love stories, which I thought were failed romances, but which I now see were all just stages of the journey. Maybe it's divine love, I don't know, but it feels like something beyond what I've ever imagined, this feeling that I'm okay just as I am.

And then, a sense of urgency hits me. This lightning bolt of certainty. I'm ready to love Jamie and be loved back by him. And I don't want to waste one minute of our second chance.

I come up for air and swim, hard, toward the shore, joy and confidence pumping through me like I've never felt before. I race out of the water and onto the sand, grabbing the dress I left lying in a clump on the shore and picking up my towel, sending sand spraying everywhere. I'm in such a rush, I don't even have the patience to shake it off and wrap myself up—I just start jogging up the beach toward the resort. As I do, the wind picks up—there are still gusts left over even though the storm has long since left—and my towel flaps into my face. I cough sand and twist around, trying to detangle myself from the mess, when I bump backward into a stranger.

I nearly tumble into their arms. "I'm so sorry!" I exclaim, still trying to unwind myself when I look up.

I'm so shocked I almost fall over—again. "Jamie!" I squeak.

He's standing there, laughing his warm, sunshine-filled laugh. "Where were you off to in such a hurry?" he asks. "Did you find out the breakfast buffet was about to run out of French toast?"

"I . . . I was—I was actually hurrying to get back to my room so I could check out early, because I was in a rush to see *you*."

Jamie beams. I reach out a hand to hold his, as if looking for proof that he's really here and not just a disturbingly realistic hologram.

"But I thought you flew home to LA—the meeting with the board?" I wrinkle my brow in confusion.

"I did fly home. The meeting was quick, but I really went because I had something else that I needed to discuss with my family in person." I feel a chill, but it lasts only a moment, as another bright smile breaks out across his face.

"About us?"

He nods. "Sybil." There are tears in his eyes. I hold my breath, some tiny part of me still afraid he's going to tell me that they didn't approve of his choice. Even though I know by now that Amelia, at least, has been rooting for us. "They were surprised, but happy for me." I'm even more shocked when he goes on to say, "And, apparently, Grandma G laid into each of them before she passed away, blaming them for our break-up and for not being kind and accepting enough toward you."

"Really?" I don't even realize there are happy tears trailing down my cheeks until Jamie brushes one away with his thumb.

"Really," he answers. And then he kisses me.

His hands come around my waist, pressing me to him. My hands twine into his hair, and I don't know that I'll ever get enough of him.

But he pulls away and bends down to pick up the towel and cover-up that I dropped in a puddle on the sand.

Except that's not what he's doing, I suddenly realize, as he looks up at me, propped on one knee. Right here on the sand. With the sun blazing brilliantly behind him, still low on the eastern horizon.

"Sybil Rain," he says, taking my hand. Gone are the crazy nerves I had, the rushing anger and the raging insecurities I felt the first time he got down on one knee before me. I'm filled with a happy sense of calm as I listen to his words. "I need you to know that I am all in with you. Whether it takes us six months or six years, or forever. I don't care if or when we walk down the aisle again. What I know is that I want to walk through *life* with you, and I don't have any ambiguity about that. I'd like to give you this ring—it was Grandma G's ring, and she would have wanted you to have it—"

"Oh, Jamie." Tears rush to my eyes. It's the Toi et Moi ring with a ruby and a round, antique-cut diamond bracketed by two sprays of tiny marquise diamonds arranged to look like branches. The ring I saw Grandma G wearing the first time I met the Kauffmans. And I realize now that I'd seen it before then, too...

The gems are smaller than the last ring Jamie got me, but this one has soul that the other one never did. It was worn for decades by someone else who loved Jamie, and even if Grandma G had gotten it out of a Cracker Jack box, that would make it more precious than the four-karat platinum ring still tucked away in my jewelry pouch.

"Jamie, are you sure? That ring has been in your family for a long time. Are you sure your parents—"

"I went back to tell them about us, and to ask for the ring," he says. "Technically, I didn't have to—Grandma G left it for me in her will—but I wanted them to know why it was so important to me. Why *you* are so important to me. This ring symbolizes my promise to never run from us, and to always be waiting for you, no matter what. If you'll have me back. If you'll choose me."

His eyes glisten with tears, and I see the hopefulness written across his face, mixed with vulnerability. And it hits me for the first time just how scared Jamie has been all this time. Scared of losing me. Scared of not being chosen, or not being good enough to stay for. Scared of all the same things I was scared of too.

And I know that I can't let him feel that way for a single second longer. "I choose you, Jamie. I will always want *all* of you," I say, repeating the words he said to me yesterday morning back to him. "I love you. To the moon and back."

25

THE FOURTH RING...
THE FIRST TIME

IT FEELS STRANGE TO SAY, BUT I DON'T ACTUALLY REMEMBER THE VERY first time I met Jamie.

He was friends with some of Nikki's friends, and apparently when I first moved out to LA, we found ourselves at some of the same parties. But the first time I took note of Jamie, the first time I had an inkling of just how important he would become to me, was at an art gallery in Downtown Los Angeles.

It was a few months after Tokyo, and Sebastian and I had broken up, officially, for the last time. Still, that itch to text him was constantly niggling beneath my skin. I knew I was playing with fire, trying to maintain a friendship with him, but I couldn't help myself. I kept looking for excuses to reach out just so I could feel the thrill and terror of sending off a text and waiting for a response. Sometimes, he'd get back to me in seconds. Other times, hours would go by. Sometimes, he wouldn't respond at all.

One night, when I was finally starting to emerge from the rot-in-bed phase of my heartbreak, my friend Chloe had her first solo show. Normally, I would've dragged Nikki along with me, but she'd been cloistered away for her first season of *LovedBy*. So, I'd gone to the gallery by myself. It felt good to be out in the world again. The crisp white walls held a dozen of Chloe's paintings, each a different arrangement of bright, juicy jewel tones splashed across a wet canvas. After taking a heavy pour of free champagne, I came to a stop in front of one with gentle swashes of marigold and periwinkle and one ominous splotch of bloodred that cut through the prettiness of the colors.

A deep voice came from beside me. "You're Sybil, right?"

He looked familiar. Tall and rangy and handsome in a way that most men in LA weren't, but I couldn't place him, so I decided to bluff my way through. "Right! And you're . . . Tim?"

"Jamie," he corrected, but he didn't seem upset. "I have some mutual friends with your friend Nikki."

The realization of who he was clicked into place. I had seen him at a few parties, but I'd been so tangled up about Sebastian, other men hadn't really registered for me. "I was so close to saying 'Jamie.'"

"Were you?" He smiled down at me in genuine curiosity.

"Absolutely. It was my next guess."

I expected him to come at me with a line—*come here often?*—but he just turned back to the painting. I wasn't sure if I should fill the silence, but Jamie seemed content just to stand beside me and look at the piece. With most art, I usually felt a zing of recognition immediately or not at all. I hadn't felt that initial sizzle with this painting, but still, something about it made me want to keep standing here. Like maybe if I took my time, gave it a second look, I'd uncover something magical about it I'd missed at first glance. I took another sip of champagne and let my eyes rove over the painting. The rhythm of the pigments exploding across the canvas tugged at something within me. I stood beside Jamie, letting the tendril of sensation dig deeper until I felt the work unfurling.

"It's really quite lovely," I said softly.

"It really is," Jamie agreed quietly, not taking his eyes from the piece. I pulled my attention away from the painting and let myself look at him, feeling another tendril begin to work itself through my chest. But before it could grow any further, a warm arm came around my shoulder.

Chloe, whose chic bob of straight black hair made me, with my pale blond frizz, look like a dandelion, pulled me into a hug. "Thanks for coming, Sybil."

"I wouldn't miss it. I'm so proud of you!" I returned her hug. It was amazing to see all of my friends' potential start to get realized. Emma had just gotten a promotion at her design firm back in New York, Willow had eloped with her boyfriend the year before, and Nikki was going to be on national TV! Chloe and I pulled apart, and I turned to introduce her to Jamie.

"Oh, this is your piece?" He gestured with his wine glass. "It reminds me of one my dentist has."

I watched Chloe's face shut down. "Gee, thanks," she said tightly. "Sybil, I'll catch you after, okay?" She gave my hand a quick squeeze and pivoted away from us to begin talking to someone else.

Jamie looked horrified as his eyes darted from me to the painting to Chloe's disappearing back. "I feel like an ass. I meant—*oh god*." He ran a hand down his face. "My dentist is a big collector."

"You probably should have led with that."

"Her piece reminded me of a Frankenthaler he has. God, why did I *say* that? I just...panicked." He took another long pull of champagne.

"Chloe loves Frankenthaler. She's definitely an influence. You should have just said that."

"I know. I know." He dragged his fingers through his hair. "I always get nervous talking to strangers."

"I'm basically a stranger, and you don't seem nervous with me," I countered.

"Maybe you're just special, Sybil Rain." Something about the way he said my full name made me feel fizzy, like the champagne bubbles in our glasses. Then Jamie's smile grew wider as he added, "Plus, I'd hardly say we're strangers. Just last weekend at Lizzie's twenty-fifth, you used my lap as a step stool to climb on the kitchen counter and perform that Sabrina Carpenter song."

"I did?"

"I don't think you even noticed there was someone sitting in the chair."

Clearly, I hadn't. But Jamie didn't seem offended, more just amused. "Chloe is a very sweet person," I said, turning back to look at her painting, which Jamie had accidentally likened to dentist office art. "I'll tell her what you meant to say, and that you were *devastated* to have offended her."

Jamie downed the rest of his champagne in one go. "Thanks. You know, the nice thing about art is that it—usually— doesn't talk back to you. So you don't have to worry about sounding like an idiot."

"A great cure for feeling like an idiot is more champagne." Maybe it was that this was my first night out and about as a single person since Sebastian, or maybe it was the easiness I felt being around Jamie, but I had a sudden compulsive urge to keep the night going, to add a little excitement to it. "Do you want to swipe a bottle of champagne and sneak up to the roof?"

He tilted his head like he wasn't sure if I was being serious.

"Come on, live a little, Jamie..." I paused. I had no idea what his last name was.

"Kauffman," he supplied.

"Thank you. So? What do you say?"

Now it was Jamie's turn to hesitate. I took in his crisp blue suit, the briefcase in his left hand. Clearly this guy had some kind of corporate job. He was polished, clean-cut. A little awkward, in an adorable way. Basically, he was the exact opposite of Sebastian. There was no way this guy was going to jump on board with my spontaneous plan.

Sure enough, when Jamie spoke, he said, "Wouldn't that be stealing? And, you know, trespassing?"

"Probably." I shrugged.

A palpable silence descended upon us. I could just picture Jamie calling his friends on the way home, telling them about running into Nikki's crazy friend, who used him as human furniture and then tried to get him to commit a felony.

I put down my empty champagne glass on a high-top table and made to leave. "Okay, well, I think I'm gonna—"

"Wait," Jamie said suddenly, his hand shooting out to grab mine. His hand was warm and soft. "Come with me."

I was so surprised, I let Jamie lead me toward the front door of the gallery, and nearly tripped when he stopped short a few feet shy of the entrance.

"Oh, sorry. Did you want to say bye to your friend?"

I shrugged. "I'll text her."

And with that, Jamie led me outside and over to a tall glass building a block away.

"So... you want to break into a totally different building?" I asked.

"You'll see," Jamie said, ushering me through the revolving door.

The lobby was empty except for a security guard sitting behind the desk who waved at us. "Burning the midnight oil again, Mr. Kauffman?"

"Just popping up to grab something, Henry." The security guard, Henry, nodded and turned back to a crossword.

In the elevator, Jamie swiped his key card and pressed the button for the top floor. The doors closed, wrapping us in that particular intimacy of being alone in an elevator with only one other person. I could feel the hairs on the back of my neck prickle as we rode up the thirty-five floors in silence. Should I say something? Ask him about his job—because clearly this was his office building that we were not-breaking into? For his part, Jamie seemed completely at ease. That bashful awkwardness he'd displayed at the art gallery was nowhere in sight.

When we reached the top floor, the elevator deposited us into a little corporate lobby, with the words *The Kauffman Group* in steel letters on the wall.

He swiped his key card to unlock the glass doors, and I followed him down a long hallway. "Give me one sec. You can wait in here."

It was a large, extremely tidy office. The only thing on the desk beyond screens and a keyboard was a photo of an older woman with a dark brown bob beside a clearly recently graduated Jamie. She was a good foot shorter than him, her arm wrapped proudly around his waist. I picked up the picture to get a closer look, noticing how the ruby and diamond of her ring matched Jamie's cap and gown.

Then, Jamie was back. I put down the photo and met him in the hallway. He was holding a dark green champagne bottle in one hand and then moved over to a bar cart that I hadn't noticed in the corner of the room, grabbing two wine glasses. "The roof is this way."

He led me to the left, and we walked up a narrow, short flight of stairs. The intimacy from the elevator settled around me again. Jamie tripped a little on his way up the final step. So maybe he wasn't immune to the slight awkwardness of the situation after all. "Whoopsie," he muttered to himself, and then, seeming to realize that he'd just said this adorable thing out loud, he coughed and said, "Here we are."

All of LA opened up before us. It was glorious. Far better than the view we would have gotten from the art gallery across the street, which was only two stories tall. The last rays of sun shimmered across the high-rises of downtown, and the lights from their windows were just beginning to twinkle.

"Wow. This is stunning. I bet you bring all the girls up here." I said, stepping toward the edge of the roof.

Jamie barked out a laugh. "This is the first time I've been up here, outside of company parties." Jamie came up beside me, setting the wine and glasses between us. "But I'm thrilled you think I have that kind of game. I guess it would be a good move. I'll have to keep that in mind."

His honesty was so refreshing. He wasn't posturing like Liam used to do, or even playfully showing off like Sebastian. He was just himself.

"Okay, Mr. No-Game, if you've never brought a girl up here before, how come you just happen to have a bottle of champagne at the ready in your office?"

"What if I need to urgently celebrate a great fiscal quarter?" His eyes were playful. "Or, you know, what if I need something to drown my sorrows when I'm working late on a Friday night? Again." He twisted the cork off with a small pop, pouring a glass for each of us. "The truth is, I swiped it from my dad's office. He's the one who keeps the good stuff on hand."

"Jamie Kauffman!" I let my face contort with mock outrage. "You are a thief after all!"

"I guess I am," he said with a small smile, handing me a glass.

"So your dad works here too?" I asked, taking a sip of the champagne. The bubbles burst along my tongue. I was hardly a champagne expert, but even I could tell that it was remarkably better than what they'd been serving at Chloe's show.

"Yeah, it's kind of a family thing."

"Are you guys close? I saw that photo of you and your mom on your desk."

He cocked an eyebrow at me. "That's not my mother. That's my grandmother."

"Okay, that's even cuter."

"She's the greatest," he agreed.

"I mean, seriously, you guys even had matching red-and-white outfits!" Jamie looked confused, so I clarified. "Her ring matched your graduation robes. What a cool piece of jewelry."

Jamie smiled. "My grandfather gave her that ring. It's called a 'Toi et Moi.'"

"You and me," I translated.

"Oui," Jamie said with a flawless French accent that sent a zing straight to my lower belly. "The ruby and diamond represented their birthstones," he told me. "My granddad died before I was born, but Grandma G tells me plenty of stories. They were one of those rare 'opposites attract' couples that actually worked."

I sighed, leaning back and letting the warmth of Jamie's affection for his grandparents wash over me. "It must be nice to work with your family."

"It is. Usually." Jamie turned toward me, one elbow still resting on the ledge of the building. His face was thoughtful and open.

Something in my chest blossomed, an unfurling. I'd kept myself so tightly wrapped up since Sebastian, but it felt good to just open myself up to a new . . . friend? Jamie turned back toward the view, his arm grazing mine, but neither of us moved away. We lapsed back into silence, and I realized in that moment that I wanted him to kiss me.

"What are you thinking about?" I whispered with a slight toss of my hair. I was giving him the perfect excuse to lean in and *show* me what he was thinking about, like many a guy had done before.

But Jamie surprised me again. "How beautiful LA looks from up here. And how I never stop to appreciate it. I was thinking that I should look at the view more often." He turned to look at me, and in his gaze, I just knew somewhere deep down that this was the start of *something*. "Maybe I just need someone to remind me."

EPILOGUE

IF YOU REALLY WANT TO GET TECHNICAL ABOUT IT, MY FIRST ENGAGEMENT ring actually came at the age of seven. I can still remember the giddiness I felt as Ryan Briggs slid the plastic band with its bright red candy gemstone onto my finger. The feeling that all my dreams were about to come true. Our betrothal was tragically ill-fated—the romance cut short by the recess bell—but right from that moment, I knew exactly how my future wedding would go.

I'd walk through a meadow of wildflowers, a gentle breeze tugging at a gauzy dress shimmering in the soft light of a golden hour. There'd be a cotton candy machine and a vintage carousel. After we'd said our vows, there would be a choreographed release of monarch butterflies as I walked down the aisle with my new husband.

As the years went on, I traded out the guys in my fantasy the way I updated the mason jars in my imaginary wedding for the vintage champagne coupes I saw trending on Pinterest, adapting the vision to suit my current tastes. The specific husband wasn't an essential part of my planning.

Until Jamie.

IT'S BEEN A YEAR and a half since we were last at Halia Falls, and it hasn't changed at all. The beaches are still awe-inspiringly gorgeous, the pools are perfectly pristine, and the rooms are still elegant and cozy. But this time, Jamie and I arrived together.

And we brought all our wedding guests.

It's a smaller affair this time around. We only invited our nearest and dearest—our parents and Jamie's sister and her kids. Jamie's best friends, Vittal, Chris, and Mike, and their wives. The Core Four and their plus-ones.

Nikki joked that after everything that went down at her brother's wedding last summer, she was officially swearing off bridesmaid duties, but nevertheless, here she is, sitting beside me on the golf cart as we rumble up the mountain trail toward the ceremony site. And despite all the drama that unfolded over the summer, Nikki seems to have acquired a new sense of inner calm. Things that would once send her into a tailspin of perfectionist anxiety don't seem to faze her anymore. For example, the ride in the cart is turning her once-flawless updo into something decidedly more wind-whipped, but she doesn't seem to care in the slightest. Her boyfriend—another newly acquired development from that wedding—is already gathered with the rest of our guests.

The last week has been a whirlwind of wedding activities. We had a welcome party (which I was on time to) and a rehearsal dinner last night (which I was late to). And now, with the wedding in ten minutes, we're hustling up the mountainside to make sure we don't miss the sunset.

When we'd emailed back and forth with Ash about the ceremony location, she'd suggested the outcropping where we watched the lunar eclipse, and I immediately knew it was perfect.

The wind picks up as we reach the end of the trail. I slip off my heels and let my bare feet sink into the soft green moss. There's no string quartet, no planned butterfly release, and the only flowers are the small bouquet Nikki holds for me and the hot-pink plumeria crown that Willow carried up separately, worried that it might blow off my head before we reached the top. Willow places the flowers on my head now and kisses both of my cheeks. "You look like a mermaid princess." She squeezes my hands and steps away.

Emma drops the train of my dress—a vintage gem that she found for me back in Dallas—to the ground but can't resist giving it one last fluff. The dress flutters in the breeze, the thousands of iridescent beads shimmering the palest hint of seashell pink in the fading light. The neckline drapes delicately across my chest, the straps settling on my shoulders. I *do* feel like a mermaid princess, stepping from the sea straight into the arms of my one true love.

Nikki hands me my bouquet. She pulls me to her in a hug, and whispers in my ear, "This is the happily ever after you deserve, Sybs."

My dad steps forward and threads my arm through his, patting my hand twice.

I glance out at the small crowd and spot Jamie's parents, looking glamorous yet stiff as always. His mother presses down the pashmina covering her shoulders, as if afraid the wind will carry it away, and I smile, realizing how foolish it was to fear the Kauffmans. They might be a little repressed, a little guarded with their emotions, but then again, they haven't had the benefit of a Gwendolyn Green in their lives. I no longer see them as daunting and terrifying; they're just people, doing their best.

Beside them stands my mom, her chin wobbling, and I no longer see a strict parent who doesn't know what to do with her wild, wayward daughter. Now all I see is someone who is fragile, afraid of seeing me get hurt again. And my heart swells with gratitude.

Then the crowd parts, and all I see is Jamie.

I couldn't convince him that he didn't need to wear a jacket, but I did manage to convince him to ditch a tie. If I look like a mermaid princess, he looks like a recently reformed pirate—a reference I know Grandma G would have approved of—his brown hair tousled by the wind and the short hike, and his skin bronzed from the days we've spent here before the wedding basking in the sun.

Amelia stands beside him at the edge of the cliff. Her dark hair, a match to Jamie's and out of its customary bun, whips up behind her, and this time when her eyes land on me, they're warm.

At last night's rehearsal dinner, she came up to us both and tried to apologize for ever having influenced Jamie to doubt me. "You know, I was still reeling from my divorce. I was feeling protective and—and cynical. I should never have put that on you—"

But Jamie stopped her before I even could. "Amelia, the thing is, *I* wasn't marriage material then. If I had been, I couldn't have been swayed. But clearly, I had some growing up to do still. I hope I can prove to you that now I have."

"You don't have to prove anything," she said to him. "You— both of you," she added, including me in her gaze, "you've inspired me. You've made me want to believe in love again." She wiped away a tear. "I may be your older sister, Jamie, but I still look up to you sometimes."

She hugged him, and then me, and then I started to cry openly, which clearly made her uncomfortable because she dabbed at her eyes and returned to her table, ending what had been a beautiful moment.

Ah well, perhaps I'm never going to fit completely seamlessly into the Kauffman style of affection, but that's okay. At least I know now that it's there.

My dad and I pass through the gathered crowd and reach Jamie in just a few steps. My dad releases me, dropping a kiss on my cheek. He blinks away tears and clears his throat before turning to Jamie. "Take care of my baby."

Jamie nods solemnly and takes both my hands in his. "I will, sir."

Dad seems to have lost his ability to speak, so he just nods in reply and steps to stand beside my mom, who quietly slips him a tissue.

Jamie and I both turn toward Amelia. Behind her, the sun has just begun to dip below the horizon, and the ocean billows out before us with sparkles that put the glitter of my wedding dress to shame. The whole island spills out before us as Amelia begins reading from the Bible in her hands, "'Place me like a seal over your heart...'"

I try to pay attention to Amelia's words, but all I can think about is Jamie. Everything he is to me comes crashing over me. My partner, my cheerleader, the one person who's always loved me just as I am. All of the missteps I've made along the way, everything we've been through has been worth it to get this one moment with Jamie.

Amelia asks for the rings, and Emma places both of them in her hand.

Amelia turns to Jamie and reads off our vows.

"I do," Jamie says with a smile as he slides the cool metal onto my finger.

Amelia repeats the vows for me.

"I do." I slip a simple gold band onto Jamie's hand, and we both turn toward Amelia. With a wide smile, she says, "I now pronounce you husband and wife. You may kiss the bride!"

Jamie's lips are on mine in an instant, and his arms are firm around my waist. Familiar flames of desire lick through me, but more than that is the overwhelming feeling of coming home. Jamie has always been my safe haven, my port in the storm, and now he's mine forever.

The kiss ends, and Jamie presses his forehead to mine. We give ourselves a few breaths in this perfect moment. As cheers go up from the crowd, I look down at our clasped hands, Jamie's fingers twined through with mine. My new ring, a simple gold band, flashes in the sun. My first—and only—wedding ring.

ACKNOWLEDGMENTS

Sybil's winding path to love was quite a journey to write—full of unexpected detours and surprising second chances. I could not have done it without the indomitable support and vision of Lexa Hillyer, the remarkable (and detail obsessed) focus of Jenna Brickley, and the true creative magic of Emily Larrabee. I feel lucky to have such talented collaborators every step of the way.

To my editor, Madeleine Colavita: Thank you for pushing this story in the ways it needed to grow, and for always rooting for the right guy to triumph in the end. Huge shoutout to Estelle Hallick and Alli Rosenthal—you two are an unstoppable force! And many thanks to the rest of the remarkable team at Forever, including Grace Fischetti, Stacey Sharp, Daniela Medina, Angelina Krahn, and Marie Mundaca.

Sarah Trilla, thank you for helping it all run so smoothly—I'm so beyond grateful! And of course, thank you to Natalie Jones, without whom I would be a complete and utter disaster—possibly even worse than Sybil—but you help me make it all look seamless!

To Nicole Perez, Taylor Rodriguez, and Paige Alvarez—you guys are truly incredible. You've helped me connect with so many readers. Working with your team has been a total game-changer.

To Stephen Barbara, as well as Gwen Beal, Albert Lee, and Jamie Youngentob, thank you for always being in my corner and believing in these books—not to mention helping them find publishing homes around the world.

To Holly Ovendenfor: Thank you for this gorgeous cover. You've captured the essence of the story perfectly—and created the romantic pink beach of my dreams!

To everyone who has embraced Sybil and Jamie's story, I can't thank you enough! Your support means the world to me. I hope you come away with renewed faith in the magic of second (and third, and fourth...) chances.

To my family and friends, your love and encouragement have been my constant source of strength, and I'm so grateful.

And finally, to Adam. By the time this book comes out, we will be weeks away from saying "I do"—and there's no one I'd rather spend forever with.

ABOUT THE AUTHOR

HANNAH BROWN is a television personality, lifestyle expert, and two-time *New York Times* bestselling author. Born and raised in Tuscaloosa, Alabama, Brown was awarded Miss Alabama USA in 2018 and used her platform to advocate for mental health awareness. Brown then appeared on season 23 of *The Bachelor*, becoming a fan favorite, and was featured as *The Bachelorette* on season 15 of the franchise—even winning a People's Choice Award. She went on to win season 28 of ABC's *Dancing with the Stars* and compete on FOX's *Special Forces: World's Toughest Test*, where she outlasted the other 16 contestants, most of whom were professional athletes.

Brown continues to inspire and empower others by advocating for mental health awareness and emphasizing the importance of self-love.

Brown currently resides in Nashville with her fiancé, Adam Woolard, and dog, Wally.